IN THE DEFENSIVE ZONE
with My Enemy

DINEEN MILLER

BOOKS

To my favorite uncle (Funcle) Mike.
Thank you for all the tickles and encouragement through the years.

Vinci Books

vinci-books.com

Published by Vinci Books Ltd in 2025

1

The EU GPSR authorised representative is Logos Europe, 9 rue Nicolas
Poussion, 17000 La Rochelle, France
contact@logoseurope.eu

By Dineen Miller

Romancing the Sun Kings

In the Defensive Zone with My Enemy

In the Offensive Zone with My Fake Bride

Messy Love on Mango Lane

Bloomed to Be Messy

Rescued to Be Messy

Tamed to Be Messy

A Very Messy Christmas

Chapter One

LUKE

"Isn't that the team that had that scandal last year?" I cross my arms and sit back in the coffee shop chair that barely fits my six-three frame, but the coffee's decent, and the place is close to home here in Clearwater, Florida. When Gabe reached out, asking if we could meet, I assumed he wanted to catch up since we hadn't really talked much over the last few months. Never expected he'd offer me a spot on the team he was recently hired to coach without even trying out.

We both left hockey roughly a year and a half ago, but for different reasons. Gabe had been playing for a while before I showed up on the scene. A bit of an old-timer, as we sometimes called him, because he had a good ten years on most of us. But then a third concussion, and his wife convinced him it was time to exit while he was *ahead* of the game. Pun intended.

My departure had nothing to do with an injury. A fatal car accident took the life of my mother, leaving me in charge of everything, including my sixteen-year-old sister.

Our father checked out when I was eight—shortly after Kinsley was born. I didn't see any other choice at the time, and I still think it was the right one.

"That's why I'm here. The Florida Sun Kings are under new ownership. They brought me on a couple of months ago to help bring the team together to up our game and our rep." Gabe turns his six-foot-two frame toward me, his expression imploring. "But I need you, Jammer."

I rub at the growing tension in the back of my neck—the one that's telling me to get up and walk away now. Gabe slid easily off the ice and into coaching. I've spent the last year or so taking care of my sister, getting her off to college, and logging as many hours as I could at the local hardware store where I used to work through high school and college before landing on an AHL team in California. That's when I first met Gabe. I don't even know if I can handle returning to the ice. I used to love the game, but now...

Yet the last thing I want is to disappoint Gabe. He took me under his wing from day one and became not only a friend but a mentor as well. "I don't know, man. It's been a while since I played."

"You're still young enough." He lets out a derisive laugh. "Unlike some of us."

I smirk. "Maybe old for hockey. Not in life." I'm sure his wife would say the same.

"I know, but my point is, you still have time. And now that Kinsley is off to college..."

He doesn't have to finish his sentence because he's right, but I'm keenly aware of the guilt that chills me more than the ice ever did. Always there, always telling me I'm the one to blame. If it weren't for me, Kinsley would have had a mother to take her shopping for her prom dress. Instead, she got stuck with an older brother who hadn't a clue about things like dresses, hairstyles, and makeup. Thankfully, my mother's best friend stepped in to help with all that, because I didn't have a clue. However, I did a pretty good job making her date squirm in his tux.

Unfortunately, finances are fast becoming an issue in light of Kinsley's hefty college tuition—the brat had the nerve to get accepted into Columbia, and I couldn't be prouder of her. But what I managed to squirrel away during my three-year stint in the AHL and working won't last much longer. No job is going to pay a former hockey player with an unused degree in business enough to cover our expenses. The next option is to sell our house, which would be like losing Mom all over again.

But my sister missed out on so much already. I drop my arms and sigh but say nothing. Somehow, I have to find a way to make this work.

Gabe clears his throat. "Did Kinsley get a scholarship?"

"Partial."

He leans forward in his too-small chair. "Luke, you were on the fast track to the NHL before…" His chest expands as he takes in a weighted breath. "You could still make that happen. I told the new owner we needed a good anchor for the team. We need a strong captain."

My pulse spikes as I frown. "Captain? I only played defense for three years."

"And, in my opinion, you were one of the best."

I shake my head. "The team won't like it."

"They'll get used to it," he shoots back.

"Yeah, they'll *love* the brand new coach choosing a newbie as their captain." I make sure there's plenty of sarcasm in my tone.

He smirks. "Most of these guys are younger than you. That'll carry some weight."

I grunt. "But they won't trust me."

"Not in the beginning, maybe. But you're a natural-born leader, Luke. I bet you'll have them following your lead within two weeks."

My brows attempt to shake hands with my hairline. "That's overpromising."

He moves his coffee cup to the side. "Just think about it, okay? The position comes with a signing bonus and a second bonus if the team makes the finals in the division. That should help pay Kinsley's tuition."

He's right. It would. Even with the increase in my hours at the hardware store, we'd have to do something drastic... like sell the house.

"And this is the ECHL. Their track record for shooting guys up to NHL is growing." Gabe leans over, pulls a folder out of his satchel, and slides it across the table toward me.

My coffee cup blocks it like a goalie. Kind of poetic when you think about it.

"That's the offer. Look it over and let me know what you think."

I'm tempted to shove it back at him. Probably would if it weren't for my sister. I move my cup and slide the folder closer. Score one for Gabe.

"When do you need an answer?"

He rises from his chair. "The sooner the better. Practice starts in two weeks. If you don't want to make the commute to Sarabella, you can stay with me and Olivia until you find something local."

I snort. "Did you clear that with her? Aren't you two expecting?"

His grin widens. Fatherhood looks good on Gabe. Real good. "Yeah, another girl. But not for a few months yet. We haven't started on the nursery, so the room is yours if you need it."

Gabe stops next to my chair and rests a hand on my shoulder. "This is a great opportunity, Luke. A chance to go after your dream again."

The unspoken message in his tone is clear. He had to give up his dream to go national, and he doesn't want me to miss my shot. A curt nod is all I can manage. I press my lips together but keep my head down, waiting for him to leave.

How can I tell him I'm not sure I want it anymore? The idea of returning to the ice makes me queasy to think about it. It's my fault my mother isn't around today because of the game. That's too much baggage to carry back into the game.

After a minute or so, I glance over my shoulder to make sure he's gone. I finger the corner of the folder, then flip it open and start reading.

My options are limited at this point, and Kinsley deserves to go after her dream now.

Even if it means I have to live my nightmare.

My phone vibrates in the cup holder of my SUV. Kinsley's name shows on the Car Play screen. I tap the accept button.

"Hey, Kins, what's up?"

There's a brief pause before her voice fills the cabin, which spikes my pulse. Since we lost Mom, anytime Kinsley calls, my first thought is that she's in trouble. Not sure why I do that, but I seem to always expect the worst.

"Kins? You there?"

"Yeah, sorry." She sounds breathless.

"What's wrong?" My tone sounds more forceful than I intend, but I'm on pins and needles here.

"Sheesh, relax, big bro. Just needed to catch my breath from sprinting across campus. This place is freakin' huge."

I'm glad she can't see my head-shake, eye-roll combo. The one she calls me out on any time she gets the chance.

"Maybe catch your breath first next time?" I bump my turn signal on with a little more force than necessary.

She snickers. "There he is, The Lukinator."

When Kinsley turned thirteen, she started calling me that anytime I got in her face about something. She entered adolescence with a ferocity that rivaled the Kardashians, and Mom needed help with her. I don't know if she learned her sarcasm from me or if I got it from her. Either way, she wins.

"Just get on with it, already."

She blows out a noisy breath, creating a static sound. "I hate to ask, but I need money for books."

"I thought we took care of those at the beginning of the semester."

"These are additional recommended readings for that investigative class I'm taking in the evening."

"Sounds so official."

"Nah, just intense."

After I pull into our driveway, that familiar heaviness creeps in. The roses Mom planted still have some pink blooms, and several of the hanging baskets of orchids have flowers on them. I can picture Mom standing on the porch, misting her orchids or clipping roses from her bushes in the yard, enjoying the subtle drop in humidity that early fall brings. It's all a reminder of the past, and a happier time.

I rub a hand over my mouth, making a scratchy sound. "How much?"

"A hundred? That will give me a little money for food, too." Her voice squeaks out. "Sorry."

I take a deep breath against the tightness in my chest. Gabe's offer is looking more and more attractive. "It's okay, Kins. Don't apologize. I'll transfer two hundred now."

"I said a hundred."

"Food's not cheap."

She hesitates so long, I lower my phone to check if the call dropped. "Thank you. It means a lot."

"Don't worry about it." I swipe the screen on my phone to get to my bank app. "Whatever you need, let me know."

"I could get a part-time job and work weekends. You know…to help."

Even though she can't see me, I shake my head. "No, stick to your plan. I've got this covered."

"Are you sure?"

I can hear the subtle relief in her voice, and that right there confirms what I need to do.

"Surer than sure."

An ache hits my chest with the words—a phrase Mom always used to reassure us whenever things got tight or difficult. Now, being on the other end of it, I have a better understanding of what she dealt with, holding our little family together. Makes me miss her even more. I wish I'd known and could have told her how much I appreciated all the sacrifices she made for us.

Especially for me and hockey.

A soft sniffle punctuates the silence. "I miss her."

I clear the emotion from my throat. "Me too. She'd be proud of you, ya know?"

"I know. Just wish she was here to see it."

Like Mom had been for me through all the years of

hockey…more reason for me to do whatever it takes. "She is, Kins. Mom is always with us."

She sighs. "You know what I mean."

"I do." That ache in my chest doubles. I grab the folder from the passenger seat. "Listen, kid, I gotta run. Got some business to take care of."

"Yeah, go sort those hammers." And the sarcasm is back.

"You know it. Call me in a day or two and let me know how things are going, okay?"

"Will do."

Once Kinsley ends the call, I blow out a noisy breath and drop my head against the headrest. Gabe asked me to think about his offer, but I don't have that luxury. Hockey is my best option—my only option at the moment—and the optimal solution for our situation.

With a sigh of resignation, I pick up my phone and open my contacts. Might as well get it over with and start planning.

Gabe answers after one ring. "That was fast."

"Kinsley needs books." Heat travels up the back of my neck again. Might be the Florida heat still lingering this time of year or this decision. Probably the latter.

"College is expensive. I'm already saving for both my girls."

"Smart man. I'll send the signed contracts tonight."

"That's great, Jammer. You won't regret it."

I won't tell him I already do. "I'll drive down in a couple of days so I can start practicing ahead of time."

"Good idea. Olivia and I look forward to seeing you."

After a few more exchanges, I end the call and trudge up the front steps of the porch. The contract folder weighs my hand down like one of the rocks Mom used to edge her rose bed, but I know it's the best solution for us. And it's temporary. That's what I'm telling myself to make the choice more palatable. Once Kins graduates, I can move on to something...

Something.

I guess I could say there's a silver lining to all this. I won't have to sell the house. Now, I just have to figure out how to get on the ice without drowning in guilt.

Chapter Two

SOPHIE

I used to think love was the most powerful force on earth.

Until it let me down.

Don't get me wrong. I haven't totally given up on love in general. Just...when it applies to me. Three failed relationships are like that saying: fool me once, shame on you; fool me twice, shame on me; and my addition—fool me three times, shame on love. A girl can only endure so much disappointment in her life, you know?

"Soph?"

I jerk my attention back to my best friend Mia, who, at this very minute, is standing on a platform in front of floor-to-ceiling mirrors, wearing the most beautiful wedding dress I've ever seen. The lace, the beading, the drape of the fabric —perfection.

She lifts her finely shaped brows in question. "What do you think?"

I grin more for her benefit than mine. "I don't know. Do they have it in a different color?"

Mia snorts and scowls all at once. "Seriously? This is like

the most important event in my life, and you're cracking jokes?"

I hold my hands up in innocence. "That's why you love me so much."

She rewards me with one of her epic eye rolls. "Save your humor for your articles."

I hunch my shoulders, but this time, my smile is real. "It's perfect."

She meets my gaze in the mirror, her eyes glassy and her voice soft. "It is, isn't it?"

If you looked up the definition of soulmate, I'm convinced you'd see a reference to Ethan and Mia. They are the epitome of the phrase 'meant-to-be.'

Not only do the two of them look like they walked off the cover of a fashion magazine, which that alone would make me hate them if I didn't love them both so much, but they're also so perfect for each other, it's nauseating.

But in a good way. A great way. The best way possible.

They're like Kate Winslet and Leonardo DiCaprio in the Titanic or Elizabeth Bennet and Mr. Darcy in Pride and Prejudice—drawn to one another with a longing and passion that sucks everyone in around them.

Including me...especially me, seeing as I'm kind of responsible for their meet cute.

A few months ago, Mia tagged along with me on an assignment to interview the new owner of Florida Sun Kings, based here in Sarabella. While I was interviewing the formidable Rebecca Piedmont, who started out as a sports-caster with a dream of someday owning her own team, Mia fell hard and fast for one of the players.

Their love story turned into a whirlwind, and now I'm helping her plan their wedding.

But this is where the romance ends for me, as a pseudo-matchmaker. And I can live with that. If I can't have true love of my own, I will find peace in helping others discover theirs. Or write stories about it.

That is if my editor-in-chief buys my idea of a "Romancing Sarabella" column. I envision it as a source to find out the best places for things like a first date, a marriage proposal, a cozy, intimate wedding, or even just a sunset picnic on the beach. Followed by a walk, of course.

Sarabella is known for its beaches and the arts. There's a plethora of material to write about, highlighting the most romantic and creative parts of this somewhat sleepy but growing beach town. Like this boutique bridal shop I talked Mia into trying.

The dream of Tulle by Tulard started ten years ago when Madam Tulard—she insists we call her that—retired to Sarabella. All her years of apprenticing and working in France ached to be shared—her words—so she opened her own shop. I knew it would be the perfect place to find a one-of-a-kind dress for Mia, and I'm convinced readers will flip when they read Madam Tulard's story. Doesn't hurt that she's giving Mia a discount.

The entire concept for my column idea came from helping Mia plan her wedding. I've lived in Sarabella my whole life. Who better than me to write about the gems hidden amongst swaying palms and gorgeous beaches?

I'm so lost in my train of thought—and checking my phone to see if my boss, Marty, has texted me yet with an answer—that I don't notice right away that Mia has changed dresses and walks out wearing a monstrosity that looks more like a cream puff than a dress. Every bit of the gown is covered in satin rosettes, and the skirt is big enough to accommodate a large family of gnomes.

She holds her hands out to her side and gives me a smile

I find rather suspicious. "Well, what do you think?" She claps her hands together and does a little bounce on her toes. "I know I said the other one was perfect, but now I think this is the one!"

My BS radar goes off—a required talent I've honed as a journalist—but I don't want to say outright what I think to Mia, in case she's genuinely serious. She better not be because I don't want to go to jail for murdering a dress that borders on the Disney spectrum.

I rise to my feet and suck in a noisy breath, and then I bring my hands to my chest as if I'm so moved I can't find the words at first—something I would NEVER do because I'm a journalist. We ALWAYS have something to say.

"Oh my gosh, Mia! You're right! It's the one." I smack my hands to the sides of my legs like a cheerleader. "Please tell me you're planning to buy it because if you don't, I'll never speak to you again."

Mia's shoulders drop as she tugs her mouth to the side. "Will I ever be able to pull one over on you?"

I giggle. "Not on your life. Now take that thing off so we can tell Madam Tulard what you need altered on the real one."

She does this little stomp with her foot—something she's done as long as I've known her. "Fine." She heads toward the dressing room, then stops to face me just before she pulls the curtain closed. "That other one really is THE dress, isn't it?"

I grin. "You know it, I know it, and I think the dress knows it too."

Her turn to giggle. She snaps the curtain shut with a noisy scrape of metal rings on the bar while I check my phone again.

This time, there's a text from Marty.

> MARTY: Whatever you're doing, stop and
> get back to the office. I have a new project
> for you.

All kinds of wonderful shivers travel up and down my back and neck. This is it, isn't it? It has to be. Marty loved my idea and wants to push forward with it. My very first piece could run by next week. I send a quick reply to let him know I'm on my way.

Mia emerges from the dressing room, wearing the actual dress of her dreams, and steps up onto the platform again right as Madam Tulard floats in. Her wrinkled lips pucker as if she just sucked on a lemon, causing Mia and me to glance at each other in concern.

Madam Tulard's face breaks into a proud smile. "Yes, that is the dress for you. It was made for you, *mon chéri*."

Mia giggles with delight, and I blow out a noisy breath. My work here is done. For now, anyway. Plus, I need to get back to the office.

I hop onto the edge of the platform and lean in to kiss Mia on the cheek. "Just got a text from Marty that he needs to see me ASAP."

Her eyes widen. "Your proposal?"

I nod in the most exaggerated way I can muster. "Yeah, baby!"

We both squeal and jump up and down.

"Do not rip the dress!" Madam Tulard glares at us, resembling a German sergeant more than the petite French woman she is.

Mia's cheeks turn pink, but I grin and squeeze her hand. "Can you finish up here without me?"

She waves me away. "Go, go!" She tips her head toward

me and whispers, "Just be sure to check on me later and make sure she didn't eat me, okay?"

I snort. "Of course. And I'll give you all the deets."

Madam Tulard's a parody of disapproval as I hop off the platform. Mia grins and waves as I dash off, already picturing the column header with my byline underneath. I'm about to meet my destiny, and nothing is going to get in my way. Not even a French sour puss who happens to be a world-class wedding gown designer.

This may not be the happily-ever-after I'd hoped for three times, but it's certainly close enough.

———

I make a run from the parking lot but slow my pace once I step inside the Sarabella Herald Tribune offices downtown. Marty said ASAP, but he doesn't need to see just how hungry I am for this.

Charlene waves to me from the copy desk. I require a few more seconds to catch my breath before I walk into Marty's office, so I make a detour.

"I didn't think you were coming in until this afternoon." A slight frown puckers her mouth. Char and I were hired on around the same time, and became close friends almost immediately. But where I'm in it for a byline, her end game is copy editor because she enjoys telling people what to do.

"Marty asked me to come in sooner." I lift a single brow, knowing she'll get my point.

Her eyes widen, and her lips make a circle, making her resemble that surprised emoji face she loves to use when she texts. Anytime she sends it, I invariably picture this image and laugh.

"Yeah, wish me luck." I flash her a smile before striding toward Marty's office.

He lifts a finger as I walk in to inform me he's on a call. The man always wears his AirPods, so we never know if he's talking on the phone or listening to a news feed.

I slip into the chair in front of his desk and fold my hands in my lap to wait. I may have caught my breath, but my heart's still pounding like a percussion drum. For once, I'm glad he has those things in his ears because I'm almost convinced he could hear it, too.

"Great. We'll get this started tomorrow, then." Marty ends the call, then faces me and actually removes his AirPods—something he only does when he has big news.

And me getting my own column is big. Huge. Ginormous. This is it! The moment I've been dreaming about for weeks.

I take a deep, relaxing breath and put a smile in place. "You said you needed to see me?"

His gray-blue eyes sparkle as he grins. "I have some fantastic news for you, Sophie."

I let out a nervous giggle as I clasp my hands to my chest. Who cares if I make a fool of myself? I got THE COLUMN.

"This is so great, Marty. I can't tell you how grateful I am."

His smile dips a little. "But I haven't even told you the news yet."

I stretch out my palms. "I assumed it's about my proposal."

He waves my words away. "Oh, that. No, we'll discuss that another time. This is bigger. A specific assignment just for you."

Talk about the bottom falling out. But I'm not ready to

give up. "So is a column about the undiscovered gems in Sarabella. From food, to shops, to the arts—"

He tilts his head. "I'm aware of the slogan. I read your proposal."

"And?"

Marty gentles his voice. "Not yet, Soph. You need a little more experience under your belt."

I shift to the front of my chair and lean over the edge of his desk. "I have lots of experience, Marty. At this rate, I'm going to need another notch to loosen it. Please, I really want this."

"I know you do, kiddo. But I promise what I have for you will go a long way in helping you get there. Trust me, okay?" Hard to resist the man when he uses his fatherly tone.

Marty has known me since I was a baby. He and my father worked together as reporters in Washington, DC. Then, after years of working on various papers, they both landed here in Sarabella. I grew up in this newsroom and caught the journalism bug while watching my father hammer out his articles. Marty and his wife, Clara, did a stellar job filling the gap left behind after my mother died when I was five.

So, of course, I trust him. But I'm desperate for this dream. Borderline psychotic, one could even say. Letting go of it in any small way feels so risky…like a setup for disappointment. But Marty has been like a father to me for the last five years since Dad passed away without warning. I know he has my best interest at heart.

I flop back in my chair. "Fine. Let me have it."

"Remember the piece you did about Rebecca Piedmont?"

"Yes, of course."

"She wants to up the team's reputation and build a connection with the fans. She was so impressed with what you wrote that she's requested you follow the team and do profiles on the new coach, the staff, and the players."

I slap my hands on the chair's arms and push up from the seat. "Nope, don't want it."

He stares up at me with mild shock. "But she asked for you, Soph. This is a big deal. Besides, you covered sports in college. You have experience."

I lean my hands on the edge of his desk. "And I hated it. I've no interest in sports. Give it to Simon. He follows everything that includes a ball, a bat, or a stick."

And a skirt, but I don't say that part out loud.

"Did you miss what I said earlier about this assignment helping you get that column you want?" His brows arch in that authoritative expression I've come to recognize when I've lost.

I drop back down into the chair. "There has to be some other way, Marty. Please. Just thinking about that locker room smell makes me want to gag."

"You're not thinking this through, kiddo. You want to do a column about Sarabella. Well, right now, this is the big news here. Big enough to wake up this sleepy beach town in a massive way. And your name will be on the byline. When you think about it, it's really not that far off from what you proposed. And doing this assignment will go a long way in selling the board of directors on your column idea."

Now he has my attention. "Okay. I think I'm beginning to see your point."

"Good." He gestures to his phone. "That was the new coach, Gabe Markelson. He's expecting you in the morning."

"That soon?! Don't I get any time to do some preliminary research so I can compose my interview?"

"Soph, this isn't a one-shot deal. You're going to observe the team over the season and write a series."

"A series?" I can't even imagine there being enough content to warrant following a team for the entire season, but I may not be trying all that hard, either.

He nods. "The team needs positive exposure to help undo the controversy from last year."

"That's months, Marty. I don't know if I can handle that." To be around sweaty, spitting, and sometimes arrogant hockey players for that long makes the salad I had for lunch feel like nettles in my stomach. Mia's fiancé, Ethan, is the exception—him I can stand—most of the time.

"Will I be able to work on anything else?"

"Nope. The idea is for you to follow the team. Get to know them so we can run profiles on the players and the managers and cover the home games, of course. That's what will bring the fans back. You can even write about the renovations done on the old rink. Ms. Piedmont is giving you full access to everything."

"Wow..." Marty could be right. If I structure this series similar to how I imagined my column, I could establish a reader following, which would back up my proposal.

But it's hockey... And only hockey for months.

I tilt my head back, covering my face with a groan. "Somebody please wake me up from this nightmare."

"Sophie."

"Yeah?"

"Look at me."

I drop my hands as I lower my chin. "What?"

"This is how it works. You pay your dues and prove you've got what it takes. Trust me, this is going to do great things for your career if you handle it right." His earnest expression conveys his belief in me.

Nothing will make me love this assignment, but I don't want to let Marty down. He's not only an amazing boss but one of the biggest sources of encouragement in my life. The only source, really. I drop my hands to my lap with a moan. "Fine. But I'm not changing my plans for Mia's wedding."

"Of course not. I'm not asking you to live at the rink twenty-four-seven. Just attend practices and games."

"Away games, too?" I'm softening. I can feel it in my chest, and I hate it.

"Not all of them. We'll cover your expenses for the ones you do."

I've always wanted to travel, but not with a hockey team. Guess I can't be choosy. Not yet, anyway. "And I do my own photos."

"I wouldn't have it any other way." Now he's placating me.

Still feeling somewhat petulant about the whole thing, I tuck my chin. "Can I stop in tonight to get the lay of the land?"

His grin stretches, pushing up his cheeks. Probably because he knows he's won. "I had a hunch you might want to. The coach said no one would be there except for the construction workers. Take a look around and start envisioning your plan of action."

Envisioning. One of Marty's favorite words.

"Don't get all woo-woo on me now, Marty." I shove myself out of the chair and start to leave.

"Sophie?" His voice calls me back.

I stop and turn around. "Yeah?"

"This is going to be fun."

A nod is all I can muster. But as I leave, I mutter, "If you say so."

"Heard that." Marty's voice rings out behind me, but I don't stop. I trudge back to my cubicle and flop into my chair like a deflated balloon at a party gone wrong.

Charlene glances side-to-side, then slinks over like the Grinch. "Well, how'd it go? When does your first column publish?"

"No column. Not yet, anyway."

She crouches down, resting her chin on her hands on the edge of my desk. "Then what was so important that he wanted you to come in?"

I sit up and lean toward her. "You're looking at the new sports journalist for the Florida Sun Kings hockey team."

Her brows do a little wiggle. "Could be interesting being around all those sweaty, muscled players."

Her eyes take on a dreamy look, while mine prefer to slam shut in disgust. Been there and done that in college, and it was pretty rank then. But if Marty thinks this is the optimal approach to land the column I want, then what choice do I have?

I'll do my time, like he said. Do the gig, get it over with, and move on to the real and meaningful stuff.

Until then, hockey, here I come.

Chapter Three

LUKE

When I gave my notice to the owner of the hardware shop, he flat-out offered to make me the manager of the place. Mr. Tempe said he'd planned to do it at some point, anyway. I thanked him and politely refused, telling him this was what I really wanted, even though it wasn't. I didn't want to embarrass him by saying the pay bump wouldn't be enough, although I'm pretty sure he already knows that.

Regardless of Clearwater's close proximity, I'd never spent any time in Sarabella. Kind of one of those places I wanted to visit at some point, but not high on the list. But I think I'm going to like it here. The town seems to run at a slower pace, and the people are friendly.

Doesn't hurt that Gabe and Olivia's place isn't far from the arena and a quick ride to Mango Key Beach, which is fast becoming my favorite beach of all. And I can drive back home on the weekends to make sure the house, lawn— and Mom's roses—stay in good shape.

Practice starts in a week, but Gabe said I had free run of the place to get a jumpstart on training. A year and a half away from the ice put a definite dent in my endurance. These pockets of time, alone on the ice, have helped bring my anxiety under control. Plus, I got first dibs in the newly renovated locker room.

Most days, I come in early, but today, the workers needed the rink clear to work on the boards and plexiglass upgrades, so I waited to practice until after they left. Surprisingly, getting back on the ice wasn't as hard as I expected. Thank goodness for muscle memory, even if they're sore and cranky at the moment. But this is a far cry from playing with a team who may or may not accept me as their captain in front of spectators.

Despite my progress, that challenge stirs up a sick feeling in my gut. I just need to push through. Then, I'll adjust and fall into a daily pattern I don't have to think about. That's what I tell myself every day as I leave the ice and head to the locker room.

That, and I'm doing this for Kinsley.

When I open the locker door to stow my skates, the bottom hinge comes loose. I gained some handyman skills working at the hardware store all those years, so fixing a hinge is child's play for me. Unless the screws are stripped, which I'm thinking might have happened when they installed it.

The workers left several toolboxes around, so I bum a Phillips head from the one sitting on the end of the bench. It's after hours, but I figure they won't mind as long as I return it. Putting pressure from behind with my free hand, I put more force into the screwdriver, hoping to get a better grip, which makes me grunt.

"Need some help with that?"

I turn toward the unexpected sound of a woman's voice and become entranced by the biggest brown eyes I think

I've ever seen perched under a fringe of glossy, dark bangs. Then she blinks her long lashes.

The screwdriver slips and stabs my palm, making me hiss.

She dashes over. "Hey, are you all right?"

Out of curiosity—yeah, let's call it that—I do a quick appraisal of her long hair pulled back into a ponytail to see if the rest of her hair is as lustrous, which it is. And probably silky to the touch. I drag my attention to my hand, which has started to bleed a little. Nothing serious, but I may have bruised my thumb muscle.

That'll be fun holding a hockey stick in the morning. "Just a scratch. No worries."

"I didn't know anyone was here." She lifts one shoulder as if she's embarrassed. Or maybe she's shy.

"I was just finishing up."

She leans in for a closer look. "You're bleeding. Got any Band-Aids around here?"

Her delicate fragrance of orange blossoms and clove fills my nose, tempting me to inhale her scent until it fills every inch of my lungs and imprints her on my brain. I want to reply, but my mouth seems paralyzed.

She blinks those long lashes again. "I might have one in my car if you don't."

A vague memory of seeing when I pinched the screwdriver floats in. I blink and clear my throat. "I think there's some in that toolbox."

I've scarcely taken a step in that direction when she darts over, finds the box of Band-Aids, and plucks one out.

"Great. Neosporin, too." She pulls apart the backing and adds a dab of antiseptic cream, then gestures toward my hand with it. "May I?"

I swipe away the bit of blood with a clean towel, then hold my palm up. "Sure."

Her fingers brush my skin as she applies the Band-Aid, making me acutely aware of the warmth of her touch.

She holds out her hand. "Sophie Adams. I'm a journalist with the Sarabella Herald Tribune."

"Luke Jameson." I shake her hand but don't add that I'm a hockey player. A key lesson I learned in the short time I played in the AHL was to keep my mouth shut around reporters. I'd witnessed too many guys getting misquoted or targeted for little to nothing. Then, my own run-in with one of them after my mother's accident confirmed they couldn't be trusted with anything personal.

Her smile spreads, making her eyes tilt. "Pleasure to meet you, Luke Jameson. Have you lived in Sarabella long?"

I shake my head as I lean over to pick up the screwdriver I dropped. "Just moved here recently. New job."

"I grew up here, so if you want to know where to go for the best burger or which beach has the best shells, I'm your girl."

My girl? Why does that make me want to return her grin in the worst way?

Doesn't matter. I don't have time to date anyone. Besides, she's a reporter. I never was a fan of the limelight, but even more so now. I have my reasons for not drawing attention to myself. Just let me play the game I love—used to love—and stay out of my face.

As beautiful as I may find Sophie Adam's face, I don't want her in mine.

I hold up the screwdriver. "I should get back to what I was doing."

Her smile slips, and she blinks as if she's startled. "Oh,

right. Me, too. I just wanted to get a feel for the place before tomorrow. I've been assigned to report on the team for the entire season, so I figured I'd get a jump on things. Not exactly the assignment I wanted, but I'm hoping it will open the door to what I really want to do."

Takes me a moment to digest her rapid spew of words. However, the way she emphasized 'entire' with that adorable eye roll, as if she's not looking forward to it, sets off warning signals. And that she sees this as a way to get what she really wants makes me even more cautious. All the more reason to keep my head down. She's most likely searching for any dirt she can find to disparage an already less-than-stellar team that's been under some shaky management in the past.

I did some digging out of curiosity after I let Gabe know I was accepting his offer. Something about inappropriate behavior between the previous owner and one of the trainers. None of my business, but regardless, I recognize a hungry shark when I see it. And Sophie Adams fits the bill. Nothing like a little scandal to get your name recognized.

"Okay, then. Have a good evening." I drop the screwdriver back into the toolbox.

Sophie waggles her fingers to say goodbye.

I nod, then wait as she heads out the door leading to the tunnel.

She'll find out soon enough that I'm on the team. Tomorrow, by the sound of it. But I think I've made it clear I'm not the talkative type. With reporters, that's just common sense in my mind.

My gut, on the other hand, can't seem to let go of her fruity-spicy scent or the sensation of her touch.

And those eyes—I have a feeling those will haunt my dreams tonight.

The locker room sounds more like a high school reunion, with all the guys reacting to seeing each other after the break, except for me. They just keep side-eyeing me as I lace up my skates until one of them steps forward, hand out. "You must be the new guy. Luke, right?"

I shake his hand, which only reminds me of my encounter with Sophie last night. I haven't seen her, so maybe she's not here yet. "Yeah, Luke Jameson."

"Ethan McKennen."

"I remember." Specifically, playing against him a few times right before I left the game. Recently recruited, Ethan still had a greenness about him then, which had nothing to do with his team colors.

"Oh, yeah?"

I nod. "You were just recruited."

He cringes. "Was I that memorable?"

"You really want me to answer that?"

He laughs, then bumps fists with me. Not a bad start for the day.

One of the other guys walks over with a cocky grin as if he's ready to compare notes. Based on his very youthful appearance, I'm guessing he's a rookie. Most likely recruited straight out of the junior league, which means two things: he's good, and he knows it.

His expression slips into a moment of confusion, then surprise. "Hey, you're Jammer. You used to play for the Barracudas." He shakes my hand next. "I watched you when I was playing junior league. Luke 'Jammer' Jameson. You melted the ice, dude."

Called it. "Thanks."

"Jayce Brady." He puffs his chest out and lifts his chin as

if about to make a challenging comment, but Gabe walks out of the coaches' office and calls for everyone to listen.

He stands with his hands on his hips. "Welcome back, everyone. Besides Derek and me, we have a couple more additions to the team this season."

The guys in front of me meander to their benches, giving me a clear view of Gabe and his assistant coach, Derek. Then Sophie steps out from behind them and stands on Gabe's other side.

Gabe holds his hand out toward her. "This is Sophie Adams, a journalist from the Sarabella Herald Tribune. She's going to be with us for the season, doing profiles and reporting on the games. So, be respectful and cooperative. This is about our reputation, and we all know that needs some help right now."

A low rumble of conversations breaks out between the players.

Sophie does the same finger waggle she did with me last night. "Hi, guys. Great to be here."

I restrain a snort at her words, remembering what she said about this being her gateway to something better. The rest of the guys murmur and nod, but I see some of the same wariness I'm feeling in some of their expressions.

Gabe shifts his focus to me. "Second piece of news—we have a new player. Luke Jameson, also known as Jammer, just signed on with us."

A few of the players applaud and let out whistles. Then there's Jayce with his buddies I've yet to meet, staring at me like he's trying to figure out what makes me tick.

I lift my hand in thanks for the welcome, then slide my gaze to Sophie because she's hard to resist looking at dressed in black pants that hug her hips to perfection and a bright pink blouse that brings out the blush on her cheeks.

She's studying me with a confused expression that does little to diminish her beauty. If anything, it heightens it because I'm betting she's unaware of how that borderline frown makes her lips appear puckered for a kiss. But then her eyes narrow as she presses them together. Maybe that blush has more to do with anger now.

"He's also your new captain."

This draws a louder mumble from the guys and a few sharp looks. I warned Gabe this wouldn't go over well. New coaches and a new captain—that's a lot of change for these guys all at once. Guess I—we—have our work cut out for us.

Gabe lifts his hands to quiet the grumbling. "There's no one else I'd want to have my back if I were playing."

"But you're not." Jayce's pointed stare bounces from Gabe to me. "And he hasn't played in over a year."

Several of the guys around him nod and murmur. Sophie is jotting notes down on a small notebook she must have had stashed in that oversized bag she's carrying. The rest of the guys are talking between themselves in a steady hum.

Already a bad start. And I'm not sure precisely what to do at the moment. Do I take a stand and say something to back Gabe up? Or do I keep silent and hope all the wrinkles in this tattered crew get ironed out over time?

Gabe turns and nods at Derek as I rise to my skates, but before I can say anything, Derek raises his voice over the din. "Head to the ice."

While the guys file out, I lag back to speak to Gabe, but Sophie approaches me first.

She frowns up at me. "You're a hockey player?"

I hold out the bottom of my practice jersey with the

blazing sun logo and crown that represents the team. "It appears I am."

"You didn't tell me that last night."

I grunt. "You didn't ask."

She glances back and forth as if to check who might be listening in on our conversation, then lowers her voice to a rough whisper. "Because you said you were one of the workmen."

"No, I didn't."

She crosses her arms and tilts her head. "You had a toolbox."

I give her my best noncommittal expression. "I never said it was mine." My sarcasm creeps in before she can reply. "You know, for a reporter, you don't seem to be able to keep your facts straight."

She lets out a soft gasp. "I'm a journalist."

I immediately regret my words—I really didn't intend to insult her, but there's something about her that seems to bring out my defense mechanism. Probably because she's already jotting down who knows what about us.

"Sorry. Journalist."

She drops her arms, blinking those big eyes as if she's suddenly unsure of herself. "You were fixing a locker door, so…"

She really doesn't want to let this go.

"So you made an assumption. I didn't think reporters—pardon me—journalists were supposed to do that."

What is wrong with me? Why does this woman bring out the snarky side I normally only share with my sister? But Kinsley's required to love me since we're family. If I keep this up, Sophie will use that pen of hers to slash and burn me. It's happened before.

Sophie straightens her back and lifts her chin, looking

unfairly cute yet provocative in a bristly way. "I won't make that mistake again."

She spins around, and speed walks out of the locker room. The oversized bag she's carrying swings behind her as if she's toting something heavy inside, which adds to my curiosity about her. Maybe she carries an arsenal of notebooks and pens in there for backup.

Gabe chuckles as he approaches. "Still wearing that barbed wire, I see."

I drag my attention away from the empty doorway. "She's a reporter."

"Journalist." He considers my words, then nods. "And we need her right now."

I turn and grab my gloves. "Wasn't it you who told me to watch my tongue around them?"

He smirks and puts his hands on his hips. "Yes, and that includes not insulting them."

I press my lips together. He's right. That wasn't my finest moment. "You're right. I'll apologize when I get a chance."

Gabe bumps his fist against my upper arm. "I appreciate that. You're the captain, so the guys are going to take their lead from you."

I want to counter with a negative comment. It's obvious Jayce and his buddies already have a problem with my presence. Somehow, I don't think they're going to accept directions from me anytime soon. But I'm here, and I made a commitment to Gabe. I'll do my best to show up like the man he expects me to be.

Even if it means talking to a very attractive journalist with a secret agenda.

Chapter Four

SOPHIE

To say I'm mad would be an understatement. Fuming is a better word. Actually, I quite like that word.

Fuming. *Fuuuuuming…*

I can hear it in my head, drawn out like that, which describes my current state of mind perfectly. I'm just not sure what ticks me off more—that Luke intentionally avoided telling me he was a hockey player or his comment about my journalism skills. The man clearly doesn't understand the difference between a reporter and a journalist. He's the one who should be fuming at the moment—over his ignorance.

With a satisfying *harumph*, I take a seat a few rows up to observe the team doing warm-ups and snap some pictures. After a few distant shots, I switch to a telephoto lens to get more close-ups of the guys as they stretch and practice shuffling pucks down the ice. Bet Mr. Sarcasm doesn't know that some journalists do their own photography. Not all of them, but I prefer to have creative control over the imagery that goes with my articles—kind of like an extension of my art—so I studied photography in college, too.

Since the guys are on the ice, I'm standing behind the wall in front of the players' bench so I can take some preliminary pictures without the plexiglass in the way. Gabe and Derek are with the players, giving the team drill instructions, so I have the space to myself.

I shift the camera to the other end of the rink and focus. A fuzzy image sharpens to reveal Luke's side profile, and since my traitorous heart has decided to wig out over the man's attractive looks, I have to hold my breath to get the shot, or else it will be blurry.

After a couple of clicks, I check the images, enlarging them on the small screen. They're mostly good. The one of Luke and two other players framed in motion as they pass the puck has a dynamic feel, and the colors are sharp. Once cropped, the picture will pop on newsprint and digital.

My imagination takes a detour to imagining Luke's face when he sets eyes on the spreads about the team. That'll prove to him I know what I'm doing. It'll blow his mind like that emoji with his brains blowing up.

Derek blows his whistle, signaling the end of warm-ups. After jotting down a few ideas for an intro article and head-lines in my notebook, I get more shots of the players doing scrimmages. I chose a special journal from my stash for this assignment last night and made a checklist of players with their numbers beside their names—something I used to do in college so I had a reference when it came time to write my articles.

I focus in closer on a player with his back to me near the glass below where I'm sitting. Number twenty-four. I know that one already. It's emblazoned on my brain from the locker room when Luke pretty much dressed me down.

Before I can shift the camera away, he turns and stares as if he's looking for something, then seems to zero in on me. His smirk flatlines into a grimace.

I lower my camera so fast I almost drop it. Shaking his head, Luke spins around and launches forward to intercept a pass. Marty said he wanted profile pieces on each player. I can already tell Luke will be the one I'll dread doing. If he'll even comply, seeing how he seems to dislike reporters.

Which I'm not.

Maybe I can get what I need from Gabe. Then I wouldn't have to engage with Luke at all. When I did a preliminary interview with Gabe this morning, he mentioned knowing Luke back when they were on the same team out in California. Writing about how he transitioned from playing to coaching hockey will make a great introduction to the Sun Kings because I can mention what necessitated the change in leadership without making it the sole focus. The team's had enough coverage in the way of criticism last season, and I'm not here to rehash the past.

Hopefully, all the interviews will go smoothly. I'm most wary of the flirtatious ones. Back in college, players often fixated on me being a woman, which made the interview challenging. I had to remind them I was a news journalist who happened to be female. Most got it. Some didn't. Those were usually the masochists I learned to avoid.

Thankfully, Luke doesn't strike me as one of those. Just untrusting. Something about that intrigues the journalist in me. Makes me want to dig deeper and find out what's underneath that bristly exterior he wears like his gear.

What is he protecting?

Derek blows his whistle again, signaling the guys to return to the locker room for the next phase of practice, which is strength building. I drop my journal into my bag and pack my lenses into their padded cases.

The new team owner went all out in revamping the facility to not only accommodate an ice rink but also add some NHL-level perks like an updated and enlarged workout room, a treatment room with several tables to assess and treat the players when they're injured or need physical therapy, and a smaller dressing room for the guys to keep their suits and regular clothes free of the usual locker room stench. There's even a lounge area with comfy couches and chairs, a large flat-screen TV, and a well-stocked fridge.

Now that the team and staff are moving about the facilities, I can take some shots of the different spaces in use instead of taking real estate type images. Way more interesting. I'm sure the fans will love seeing what happens behind the scenes. They eat that stuff up.

I hang back to follow some of the guys, figuring I'd have short convos with them and the trainers so they can get used to me being around. Ethan knows me, so I know his interview will be a breeze, considering I kind of already know what some of his answers will be. I may not have the years in this field like my father had, or Marty, for that matter, but I learned early on how to not only read the room but to read the person, too.

I calculated twenty players, plus the two coaches, three trainers, and one or two physical therapists, who, I found out, are being contracted locally. I'm especially excited about interviewing the owner of that facility, Hannah Lawless, because she not only started out in sports rehabilitation, but she also treats animals.

That right there will be a great example of highlighting the nuances of our little beach town, which is growing by the day. Fans will love a behind-the-scenes glimpse of what these guys deal with and the professionals that work to keep them safe and well.

Marty didn't specify which ones to interview, and knowing how it takes as many behind-the-scenes as on the ice to keep a team functioning in top form, I figured covering everyone involved would connect readers and fans more to who the Florida Sun Kings are and what they're about.

I stop to shift my bag to my other shoulder as Ethan passes by and winks at me, making me feel like less of an outsider. Luke seems to be lagging behind. Intentionally, too, I think, by the way he keeps glancing back at me. He clearly has something on his mind—those lips of his are still flatlined.

Did I mention he has sculpted lips? I took an art course in college for fun during my senior year as a way to feed my creativity. Turned out that studying the human form helped enhance my photography skills. But the class made me very aware of lips.

I know that sounds weird, but when you think about it, our lips are one of the most multifunctional parts of our bodies. We use them to speak, express emotion, consume food, drink liquids, and…kiss.

Luke's bottom lip dips down in the middle just above a small curve leading to his strong chin and jawline. His upper lip is almost as full, with a shallow divot beneath his nose. And then there's that hockey hair—his dark waves will reach his shoulders before the season ends, I'm sure. I wonder if he'll grow a beard, too, when the Stanley Cup finals start as a way to show his support.

I shut down the reel of distracting thoughts as he approaches. The last thing I need is for him to think I'm attracted to him. I mean, I am. I have a pulse. I am a woman. And Luke Jameson is a very attractive man, even if he leans toward the broody, grumpy side and never seems to smile.

Which brings me back to his lips... I wonder what they look like when he smiles. I bet they're great for kissing, too. But I'm not interested in finding that out.

Not. At. All.

In fact, the thought repulses me. Why would I want to kiss lips that have already insulted me? I'll remember that next time I'm drawn to his mouth.

But now he's heading toward me, and heat is rising from my neck to my cheeks. What are the chances that he'll think it's just warm in here? It's unlikely since we *are* in an ice rink. I could make up an excuse about forgetting my camera and flee back to the players' bench, then hide there until the coast is clear.

Or I could behave like a grown adult and stand my ground. I have nothing to prove to Mr. Sarcasm, right? Now, if I can stop staring at those gorgeous lips...

He stops in front of me, appearing as uncomfortable as I'm feeling right now. "Listen, about earlier...I want to apologize for being a jerk."

Hmm, that's unexpected, but I'm uncertain which 'earlier' he means. "Are we talking about last night when you intentionally neglected to tell me you're a hockey player or this morning when you insulted my journalism skills?"

His jaw tightens, making the muscle on one side pulse. "I meant this morning. I don't feel I need to apologize for last night. Unless I missed something? Did I somehow insult your need to know everyone's business?"

Wow. Did he actually just add another derogatory comment to his apology? "I don't *need to know* anyone's business, Mr. Jameson. Just their stories, which is what I've been assigned to tell."

He smirks and nods. "An assignment you're not too keen about, as I recall."

My cheeks feel like I spent too much time in the sun at the moment. Oh, how I wish life had an undo button. I have a bad habit of overheating when I'm nervous. "Had I known you were a *player*, I would have never said that."

"Which confirms my point. You made an assumption."

The man is borderline insufferable! No, I take that back. Not borderline. Just completely insufferable.

I pat my bag. "If you don't mind, I mean, if you're done insulting me, I have an assignment to do."

His voice stops me in my tracks. "About that."

I inhale a deep breath before turning around. "Yes?"

His expression softens some but shifts more to concern. "I'd appreciate it if you'd leave me out of your photos."

I hold my hands out to my sides. "I'm supposed to do profiles on you guys, which requires photos."

He nods. "Yes, I get that. But I'm asking you to at least blur me out. Or something."

I frown. "May I ask why?"

One side of his mouth quirks up. "Didn't you say you don't need to know my business?"

Now I'm the one clenching my jaw. I can't help but admire the way he threw my words back at me so deftly, but that doesn't mean I have to like it. "I won't make any promises."

Worry flashes in his eyes, and his shoulders lower, then lift as if he's about to argue.

"But...I will keep that in mind when I'm taking pictures at practices and games."

His lips tighten for a moment, then he nods and turns toward the hallway leading to the locker room.

I study Luke as he strides away. Some players look like waddling ducks when they leave the ice for the rubber-matted walkway, but not him. He moves just as confidently as he does in the rink. But that flicker of concern I saw in his eyes lingers with me as I head back to my temporary office.

Luke's hiding something. And this journalist can't resist digging a little deeper to find out what.

Chapter Five

LUKE

I chewed on this all night long and came to the conclusion in the wee hours of the morning.

Gabe needs to pick a new captain.

A week of drills and scrimmages has done nothing to make the guys accept me as captain. A few have—such as Ethan McKennen, who plays defense like me. But he's probably distracted by his upcoming wedding, which I somehow got invited to.

Two of the guys I crossed paths with during my time with the Barracudas. Wade Pierce, aka the Cowboy because he's from Texas and calls himself a 'puck wrangler.' I couldn't stop the eye roll on that one, but he's a lot of talk and mostly a marshmallow. And Mathéo Barbier, who's our center. Sometimes, they call him the Barbie Man because of his last name and his blond hair. He says he hates the nickname, but I'm convinced he secretly likes it. I share a mutual respect with these guys that comes with competition.

Then there are the ones who seem more aloof. Like Elias Brunner, but that could be because he's Swiss, and they're known for their neutrality—that's the running joke, anyway. And Payton... Payton Maxwell, the third, to be correct, which he is—very proper and polite.

But I suspect this guy has a wild side hidden somewhere. He must...to be a hockey player. Although he's only a year older than me, his British formality makes him appear closer to Gabe's age. I wonder if his reservedness has more to do with shyness. He rarely says anything unless we're on the ice.

When I approach the glass wall separating the coaches' office from the main locker room, Gabe and Derek are standing in front of a whiteboard with a rink diagram covered in red and blue marks.

I clear my throat as I walk in. Both cast looks over their shoulders before turning around as they cap their markers.

Gabe's welcoming grin encourages me to move forward with my plan. "How's it going, Luke?"

I close the door for privacy since several of the guys are changing to get ready for practice. Derek shoots a semi-concerned glance at Gabe, whose smile appears more like an attempt to stay positive than a reaction to seeing me. I'm guessing they expected this visit from me, so I'll get right to the point.

"I think you should pick a different captain."

Gabe leans on the edge of his desk thoughtfully. "What makes you say that?"

I let out a soft snort. Surely they've noticed how the guys behave around me. Maybe if they'd integrated me into the team first, gave me time to prove myself, and then made me captain, this would have worked. But as the saying goes, the cat's out of the bag, and there's no way to get it back in without getting scratched.

Derek keeps his stance by the whiteboard and crosses his

arms but says nothing. His expression remains unreadable, but I've noticed that's his MO most of the time.

"I think it's pretty obvious. Don't you?"

Gabe clasps his hands in front of him. "It's only the first week, Luke. You need to give it more time."

I run a hand over my mouth, realizing I didn't shave. As the Kelly Cup playoffs get closer, I'll quit shaving altogether, but in the interim, I prefer a smooth face. That just shows how distracted I was this morning with this decision.

"They trust Ethan. Make him captain."

Gabe shakes his head, but before he can say anything, Derek jumps in.

"Just keep playing the game. They'll catch on."

I grunt but try to contain my pessimism…somewhat. "You really think that'll do it?"

Judging by the way Derek retracts his head like a turtle, he's making an effort not to react.

I sigh. "Look, I'm not trying to weasel out of anything. I just think this isn't going to work."

More like, I'm not sure *I* can make this work. Right now, this gig feels like a dumpster fire on the verge of turning into a full-blown inferno.

"Our first game is in a few weeks. That's not much time."

Gabe nods. "I know, but I have confidence in you, Luke. As I recall, you filled in for your captain on the Barracudas for a few games when he was injured."

He's talking about himself. And yes, I filled in because we didn't have an alternate captain. "Yes, but that was different. The guys knew me. We had history."

Derek's expression turns incredulous. "Which is why I said to keep at it. Give the guys more time."

I shove my hands into the pockets of my trainers. "For how long?"

Gabe's voice is soft but firm. "For as long as it takes. You can do this, Luke. Derek and I discussed this for weeks before I approached you. In our minds, you're the best one suited for the role."

Weeks? Interesting...and both of them. I split my gaze between them, searching for any sign that they're not still on the same page, but all I see is a solid wall of agreement.

Maybe they're right that I need to give it more time. But the closer that first game comes, the more unsure I'm feeling.

Sure, I'll admit it felt kind of good to get back on the ice. Okay, it felt great. Something lying dormant came alive again. Kind of like those resurrection ferns covering a low branch on the oak tree in my backyard. My mother used to love seeing them spring back to life when the rainy season started.

"All right. Fine. Then give me some pointers here. Something that will help." I keep my eyes averted because I don't want them to see what I'm really grappling with. This isn't just about winning a bunch of guys over so they'll accept my leadership. I haven't played in almost two years. What if I've lost my edge and suck at the game? In a way, I have more to prove than the rookies. With them, there's an expected learning curve, but for me? I'm at the risk of ranking as a subpar player—a plug. That's not a good look.

And they won't follow a player they don't respect.

Derek looks at Gabe. His face splits with a grin, and his eyes have that confident sparkle that used to drive me nuts when I wound up playing opposite him in practices. "Just be yourself, man. You got this."

43

A knock comes from behind me. When I turn around, Sophie gives me a wary look, then shifts her attention to Gabe and Derek. She smiles at them, so I'm guessing she feels put out by my reluctance to go willingly into her lair of journalistic exploitation. Or she's still feeling salty about me not telling her I'm a hockey player.

But that's her reality. Not mine. So why does it still bother me?

"I hope I'm not interrupting." Even though she makes a statement, she lifts her brows in question.

Gabe rises to his feet. "We were just finishing up. What can we help you with?"

She steps inside, past the doorframe. "I wanted to thank you for the office you set up for me. It's perfect for doing the interviews."

He sits on the edge of his desk. "No problem. Let us know if you need anything else."

She appears thoughtful for a moment. "I'd like to start scheduling individual interviews with the guys, but I don't want to interfere with their schedules. What time would work best?"

Gabe and Derek glance at each other in silent communication and nod in agreement. Gabe swings his attention back to Sophie. "How about after practice when they're done cleaning up?"

"That'll work, but I would like to get some photos of them in uniform, sans sweat and stink, of course." She finishes her statement with a soft giggle that spikes my pulse.

I'm also captivated by how her eyes become more almond-shaped when she laughs, which she does a lot.

"Let's schedule a day before practice starts," Derek interjects.

Gabe nods in agreement.

Sophie does as well. "I can take those shots quickly."

I, however, am getting agitated at the idea. I'm not convinced she'll find a way to keep my face less visible. Like I told her, I have my reasons for that, and they have nothing to do with my reticence to be in the limelight.

Her broad smile firmly in place, Sophie does a little bounce and puts her hands together in gratitude. She's like a bubbly imp. "Thank you. I'll get with the guys to schedule the interviews."

Gabe gestures at me. "Start with Luke since he's our captain. I'd like to think his take on the team and where we're headed will help you with the rest."

I can read between the lines. I know what Gabe's doing—he's reinforcing my position as captain as much for my benefit as the team's. And I'm doing my best not to spiral down and walk out.

Sophie's smile slips when she meets my gaze. "Sure. Sounds good."

Her expression says she's thinking the same thing I am. The idea of my interview guiding her with the rest of the guys will be as helpful as a hurricane watering a flower garden.

For the first time, I'm in total agreement.

Stepping into Sophie's temporary office is disconcerting, to say the least. She's obviously given this project a lot of thought in creating a space that's inviting and comfortable, not only for her but for her interviewees.

Which I am now one of. I shift on the quilted gray

45

bench seat situated opposite a small window that lets in enough light to keep the place from feeling like a cave. A large planter filled with something leafy and green sits to my right. I reach out and touch a leaf, fully expecting it to be artificial, but the surface is soft and yielding.

On the wall behind me hangs a banner with the Sun Kings' blazing sun and crown logo. Not sure where she found that, but I'm kind of impressed to be honest. This feels way more professional than I expected.

To the left of the window sits a desk butted up against the wall. Sophie drags the chair out and spins it around to face me. Her hair is loose today and cascades over her shoulders like a waterfall of silk. Sunlight from the window reflects across her bangs as she sits down. My fingers twitch of their own accord with a desire to touch her hair, to find out if it feels as satiny as it looks.

She crosses her legs, bringing my attention to the hot pink toenail polish peeking out from her sandals. The first day Gabe introduced her to the team, she had on a top almost the same shade. And considering the rose pink accent pillow propped against the opposite side of the bench seat, I'm going to make a guess that pink is her favorite color.

A pang shoots through my chest as I stare at that pillow and realize the tufts of fabric are supposed to resemble roses. A wash of memories unfurl in my mind of the last rose bush I surprised my mother with for her birthday a week before the accident—her smile of pure delight at the color and scent of the blooms, how she stood by directing me where to dig the hole in her rose bed, and her warm embrace afterward to thank me for her beautiful gift.

After all this time, you'd think the pain of her loss would diminish more. In some ways, it has. I don't feel like I have a bone-sucking cave in my chest anymore. More like a dull ache that I've grown accustomed to and almost don't notice at times.

Almost…

"You okay, Luke?"

Sophie's voice snaps me back to the present.

I mentally shake myself and clear the knot of emotion from my throat. "Yeah, I'm good."

The slight tilt of her head suggests she's not convinced.

I rub my hands down the top of my thighs. The soft fabric of my trainers against my palms feels soothing. When she told us she wanted shots of us in our regular clothes as well as our gear to go with the profile pieces, I found myself intrigued. "So, how does this work?"

She opens the notebook she always carries with her. "I have a list of questions I've created so that the profiles will have a continuity and flow to them."

I nod, but my anticipation of what those questions will cover spikes my pulse like I'm back on the ice doing drills.

Then she stands up and sets the journal on her chair, open to the page she was studying, and grabs her phone off the desk. "I'll ask each question and use this to record your answers."

I point to her notebook. "You don't just jot down notes?"

She gives me a hesitant smile. "No, I need my hands for my camera. I prefer candid shots and find the best ones happen when my subjects are talking about themselves or about something they love."

The passion in her voice captivates me. And somehow being her 'subject' shoots an oddly warm sensation through my chest. Suddenly, this feels intimate and unexpected. I'm not a fan of surprises normally. Especially when I'm dealing with someone I don't know very well.

But Sophie has this way about her. She's like a free spirit, always embracing the world with a smile.

"Ready to start?"

I blink, realizing I was staring at her. And judging how she passes her camera back and forth in her hands, I may have made her uncomfortable. "Yeah, sorry. Just lost in thought."

Her mouth tilts up in this cute manner that pushes her cheeks up. "Feel free to share." Her eyes widen as she backpedals. "I mean, if it's something you think fans would want to know about you."

She jerks her camera in front of her face, leaving me to wonder if she did that more to cover her embarrassment than to snap photos of me.

I squelch the temptation to smirk and, instead, tuck my chin, determined not to give her any direct shots. Kinsley doesn't need any more drama in her life, and the press has a way of creating it. Not that what happens here in Florida would affect her in New York, but I don't want to take the risk. The more I wind up in the limelight, the more likely there will be ripple effects.

Sophie snaps a few pictures, then lowers her camera. "Let's start with the most basic question. Why hockey?"

I pinch the bridge of my nose as I formulate my answer. "I started playing street hockey as a kid, just in the neighborhood with friends. Guess it just grew from there. I played in high school, then college."

She leans over to check her notebook. "What about your family? Did they support you early on? Go to all of your games?"

My chest tightens, and a flash of heat rides up the back

of my neck. I rein in my reaction and take a breath. "My father hasn't been in the picture since I was eight, and yes, my mother would attend every game."

Every single one except the last...

She lifts her camera again. "Would you say she's your biggest fan, then?"

My gut twists. I turn my head away to keep my face shielded. "Can we talk about something else?"

"Sure." Her whisper snaps my attention back. The way she's blinking makes me realize how angry I sounded.

Inwardly groaning, I close my eyes and drop my head. "Sorry. I didn't intend to sound angry." I work more saliva into the desert of my mouth. "It's still hard to talk about her."

Sophie's eyes widen. "Oh, I'm so sorry. I forgot about the accident. I didn't get much time to research the team, so I've been trying to read up on all twenty of you. And the trainers and the staff. That's a lot of information to absorb in just a few days when you think about it, and easy to confuse which player did what or experienced..." She catches her breath. "Experienced tragedy...sorry."

The way her words tumble out in a rush, and the cute blush of her cheeks makes me want to reassure her I'm not angry, even though I am—just not at her. I'm mad at the world...and hockey. I guess blaming the world or the game is a break from blaming myself.

I rub my hand over my mouth, which sounds like sandpaper. I'm about to tell her it's okay, but then my phone chimes—the special ring tone I assigned to Kinsley so I know when it's her.

"Sorry. I need to take this." I reach for my phone in my pocket as I stand.

"Oh, sure. I'll wait." She blinks at me, still appearing somewhat unsettled.

Once I'm out of earshot, I answer my sister's call. "Hey, Kins, what's up?"

There's no answer at first, just a sniffle, which sends me into full fight mode.

"Kinsley, what's wrong?" Free hand on my hip, I start pacing back and forth.

A shaky inhale seeps over our connection. "Nothing really."

I stride to a somewhat secluded nook down the hallway. "Doesn't sound like nothing. What's wrong? Do you need me to come get you? I can leave—"

"No, just stop, Luke. I'm fine. I'm not hurt or bleeding or kidnapped, okay?" The tinge of sarcasm in her voice reassures me she's telling the truth.

I soften my tone, trying to emulate the way Mom used to handle Kinsley. "Then why are you upset?"

"I'm supposed to write a paper about someone who's had the biggest influence in my life, which you and I both know is Mom. It's just...writing about her brought up all these memories." A soft sob stops her words.

"I know." And I do. I just had a similar moment over a pink pillow. "It's okay, Kins. Write about it. About her. No better way to honor her memory."

"Just wish it didn't still hurt so much."

That knot of emotion returns to my throat, making my voice sound low and rough. "I know. Same here."

"Yeah?" She sounds genuinely surprised.

"Of course."

"You mean the Jammer has emotions?" My sarcastic kid sister is back in blazing glory.

She'll never let me live that one down. The only time I

let my temper get the best of me during a game earned me the nickname 'Jammer.' I roughed up a competing player after he elbowed a teammate in the jaw hard enough to knock him out. I got several taps on the ice and a new nickname that night.

I chuckle. "Shut up."

"Nope." She makes a loud popping sound of the 'p,' and she sounds less upset.

"You okay?"

Her reply is soft yet solid. "Yeah. I'm good now. Thanks, big bro."

"Anytime, little sis."

After ending the call, I head toward Sophie's office.

She's leaning against the doorway as if she's been waiting for me and blasts me with that smile again. "Ready to finish?"

After dealing with her questions about my mother and then Kinsley, I'm too raw. I stare down at my phone, acutely aware of her lingering weight in my chest. "Can we finish this another time?"

Sophie pushes away from the door and takes a few tentative steps toward me. "Would it help if I showed you my list of questions? I promise there aren't any more about parents. And I don't have to ask you anything about your family at all if you'd rather—"

I lift my hand to stop her adorable yet panicked rant. Again, I want to reassure her she's fine, that it's me who needs a minute to gather myself before I do something like react and show my anger. "Sure. Email me the list. I'll let you know when I'm available."

With that, I spin on my heel and walk away so I don't have to see her reaction.

Could I have done a better job telling her I needed

time? Most definitely. But I know when I'm pushed to my limit, and this is one of those times. The more I talk, the greater the risk of my anger showing. And that's something I can't let happen. Especially not with her, which doesn't make sense, considering we don't really know each other. Although she most likely thinks I'm a royal jerk by now.

Yet another thing in my life that I'll have to figure out how to fix.

Chapter Six

LUKE

Practice is nearly over, and, once again, Jayce takes the puck down the ice toward the goal like a dart headed for a bulls-eye. Except this isn't a pub filled with a bunch of half-drunk hockey players burning off steam with a friendly game of cricket. Our first game is in two days, and this team still functions more like an autonomous group of testosterone sticks.

I'm on the opposing team for this scrimmage. So is Ethan, who gives me a knowing look. I lift my chin in agreement. We attempt to close in on Jayce, but he's skating hard and gaining momentum. If hockey doesn't work out for the guy, he could easily train to be a speed skater for the Olympics.

On my other side, Elias is wide open and has a clear shot to the net.

Does Jayce make the pass? No, he does not. It's like he's completely oblivious to anyone on the ice but himself. The kid may have the potential to be a great hockey player—

hell, he's already one of our best players—but he's a lousy teammate.

Jayce pivots to the left, skating backward, then spins around and makes a slap shot, sending the puck into the air and over Wade's shoulder into the net.

Jayce pumps his fists as he skates an arc behind the goal, escalating my simmering anger into a bomb about to ignite. One, the kid totally stole my move, and two, he's still not getting the message about passing the puck to an open player for a sure shot.

When he reaches the other side of the net, I shove him against the glass, pinning him with my forearm.

His eyes go wide at first, then narrow as he spits out his mouth guard. "What the—?"

"Next time, make the pass."

"Why? I made the goal." His voice cracks.

When he squirms, I press harder against his chest protector. He's still a kid losing his baby fat, and I've got three inches and a good thirty pounds on him.

"You got lucky." Not entirely true but not a lie either.

He sneers. "You think I didn't see you and Ethan closing in?"

"You know what to expect because we're teammates. Ever heard of that word, Jayce? Teammates? We work together. And unless you've studied every player on every opposing team, you can't predict what they're going to do." With a last shove for emphasis, I let him go.

He glares at me while shifting his shoulders to get his pads back in place, then skates away.

Ethan glides over to me. "Think he'll get it?"

I shake my head. "Not before our first game."

He smacks my shoulder with his glove. "You'll convince him, Cap."

About half of the team has accepted my position now. Ethan, Wade, and Payton are starting to feel like friends, especially since we started a group text to discuss how the team's doing overall.

As Ethan skates away, I catch Gabe's wave from the players' bench. I come to a stop in front of him, unsure if he's going to tell me to back off or praise me for dealing with our wild card. "Guess you saw what went down?"

He lifts one shoulder in a half-shrug. "Just the tail end. I was on a call with Tampa's head coach."

Tampa Bay Lightning is NHL. If he's negotiating an affiliation… "Oh?"

Gabe gives me a pointed look. "I'm hopeful."

Part of me—the pre-accident part—is elated. The other part doesn't want to know. I wanted that once, to get moved up to the NHL. Now I'm not so sure. I'm still getting used to being on the ice again, and we haven't even played our first game yet.

Gabe taps his finger on the top of the boards. "Keep working on Jayce. He has potential."

"Lone candles burn out fast."

He smirks. "I kind of recall dealing with one of those back in our Barracuda days."

Of course, he would bring that up. "Yeah, you roughed me up a few times."

"You needed it. As does Jayce." He holds his hand up. "Not that I'm giving you permission to rough him up, but…" He pauses as his grin turns serious. "Great job, Luke. Keep it up."

I still don't get why Gabe thinks I can do this. Yeah, I handled Jayce today, but Ethan or Payton could have easily filled the role of captain. Maybe even better. Hell, even Wade could have reined the kid in with his wrangling skills.

Derek blows his whistle, bringing practice to a close. The guys skate toward the side boards to leave the ice. As captain, I feel the need to hang back and study each guy as he heads down the tunnel to watch for any issues like injuries...or attitudes.

Jayce glares at me as he passes, reminding me of some tough days I had early on with Gabe being the recipient of my unhappy mood. But he didn't give up on me. I didn't see it that way then—just thought he was out to make my life miserable.

However, unlike Gabe, I'm not a patient man. Somehow, I need to figure out how to deal with Jayce without losing my temper.

———

A light breeze greets me as I step outside to head home— my home. I've opted to stay with Gabe and Olivia only during the week and go home on weekends. That way, I can keep up with the house and make sure Mom's roses and orchids thrive.

Before I drive up to Clearwater, though, I agreed to join a few of the guys for a beer at a local place, the Turtle Tide, known for its hush puppies. Some seafood and relaxed conversation sounds just about right. Besides, some downtime would be good for me. And this will help me connect more with those still on the fence about me being captain.

My phone buzzes in my pocket as I'm about to get into my car. A text to our group:

PAYTON: Heads up. Sophie is joining us.

ETHAN: I knew you had a thing for her.

PAYTON: Not at all. She overheard and asked if she could come along.

I consider bowing out, but I know I'll get more flak than it's worth.

LUKE: So much for relaxing.

WADE: Why so negative, bro? She's nice.

LUKE: I used to think sharks were nice too.

ETHAN: What do sharks have to do with it?

LUKE: Never mind. Just don't forget she's a reporter, so watch your mouths.

There went my hope for a relaxing evening with friends. Now I'll have to be on guard all evening. Suddenly, a beer sounds like a bad idea, seeing as how alcohol can lower one's boundaries and loosen the tongue. On the ride over, I contemplate an array of excuses to get me out of tonight, even to the point of considering calling my sister to see if she needs to talk about something. Anything.

That would be a believable excuse—that my sister needed me. So it wouldn't be a complete lie. But I'm not a fan of half-lies either. I much prefer the truth. And this idea feels not only deceptive but manipulative as well.

I'll make an appearance and leave early. It's been a long week, and honestly, I'm borderline exhausted since my body is still adjusting to practices and workouts again.

When I step inside the restaurant, the aromas of fried seafood and spices bring my stomach to full alert. A constant hum of conversation fills the joint, and beach-themed decor and decorations add to the quaint and inviting ambiance. Ska music plays in the background, giving a lively vibe to the place.

No reason why I can't eat first and then leave. That will seem more natural, anyway. Not that I'm overly concerned with what the guys would think. Or Sophie, for that matter.

Although I'm a little curious to see what she's like in a social setting. Specifically, I'm curious to see if she whips out that pink notebook of hers to jot down notes. I bet her pen is pink, too. If I see that big bag of hers, I'll know for sure since she always has it with her.

I find my crew sitting in an oversized circular booth near the back of the restaurant. Sophie's already there, nestled between Payton and Mathéo. Her hair falls loose around her shoulders and frames her face in such a way that makes her eyes pop even more under those shiny bangs of hers. She must have gone home to change because I don't recall her wearing a floral top when I briefly saw her before practice started. I narrow my focus on the pattern.

Pink roses.

Something stirs in my gut. Not the usual pang of grief I associate with reminders of my mother, but something... warm...endearing.

Sophie lifts one hand in that waggle wave of hers and smiles. "Hi."

I nod in acknowledgment, but before I can say anything, our server appears at the open end of the table to take our drink orders. Most of the guys order a beer or iced tea. Sophie decides on a Pink Lady.

Of course, she does. The woman clearly has a thing for the color pink. Why wouldn't that apply to the color of the liquids she consumes? My curiosity about her obsession with the color brings up a myriad of questions in my head.

Like, does she have a pink couch? Pink pillows. Pink pajamas?

That last one leads to other imaginations which I shut down fast. I've allowed her room to scrutinize my career. No way am I giving her headspace.

But watching her take that first sip, how the pink of her lips almost matches the blush of her drink, is doing something crazy to my insides.

Wade elbows me in the ribs. "Earth to Luke."

I snap my head around to face him. "What?"

He gives me a subtle frown. "I asked if everything's okay."

"Why?"

He leans in so only I can hear him. "Because you looked pissed as hell."

"I'm good." I take a quick sip of the beer I didn't even notice was sitting in front of me. Until I get some food in my stomach, I'll pace myself. Luckily, the server just placed a large basket of hush puppies in the center of the table.

I nab one and pop the whole thing in my mouth. "Just hungry, bro. No worries."

Wade grins at me. "He's just hangry."

The entire group laughs at his joke. Heat rides up the back of my neck in a blaze that sets my nerves on edge. And when I skim my gaze to Sophie, our eyes lock for a moment. Her cheeks match her lips now. I didn't notice that before, so I'm guessing she's blushing.

But why?

Then, the pieces click. Wade said I looked pissed, and I was staring at Sophie when he nudged me. She must think I'm mad at her or something.

Or something…

For some reason, this stirs a deep need to know what she's thinking about me. And that worries me more than anything.

Chapter Seven

SOPHIE

I was ready to crawl under the table until Wade got Luke's attention. If he stared at me like that any longer, I'd have two holes drilled through me, thanks to that penetrating gaze of his. And that smirk on his face...I can't figure out how he winds up looking sexy even when he's frowning. Even when I'm not looking, I feel his eyes on me.

But I can't tell if he's disgusted with my profession or if there's something more going on behind that guarded facade. Either way, I'm steering clear. He's like a volcano simmering on the verge of eruption. And I witnessed his confrontation today during practice.

Granted, Jayce deserved it. He was acting like a hotshot out for his own glory. And there's a reason they call hockey a violent sport. The guys regularly rough each other up. It's an expected part of the game. I've witnessed enough to understand that aspect. But somehow, seeing Luke take matters into his own hands stirred something in me I'd rather not talk about. Or even consider.

He was just doing what a team captain needed to do.

And he used the language of the game. I get that. But just when I didn't think the man couldn't look more devastating, he goes and gets all machismo on the ice.

The effort to keep my focus on my drink is almost too much. I want to look up and see if Luke's staring at me again. I wish I knew what was going on under that mop of dark, wavy hair. I'm like a newbie on skates when he stares at me like that. Unsteady and fumbling.

Afraid to fall…

Is that what this is? Me falling for a hockey player? Oh, please, tell me I'm not turning into a puck bunny. I saw enough of those in college, and despite being in the trenches—aka, locker rooms—with the players on occasion, I prided myself on NOT being drawn to them. The smell alone was enough to nip that in the bud. Killed it, more likely.

Although, I'm not drawn to any of the other guys on this team either…just Luke.

And I'm not entirely sure why. I've felt physical attraction before, but this is different and on a much deeper level, which is terrifying, considering the man doesn't seem to want anything to do with me.

I take another sip of my drink, daring a glance up as I do, and nearly choke, not because of the alcohol but because Luke is *staring* at me again. He darts his eyes away, but not before recognition rides his gaze. He knows I saw him watching me.

What a funny game this is. Me studying him. Him watching me on the sly. Almost like dance partners trying to figure out each other's moves. But I'm certain there's something more there. I feel it in my heart.

Maybe knowing and understanding the trauma of losing a parent connects us on some deeper, unspoken level.

I mean, how could it not? Part of me wants to comfort him since he's obviously still struggling. I know what that feels like. My dad was like my best friend. His death would have destroyed me if not for Marty.

A nudge on my arm alerts me that Payton's need for the 'loo,' as he calls it, has everyone on our side of the booth sliding out. Before I can sit down again, another group of guys from the team heads in our direction.

Jayce is one of them. I bounce my gaze to Luke to see if he's noticed yet, but he's chatting with Wade and has his back to us.

I'm starting to put faces with their names without the help of their numbers, so I recognize Elias first. He's on the shorter side compared to the rest of the guys.

He stops next to me. *"Grüezi mitenand."*

I grin, recognizing his Swiss German greeting for 'hello, everybody.'

"Guten Abend."

His eyes widen. *"Spichts du Deutsch?"*

I laugh. *"Nur ein Bißen."*

"Only a little? Where did you learn?"

His accent is faint, but I remember it clearly from the year I spent traipsing around Europe after my father died. He'd always wanted to go, so I decided to fulfill that dream on my own. "I spent a year traveling all over Europe, but Zürich, Paris, and London were my favorites."

Payton stops next to us. "Did you say London?"

I nod.

"Well, isn't that a surprise? I do hope you had a chance to explore more of my fair country than just the big city." He makes air quotes with his fingers.

"I did, but I still loved the energy of London. So much to see and do."

Payton mocks a pained expression and holds a hand to his chest. "In other words, she rode the London Eye and now thinks she's seen it all."

I smack his arm in a playful manner. "Not true. Although, I did ride it once. I explored a fair bit of the countryside, too."

"Well, that's a relief." Payton chuckles, then slides back into the booth, clearing my line of sight to Luke, who's staring at me again.

No grimace this time, just open curiosity. An improvement, right? Then his eyes scan down the length of my dress. The appreciation I observe in his appraisal makes me happy that I opted for something more than the usual jeans and T-shirt I change into after work.

However, I really shouldn't care about Luke Jameson's opinion of me. That's what I keep telling myself. Hopefully, my heart will listen to my head for once.

Elias sits next to Payton, which puts him in front of my drink. He slides it across the table toward me. "I'm guessing this is yours. Sorry. Didn't mean to steal your seat."

I shake my head. "It's okay. I'll just sit at the end." But when I look down, there's no room left due to the simple fact that these guys are huge. I'm not short at almost five-eight, but these guys still tower over me. Add those broad shoulders, and it's like I have my own personal Wall of China. I wouldn't want to meet this crew in a dark alley.

Jayce's voice comes from behind me. "I've got you covered."

I turn around to find him placing a chair for me. Another one dangles from his other hand as if it weighs nothing. He sets it down next to mine and sits. We're now the two people occupying the open end of the large booth.

Won't that be fun for our server? And judging by Luke's

scowl, he's not happy about this either. Although, I'm not sure if his grumpy attitude is left over from his earlier encounter with Jayce or his mistrust of me. He still seems suspicious of my every move.

But there's no reason for me to let that ruin an enjoyable evening. This is my chance to become more familiar with some of the players and for them to get comfortable with me, which will make my interviews go much smoother.

And perhaps a more relaxed setting will give me a glimpse of what lies beneath Luke's icy exterior.

Roughly an hour later, the table is covered with empty fried seafood baskets and an array of half-drunk beer bottles and glasses. Jayce turned out to be a better conversationalist than I expected. He came across as almost vulnerable a couple of times when I asked some personal questions. I can already tell his interview will be one of the easier ones, but I suspect an insecure boy lies at the heart of his tough-guy persona. The one time I asked anything about his family, I got the impression he doesn't have the best relationship with his father. I resisted the temptation of telling him he's lucky his father is still around, but I held back, taking another sip of my drink.

I did NOT, however, miss how Luke kept darting his gaze our way despite appearing engaged in Wade's analytics of their performance at practice today. At one point, Luke used an empty seafood basket as a goal net, then positioned the salt and pepper shakers and the ketchup, mustard, and malt vinegar bottles to demonstrate a play. Wade tossed in a piece of batter as the puck and used his hand as a miniature goaltender, doing outrageous splits with his fingers to block it.

The biggest shocker though? Luke smiled a few times. Not at me, but at the other guys. I only got a side glimpse, though—enough to make me curious about what he would look like if he ever smiled at me.

Probably not going to happen. He pretty much avoided eye contact with me all evening. Thus why I talked to Jayce most of the time or to Elias on my other side, who would occasionally throw in a German word here and there with a wink.

I've lost count of how many orders of hush puppies this group consumed. There's one left in a basket near me, so I decide I'm going for it, seeing as I've only had one of those delicious fried balls of seasoned batter. A girl has to pace herself, you know?

Unfortunately, Luke has the same thought at the same time as I do, and our hands kind of smash together as if we're two awkward teenagers. The warmth of his fingers sends an interesting tingle through me that's also comforting in an odd way, like finally coming home after a long trip.

Our eyes lock for a moment before he retreats. "You take it."

"No, that's okay. You probably need the fuel more than I do." I let out a disparaging laugh, feeling more vulnerable now that Jayce isn't a barrier between us. He and Elias decided to play a game of darts near the bar, so I've lost my protective barriers. Not that I need protecting from Luke.

Or perhaps I do.

He's studying me again, but this time, his mouth lifts on one side. "Are you making an assumption, or were you watching me at practice?"

I think my face just caught on fire. And his voice sounds

almost…flirty? The slightly mischievous gleam in his eye makes me think he's flirting with me. Yet his reference to assumptions—again—sends prickles of heat all over me. I'm tempted to slapshot the hush puppy into his mouth and shut him up for good.

Instead, I nab the thing, break it in half, and hold a piece out to him. "Let's share it."

He grunts, then brushes my fingers with his when he takes it, making my pulse stutter. But he pauses for a fraction of a second, leaving me to wonder if he felt something, too.

"Sure. Thanks."

While he pops the entire piece into his mouth, I dip mine into the remoulade sauce and bite off a chunk. As I chew, I scramble for something to say, determined to see if I can engage him in some kind of conversation that requires more than yes or no answers. Or grunts.

"Not a sauce person?"

He studies me for a moment, then shakes his head but says nothing.

Okay, this may be harder than I think. I'll try a different tactic. "Beach or pool?"

He frowns. "What?"

I dip the remaining piece of my hush puppy in the sauce. "Which do you like better? Beach or pool?"

"Beach, I guess."

"How about…spring or fall?"

"Both."

"Why?" I finish my hush puppy, chewing as I wait for his answer.

He tilts his head. "Is this part of your interview process?"

I shrug. "Just conversation."

He gives me a curt nod as if he's willing to consider believing me, but I can tell he's still not sure. "I like fall because of the cooler weather…" his voice lowers, "and holidays. And spring because of flowers."

"Flowers? Any particular kind?"

His shoulders lift as he glances away.

Did my question annoy him?

But then his body settles as he studies the glass he's turning between his fingers. "Roses. Orchids. My mother had a knack for growing both."

Oh…not annoyance. The bottom of my determination falls out. "Sorry. I didn't realize—"

"No, you didn't." He runs a hand over his mouth. "I mean, it's okay. How could you know your question would wind up so personal?"

The soft look he gives me is as disarming as his question. "I didn't."

One side of his mouth lifts into a half smile. "Like I said."

His partial grin feels like a victory. I let out a short laugh. "Do you always have to be right?"

Luke pushes the tepid beer away. "I don't have to be, but I usually am."

He doesn't sound as if he's bragging. More like he's making a statement he wishes wasn't true.

I have no idea what to say next, which makes this moment feel very awkward, yet somehow…intimate, as if Luke creaked open a door kept hidden from the rest of the world. And I so much want to tug it open all the way and march in to see what's inside.

My hand shakes as I pull my credit card out of the small wallet purse sitting in my lap. "What a week, right? I don't know about you, but I'm beat. Sorry. That was silly.

Of course, you're tired. You've been practicing hard all week, getting ready for your first game. I should really get going."

For the record, I don't intend to sound like a babbling idiot. It just happens whenever I get nervous. And Luke seems to have a knack for unsettling me.

Amusement fills his gaze. That's a step up from disdain, right?

Card in hand, I swivel my head around in a desperate attempt to hide my discomfort and find our server, who seems to have vacated the premises.

Luke grasps my wrist and gently pushes my hand down. "Don't worry about it. I'll take care of it."

I can't help but frown at his unexpected offer, which makes this feel almost like a date. "Why?"

His brows lift in surprise. "Because you said you're tired and want to go?"

Or is he relieved I want to leave? Did I push the whole conversation thing too far? "I can take care of my own dinner, thank you."

He lets out a small sigh. "I'm just trying to be helpful."

Our server appears with her handheld reader and takes my card. Luke hands her his after she finishes with me.

I say my goodbyes to the rest of the guys and head toward the exit, ready for some peace and quiet to sort out the chaos in my head. Luke has a knack for muddling my brain, and I've had enough tonight.

As I reach the door, it swings open. My eyes track the large hand planted on the wood panel up a muscular forearm to the man standing behind me. Luke's clean, soapy scent mixed with a hint of something spicy fills my nose and whips the chaos in my head into high gear.

Yep. My brain is officially some kind of mousse at this

point. All fluffy with imaginations of what those arms would feel like, wrapped around me.

He lifts one brow as if to challenge me to refuse his help this time.

His gesture unexpectedly stirs the romantic in me—that's interesting, considering he seems to avoid me most of the time. He never replied to my email with the questions and suggested times so we could finish his interview.

And he could have stayed at the table until I left. Yet, he didn't. Very interesting indeed.

Instead of brushing off his chivalry, I smile up at him. "Thank you."

His expression shifts to one of surprise. Score one for Team Sophie.

"No problem." His voice is gruff but not unkind.

The night air washes over me with a hint of coolness typical for this time of year. We may not have much visual change of season in this part of Florida, but we do enjoy the subtle shift in the temperature and the break in humidity, especially in the evenings.

Luke walks beside me but remains silent as I approach my car.

I stop at my rear fender. "Are you walking me to my car?"

He points to the SUV sitting next to mine. "My ride."

My face heats, making me wish I hadn't parked right under the light. Which any sensible woman does for her safety, right?

Though muted, the deep rumble of chuckle reaches my ears, which I'm sure are the same shade of red as my cheeks by now. "Making those assumptions again, are we?"

A guttural growl rises in my throat with my words. "Goodbye."

I slide into my car as fast as I can with the intention of leaving without seeing or hearing Luke anymore, but his voice reaches me before I can shut my door.

The humor in his voice is unmistakable. "Night, Sophie."

I slam my door and grab my seatbelt, which locks up when I yank it, which I do two more times before forcing me to take a deep breath and calm down. Once buckled, I start my engine and glance out my side window to find Luke staring at me with his hands hanging over his steering wheel.

His window is down, so I get a full glimpse of his face as he watches me, and he's smiling. Not the lopsided one that resembles a smirk, but a full-on grin that reveals a single dimple in his right cheek.

I hit the gas and almost peel out on the gravel. Knowing I will spend the rest of my evening replaying every detail to my immortal embarrassment does little to calm my frustration. Somehow, I have to find a way to keep Luke from getting to me. Or else, this assignment will turn into a daily obstacle course of finding ways to avoid seeing him.

And hoping for another glimpse of that sexy dimple.

Chapter Eight

SOPHIE

I tap the thirty-second rewind arrow to listen to Luke's answers about why he chose hockey. I'm not so much listening to what he's saying as to how he says it. His words speed up at key points, revealing a hint of his passion for the game. Then it's as if something sneaks in and shuts him down. I jot down a reminder to do some research on his time with the Barracudas. Maybe that will help me figure out the enigma that is Luke Jameson.

The recording continues playing what's left of his curtailed interview. My pen pauses at the way his voice deepens and gets rougher. My chest aches, and my pulse spikes all at once. It's like his words sprouted vines that are tangling with my heart and tying knots in my chest. Maybe those vines have thorns because this is a weird mix of compassion and prickly attraction.

The memory of his smile and that dimple in his right cheek flashes in my head for the umpteenth time. I've tried to blow it off as a smirk. He was just being his usual arrogant self, insinuating that I make assumptions, which I do not. A natural conclusion is NOT an assumption. I looked it up, and Webster has two definitions for a conclusion and an assumption.

The man held the door open for me when I left and continued to walk beside me. How was I supposed to know that he parked next to me? And I *asked* him if he was walking me to my car. I didn't assume he was. That's why I asked, for crying out loud!

I growl to myself, then open my laptop to scan through the photos I have so far. Marty asked for an outline of my plan for the series so he could plan the spreads, but my eye is drawn to the images I took of Luke before his phone call interrupted the interview.

His face is turned away in most of them, reminding me of one of those angsty shots from a reality show. You know, the ones that are supposed to tug your heartstrings and capture your interest. But in this particular one, he's looking directly at the camera. His expression holds a mysterious feel—almost as if he's on the verge of saying something meaningful or, heaven forbid, a smile, which he doesn't seem to do a lot.

And his eyes…they're captivating…dark and piercing… a well of mystery in of themselves. And, of course, I search for a hint of that dimple to see if it's there all the time, which it's not.

That old expression about a picture speaking a thousand words comes to mind. I don't think I'd have much trouble writing a thousand words to define Luke Jameson. On the outside, he appears like a man of quiet strength, but upon closer look, there's something tumultuous brewing on the inside of his hot exterior.

Cue a cliche needle screeching across vinyl, bringing an end to my errant thoughts and imaginations involving one very attractive yet mysterious hockey player. A reality check moment, you could say, where the girl—that would be me—realizes she's way too interested in a guy who might not be into her.

But the way he kept watching me last night, then smiling with amusement as I left in a huff...what if it's more? What if he's attracted to me as well, but his entire issue with reporters—and journalists—is holding him back?

Oh, please tell me I'm not one of those women who's drawn to broody men. That's the last thing I need in my life. I could quickly fall down a rabbit hole here and get overly involved, figuring out why Luke is so distrusting of reporters. It's hard enough sharing his pain over losing a parent. Unlike Luke, I've had more time to recover and heal since losing Dad five years ago.

Like Luke's mother's death, my dad's was unexpected. A heart attack took him from this earth way too young, leaving me an adult orphan. All my friends still have at least one parent in their lives. I have none.

Despite his father being alive, Luke said he hasn't been in the picture since he was eight. So, in that sense, he and I are a lot alike. At least I have Marty. Even if he is my boss, he's always been in my life, like a favorite uncle—my funcle, as I call him. I never expected to wind up working for him, though. So far, it's worked out okay. Occasionally, he has to appear a little more strict with me, but I know that's his way of ensuring the other reporters and journalists realize he's not about favoritism. And I wouldn't want him to be.

That must be it—I'm drawn to Luke because I understand his loss in a very real and personal way. In college, one of my professors said my articles and photos revealed my compassion for my subject's pain and struggles, which would make me a great journalist one day.

All three of my previous boyfriends implied at some point that I was either too emotional or too sensitive. My first boyfriend in high school said I should join the drama club when he broke up with me. That was right after I told him he wasn't the inspiration behind the chivalrous and kind hero I'd written in a short story for English Lit. He threw a tantrum, slamming his locker, and stormed off. I did NOT miss the irony in that encounter.

The second one happened in college. He admitted he lacked the energy to deal with my constant perkiness. That it was him—not me. That should have clued me into his idiocy right there. Seeing him a few months later, dressed as a Goth, explained a lot. But in all honesty, he didn't like to get excited about anything. He broke up with me at an art gallery because I was so moved by a piece that I wept. I think he was more embarrassed than anything else.

That brings me to my last boyfriend, who implied I was too impassioned. Seriously? Just because I love going to the aquarium to watch the sea otters? I can't help it if their cute antics make me forget I'm an adult and act like a five-year-old. I mean, come on! How can you not squeal and laugh at those adorable furry creatures?

I realize I've stared at that picture of Luke for almost ten minutes while my brain took an analytical day trip. He asked if I could avoid capturing his full face, so I should probably delete it. But the image captures more than his appearance. His essence shines through the light reflected in his eyes, the way he's leaning forward as if he wants to have a conversation, and the potential promise of a smile tipping the corners of his mouth up just so.

There's a definitive mood to the picture as if it's alive. I can't really describe what it is, but I recognize that feeling in my gut when I've captured near perfection. And Luke Jameson is pretty darn perfect.

Bummer. This would make a fantastic introduction to the fans. I can't bring myself to delete it, so I'll just move it to another folder.

Before I can do that, though, Payton shows up in my doorway for our scheduled interview. I slam my laptop shut so he won't think I'm pining after his teammate, which I'm not.

At all.

I wave him in, then point to the bench seat. "Hey, Payton. Go ahead and sit down."

"There?" His brows lift to his hairline in that signature way I've come to recognize with him. He pushes on the surface of the bench.

I giggle behind my hand. "I promise it won't break."

He shoots me a grin, then positions himself in a series of awkward poses.

"Just relax. No need to pose." I suppress another giggle at his attempt to look like Rodin's *The Thinker*.

He chuckles yet sounds nervous. "Just a little sport there."

After starting the recording on my phone, I grab my camera and go over my process with Payton so he knows what to expect. He relaxes visibly and answers my questions with that smooth accent of his. I can tell this interview will go much easier than Luke's did. For one, he's more engaging, although he didn't seem to want to talk about his family in Britain. He would redirect and ask me a question, which I found fascinating. Another mystery to solve, perhaps?

I place my camera on my desk as we finish. "Great. I think I have everything I need. Did you have any questions?"

He gets to his feet but pauses in front of me like a shy first-grader. "Just one, if I may."

"Sure." I nod to encourage him to go on.

"Are you free for dinner tonight?"

Before I can answer, the sound of someone clearing his throat from behind me brings both mine and Payton's attention to the doorway.

Luke walks into the opening, his facial expression bordering on the dark side. At least I'm not the one on the receiving end of his impaling stare this time.

Payton bounces his gaze from Luke to me. "Right. Let's just forget I said that, and I'll be on my way."

He darts out the door so fast I think my bangs fluttered. I didn't realize a hockey player could move as fast off the ice as on. Look out, Flash. You have some serious competition.

I don my fiercest expression to give Luke an indicator of how I feel. "What was that?"

His terminator impression shifts to confusion as he walks into my office, making the limited space feel even smaller. "What was what?"

"I was in the middle of an interview—"

"Sounded as if you finished." He smirks, as if he thinks he has me cornered like a cat chasing after a mouse.

Well, this mouse just found her teeth. I cross my arms. "How long exactly were you standing there? In case you didn't notice, you're not a small man, which means your hulk filling the doorway is very noticeable. So that makes me wonder if you were listening in before you made your presence known?"

There. Take that, Mr. Cat.

His eyes sparkle with amusement as one side of his mouth quirks up. "So, you think I'm noticeable?"

I drop my arms, tempted to squeak for help. "Is that all you took away from that?"

He does a curt shrug. "All that matters."

I point to my door. "You can leave now."

"But I just got here."

"Okay, then, why *are* you here? Are you ready to finish your interview?"

For the first time since he made his presence known, his gaze wavers, dropping to his feet, then up to some spot over my shoulder.

I'll take that as a no. I'm tempted to turn around and see what he's looking at, but I have a feeling it's the photo I just hung this morning of my dad and me at my college graduation.

"Is that your father?" He gestures to the picture.

I keep my gaze forward. "Yes."

"He looks proud of you."

"He was."

"Was?" His brows pinch, and his eyes soften as they connect with mine, as if he's seeing me for the first time.

My patience appears to be limited today because I'm out of conversation points. "He died five years ago. Heart attack. Anything else you'd like to know?"

He tucks his hands in the pockets of his trainers and shakes his head. "No. Sorry to hear about your father. You must miss him."

His question almost sounds curious. I remember feeling like that after my father's death. Anytime I met someone who'd suffered a loss, I wanted to ask a million questions about how they dealt with their grief. Probably my way of looking for ways to process mine. Maybe Luke's doing the same thing.

My irritation slides into this desire to help him find some

answers, even if it means being vulnerable with him. I take a breath, then let out a harsh exhale. "Every. Single. Day. He was my best friend."

He nods before turning to leave.

I lurch forward a step. "Wait. You never said why you came."

Luke comes to a stop and pivots halfway around, giving me the full effect of very photogenic profile. "Doesn't matter."

Then he strides down the hall and turns the corner, leaving me a tad shell-shocked by our conversation. Or was it a confrontation?

What set him off more? The interview with Payton? With his clear distrust of the press, I'm almost positive he was snooping. Or did he overhear Payton asking me out?

But that would mean Luke was jealous, right?

Perhaps the bigger question I should consider is, why does that make my heart stutter?

Chapter Nine

LUKE

By the time I hit the locker room the next morning, most of the guys are geared up and heading down the tunnel to the ice. Payton, who's on the bench a few feet from my locker, finishes lacing up his skates. He glances at me but says nothing.

Which is good because I don't want to talk to him. Not yet, anyway. Not until I process this prickly feeling that's been stuck in my chest since yesterday. I suppose it could be jealousy, but that makes no sense. I'm trying to avoid Sophie Adams, not date her.

Payton saves me the trouble by leaving as I pull my shirt off and get my gear on. Practice will give my brain time to figure this out while my body works off some steam.

Coach has the guys gathered in front of the bench when I hit the ice. He pauses, giving me a pointed look, then continues his pre-practice pep talk. I make a tight arc and stop next to Ethan, who lifts a brow in question.

I reply with a curt head shake to shut him down—nothing up for discussion here. I'm late. That's it. No way

I'm going to tell him I overslept because thoughts of Sophie and her captivating eyes kept me tossing and turning until almost dawn.

We start with warm-ups and then move into flow drills. Once those are completed, Coach transitions us into competition drills. Near the end, my muscles feel like rubber, so I take a breather by the boards to shake my hands out and relieve the tension.

Payton comes to a stop next to me. "About yesterday."

"What about it?" One of the trainers passes me a water bottle. I gulp down a long slug while Payton flexes his neck, trying to figure out what he wants to say.

"Sorry if I crossed a line." He exhales as if he's relieved to finally get it off his chest.

I lower my bottle. "You didn't."

He raises his brows. "Are you sure?"

I nod.

His expression turns borderline cocky. "Then you won't mind me asking Sophie out."

I grunt. "I didn't say that."

He snorts. "Then you *do* have a thing for her."

"I didn't say that either," I growl.

"Maybe you didn't have to." He shoots me a wry grin.

Before he can skate off, I pin him with my fiercest look. "She's a reporter. Watch your back."

He tips his chin up as he says, "Journalist."

"Whatever."

He tilts his head. "Is this Luke speaking or our team captain?"

I sigh. "Both."

Still facing me, he pushes off the boards, gliding backward. "You know, sometime I'd love to hear why you have such an intense dislike for the press."

"Today is not that day, my friend." Or ever. I've tried to put that behind me—behind Kinsley and me—since what went down after my mother's accident. Just took a nosy reporter taking a deep dive into my family's history to reveal stuff about my father that I didn't even know about. Suddenly, our loss became more about him than the loss of our mother. He didn't deserve the attention, and Kins and I didn't need the scrutiny.

That's when my anger really started. Anger at my mother for not telling us the real reason he 'left.' Anger at the press for making a painful loss worse—thank goodness for the Barracuda's PR team and their hard work getting it shut down before it went viral. And anger at my father for bailing on our family. Although maybe that's a blessing in disguise.

Finding out the truth wrecked me, but explained a lot of things I couldn't understand as a kid. I know my mother was trying to protect us, and I'm glad that Kinsley has no memory of it. But it's a burden I never wanted to carry.

When I turn around, Sophie's staring at me through the glass like an angry fan on a rampage with that giant bag of hers slung over her arm. I don't know how much she overheard through the plexiglass, but I'm sure she heard Payton's last words since he raised his voice. But she already knows I have an aversion to the press, so maybe she heard me call her a reporter again.

I can't help but wonder if her timing was intentional, though. Did she leave her usual perch in the upper seats to eavesdrop?

"Guess that makes us even." I take another slug from my water bottle.

She frowns as she moves closer. "What are you talking about?"

"I heard your convo with Payton. And now you over-heard mine."

Her mouth slides into a smug grin. "So, in other words, you're admitting you eavesdropped yesterday?"

I clench my jaw. Touché, Sophie Adams, touché. Not that I intended to overhear their conversation. I just happened to walk up when Payton asked her out for dinner and interrupted before she could answer. That part might have been intentional.

She walks away while I stand there staring at her like the idiot that I am. Something about Sophie brings out my sarcasm more than I'd like.

Ethan makes a hockey stop next to me, spraying ice over my skates and nudging my shoulder. His chest rises and falls with his exertion. "Something going on there?"

Sweat trickles down the side of my face as I shake my head. "Not a thing."

He chuckles. "Yeah, not buying it."

I pin him with a look to back up my words. "No need to. It's the truth. There's nothing going on between us."

He shakes his head in disbelief. "Whatever you want to believe, man."

Ethan returns to the scrimmage while I take a moment to stuff my anger back into the metaphorical locker I created in my mind.

Some things just aren't worth revisiting.

After practice ended, Derek instructed me to go to the coaches' office right after I shower and clean up. He sounded terse, so I'm guessing something's up with Gabe.

When I get there, Sophie's sitting in one of the chairs

positioned in front of Coach's desk, and neither of them looks happy. I close the door behind me and approach the empty seat.

Did she run and tattle on me for calling her a reporter again? It wasn't intentional. In my mind, they're one and the same, so I don't understand the differentiation.

Coach gestures to the chair. "Have a seat, Luke."

I can already tell Gabe enjoys being in this position about as much as I do. His jaw is clenched, and there's a tightness around his eyes. Sophie seems to find her hands clasped in her lap very interesting. Guess she's not thrilled to be here either.

Gabe fiddles with a pen on his desk. "There appears to be some miscommunication going on. That's why I asked you both to come see me, so I could aid in facilitating this process."

I know Gabe well enough to read between his diplomatic lines. However, I don't know exactly what Sophie said.

He pins me with a gaze that means business. "Our team's reputation is sitting on a cliff, Luke, and we need your help."

I shift in my chair. "If you mean the interview, I did that."

Sophie keeps her chin tucked as she speaks. "You walked out before we could finish."

"I didn't walk out. I got an important phone call."

Gabe's expression softens somewhat. "Kinsley?"

I nod.

"She okay?"

I turn away and stare at the training manuals filling the bookcase to my left. "She was having a rough day."

"Kinsley's your sister, right?" Sophie's probing question brings my full attention back around to her.

"Yeah. She's been through a lot. Too much. Let's keep her out of this." My words sound harsher at the end than I intended. "I'm not trying to be difficult. Just looking out for her."

Sophie's smile holds a tenderness that matches her eyes. "Understood."

The tightness in my chest releases some at the genuine concern I see there. Perhaps I've gone about this all wrong. Instead of holding Sophie at arm's length, maybe I can trust her…a little.

Gabe sets his pen aside. "Now that we're on the same page, we can get this ball rolling so Ms. Adams can meet her deadlines. We're taking the bus up a day early for our game in Jacksonville. That should give you two ample time to finish your interview."

"I sleep on those long rides, Coach."

"I was planning to drive up later in the day."

Our words tumble over each other. Gabe splits his gaze between us as if he's watching a tennis match.

He focuses on Sophie first. "Ms. Adams—"

"Sophie, please."

"Sophie…you said you've had a hard time getting Luke scheduled to finish his interview. This seems like the perfect solution to that."

She fidgets in her chair again. "There was just something I needed to do tomorrow." She sends me a sidelong glance. "But I'm sure I can figure out a way to rearrange my schedule."

"Great." He turns to me. "Luke, the ride is eight hours. I think you'll have plenty of time to finish your interview and take a decent nap."

Sophie leans forward in her seat. "I emailed Luke the rest of my questions, so it shouldn't require more than half an hour...if he's prepared."

Sounds like a challenge to me. "I'll be ready."

Gabe studies us for a moment. "Good. That's all I wanted to discuss. See you both in the morning."

I stand at the same time Sophie does, but I reach the door before she does so I can open it for her. My mother taught me good manners, and I intend to exemplify the gentleman she raised me to be, no matter how uncomfortable the person makes me.

And Sophie Adams has a knack for making me itch on the inside.

"After you." Her eyes connect with mine, escalating that itch in my chest to a swarm of bees.

"Unnecessary, but thank you."

I slide my hands into my hoodie pockets, keeping my stride in pace with hers as we walk down the hall. Awkwardness walks between us like a third person.

"You could have talked to me before running to Gabe."

She stops and spins around to face me. "I didn't run to Gabe. You didn't reply to my first email about rescheduling, or the second one. I knew you and Gabe were friends, so I simply asked him for a few details about you. He put two and two together."

I run a hand over my mouth. "Sorry. I'm not great at following up with emails."

Her expression softens as she studies me. "Good to know. If I created tension between you and Gabe, I apologize. That wasn't my intention."

"Don't worry about it."

She opens her mouth as if to say something, then shakes her head and continues toward the exit.

Again, I open the door for her as we head outside. The temperature has dropped some with the onset of fall, but the lingering warmth of the day folds around us.

"Thanks." She slides a glance and a tight smile at me before rushing to her car.

I'm barely inside mine when she drives away a little too fast for a parking area, making me grin for the first time today.

Maybe, just maybe, I make her as twitchy as she does me.

Chapter Ten

SOPHIE

"Soph, this is important." Mia repositions herself on the big, overstuffed couch so she can face me. That's one serious pout she's wearing, too, which feeds the simmering irritation I'm holding against Luke. If he'd just finished his interview, this wouldn't be an issue. I could have gone with Mia to the flower shop in the morning and then driven up to join the team later in the day. Instead, I have to spend the day on a bus with a bunch of hockey players.

"I know, Mia. And you know I wouldn't miss it if I didn't have to. But I called Amanda at Bloomed to Be Wilde and told her what we have in mind for the flowers. She's putting together some ideas and sketches for you—that's almost as good as me being there, right?" I grab her hand and squeeze reassuringly. "Besides, I've seen her work. She's amazing! She'll have ideas and suggestions I haven't even considered."

Chin down, Mia nods. "Okay. But what if I'm not sure which ones to pick?"

"Just send me pictures, and I'll give you my vote."

She flops back on her couch. "Maybe Ethan and I should just elope."

"Don't you dare! That would break my heart. And I think Ethan's mother would put a hit out on you."

Mia's laugh is almost maniacal. "Probably." She turns her head on the cushion to look at me. "But you'll still be able to help me with all the other stuff, right? Ethan may be proficient with a hockey stick, but he's all thumbs with a glue stick."

I giggle at the mental image of Ethan gluing the tiny bows for the wedding favors to his fingers, then grab my notebook and slip out the multi-page calendar I filled out with the team's schedule to show her. All the games are in orange because that's one of the colors in the Sun Kings logo. Pink, of course, indicates anything personal. And since the wedding colors are lilac—Mia's favorite—and green, I used a sparkly lilac gel pen for everything wedding-related.

Mia leans in closer. "Whoa. It's like a work of art."

My turn to giggle. "Who says organizing can't be fun and creative? So, does that make you feel better?"

"I suppose." She draws her brows together in a deep frown and studies me.

I hate throwing a curve ball like this at her, but what choice do I have?

"Are you going to be okay on a bus with a bunch of noisy guys for eight hours? Two is usually your max when it comes to crowded, small spaces."

I fold the papers and insert them back into my notebook for safekeeping. That was the other reason I wanted to drive up by myself. I enjoy parties and social gatherings, but after the first hour, it starts to drain me. "I'll have my noise-canceling headphones with me if it gets to be too much. It'll be fine."

Hopefully, Luke Jameson won't throw any more complications into my process. He said he likes to sleep on the ride. If that's true of the other guys, I can take advantage of the quiet to work on the piece about the team captain since Luke's interview will be the first featured as far as the players go.

I've already written and submitted the introductory article about the Sun Kings and what they're projecting for the season and Coach Markelson's interview. Derek's will follow next, along with the rest of the trainers and managers intermingled with the players. And since we're running one piece a week, not including game coverage, I'll stay busy for a while.

So far, Marty loves the style of the photos I've taken and my plan for the structure of the series. With a few tweaks, of course. I may not have been thrilled about doing this assignment in the beginning, but now, my creative juices are going wild with all kinds of ideas. By the time I'm finished with this project, Marty will have plenty of proof that I'm more than capable of creating a captivating column about Sarabella.

Mia taps the cover of my journal. "You better not lose that. Maybe you should take pictures with your phone. Just in case."

I nod. "Great idea. I'll do that once I have it all filled out."

She sighs and stares at the ceiling. "What's it like?"

I stuff my notebook back into my bag. "What's what like?"

"Being around all those hockey players."

"Sweaty. Stinky. Noisy."

She snorts. "Come on. There have to be some perks. Like, what about all those muscles?"

"Did you miss the sweaty, stinky part? I don't go in the locker room, Mia."

"Not even to peek?"

I shake my head. "There's plenty to see on the ice."

Images of Luke gliding over the ice and doing those turns without missing a beat fill my thoughts yet again, along with those broad shoulders and graceful maneuvers. He moves like a panther, and he does this thing where he runs one hand through his wavy hair, combing it back before he puts his helmet on. I know it's to keep his hair from getting into his eyes, but I find the whole thing rather powerful...and very attractive.

Funny. I don't recall noticing anything like that with the other players...

"Earth to Sophie."

Mia's sing-song voice snaps me back to the present. "Yes?"

"Where did you just go?" She points at me, then makes a circle with her finger. "What's going on up in that head of yours? Because you kind of looked like Ethan did on our first two dates."

No way. She has to be mistaken. "What, agitated?"

She blurts out a laugh. "No, more like a love-sick puppy." Her laughter turns into a gasp as she grabs my hand. "You have a crush on one of them?"

"What? No. I do not. That's ridiculous. I just want to finish this assignment so I can move on to doing what I really want."

"But what if he's the one?"

I snicker. "Then I'll be one of those older women who carries a miniature chihuahua with her wherever she goes. And his name will be Sparky, and he'll wear—"

"A bright pink, gem-studded collar. Yes, yes, I remember." She grabs both my hands and holds them between hers. "But I want my best friend to have what I have."

"You and Ethan are not the norm."

"I don't know about that. But what I do know is there's someone out there for you. You just haven't found him yet."

I lift our tangled hands and kiss the back of one of hers. "I love you, but I've made peace with my future spinster status. I'll live vicariously through you. I'll be an eccentric aunt to your kiddos. How's that sound?"

She drops my hands and leans back against the cushions. "Sad and pathetic."

I sigh. "I'm fine, Mia. I gave it a shot. It's not for me. Let's just leave it at that, okay?"

"I still think you're crushing on a hockey player." She shoots me a mischievous smile.

I grab my bag. "Okay, I'm leaving. I have to pack and get ready for tomorrow."

She jumps up from the couch and points at me again. "See? You're avoiding the question."

I push her finger down. "I don't recall hearing a question, so how can I be avoiding it?"

Now I sound like Luke, reasoning my way out of being honest.

Can I not go an hour without thinking of that man?

"Looks good." Actually, it looks fantastic, but I stand behind Marty, looking over his shoulder as he shows me the first spread of the series on his computer screen. Coach Markelson has to be among the youngest coaches in the ECHL, but despite his youth, he appears confident and wise.

He beams one of his proud uncle grins at me. "Your photos came out great, Soph. You could have a career in that alone. If you wanted to, that is."

"Are you trying to tell me something, Marty?"

He waves me off and tugs his glasses down his nose as I take a seat on the other side of his desk. "No, not at all. Just thinking down the road when you decide to write that first book."

"Book? Who said I'm going to write a book?"

His lopsided smile warms my heart. He slips his glasses off, folds them thoughtfully, and places them on the calendar blotter on his desk. The man still prefers to keep a paper schedule in front of him at all times—a leftover from his early days as a news reporter.

"I seem to recall a young girl about to head off to college, talking about her dream of being a novelist."

"Yeah, then the reality of what it took to be an author settled in, and I didn't like the pay. Besides, I make a much better journalist."

"They're not exclusive, kiddo. I can picture you creating a photo book replete with philosophical ponderings to accompany your imagery."

Not a bad idea, actually. "I kind of like that idea."

"Good. Something for you to chew on down the road." He gestures to his screen. "This will run tomorrow. I'll need your piece covering the game the night of."

"No problem. I'll email it to you from my hotel room. That should give me plenty of time."

"Perfect. I'll make sure they hold the space for it." He steeples his fingers in front of him. "What about the piece about the captain? Luke…?"

"Jameson?"

He nods.

"I'm hoping to finish his interview on the bus ride up."

"I thought you were driving up on your own."

I groan. "That was the plan, but when I talked to Coach Markelson, hoping he could fill in the blanks for the rest of what I needed, he saw right through it. Sat us both down in his office and ordered us to get it done on the ride up."

His concern radiates in his frown and his tone. "Ordered?"

"More like strongly suggested."

"Ah, I see. Is Jameson still not warming up to the idea?"

I shake my head. "He has a serious mistrust of the press."

Marty sighs. "I don't blame him." He taps on his keyboard and brings the printer to life. "After you told me you were having some challenges there, I did some research into the articles about his mother's accident. One reporter dug up some dirt and did an exposé on his father."

"I found nothing like that when I poked around." I wiggle to the edge of my seat in anticipation of what Marty found.

He grins at me. "I have contacts."

"Of course you do." I snicker.

He reaches behind him and grabs the sheets printing out, then hands them to me. "A little homework for tonight. Maybe that will help you connect better with Luke."

I study his face as I take the printout from him. He knows something. Marty has never been one to tell me details flat out. He's like an old sage, giving me just enough direction to get started without telling me what I'm looking for.

"Thanks, Marty."

"My pleasure, kiddo."

I tuck the pages into my bag and stand. "I better get home so I can pack."

As I'm about to leave his office, he calls me back. "Soph?"

I stop in the doorway and turn halfway around. "Yeah?"

"I know this makes the introvert in you squirm a bit. I'm just a phone call away, okay?"

His words are like a hug. "Thanks, Marty."

That slanted smile of his sends me on my way. I know he has faith in me to do a good job on this. And I know I will, too, even if it is pushing me out of my comfort zone.

I stop by Charlene's desk on my way out.

She leans back in her chair as I approach. "How's life in the hockey world going?"

My trepidatious thoughts do a quick dance over being in a sardine can with a bunch of oversized fish and what I may discover in the article Marty handed me. As a journalist, I know how one rogue piece of information can change the picture of everything.

"It's…going." I bob my head affirmatively.

Her desk chair creaks in a foreboding manner as she leans on her desk. "That's…telling."

I giggle at her imitation of my answer. "Not exactly what I had in mind."

"I know, but you've got this, Soph. That spread you did on the coach was some of your best work yet."

Relief rushes over me like a wave at the beach on a hot day. "Thank you. I need this assignment to go well."

"I know that too." She leans closer, lowering her voice. "I overheard Marty on the phone with one of the execs, bragging about your piece."

"Really?" I glance toward his office. "He didn't mention that."

She shrugs. "He probably doesn't want to get your hopes up, even though we all know you're more than capable. It's all about the numbers in the end."

Deepening my voice, I don a dramatic tone. "The evil forces of greed, hell-bent on destruction and chaos."

This is a reference to a comment she made in an edit on one of my articles a couple of years ago about the county pulling funding to preserve sea turtles. But it did have a happy ending. Apparently, an anonymous donor picked up the slack. I wanted to dig deeper, but the gentleman in question asked me to keep it hush-hush when I figured it out.

She snorts at me. "Very funny."

"Just seemed appropriate."

Char squeezes my hand. "If there ever was a real-life superwoman, it would be you, Soph. Now go wield your mighty pen."

Chapter Eleven

LUKE

Funny how nerves can take on a mind of their own. I feel like I've handled my return to hockey fairly well for the most part. Practices have gone smoothly. Despite the initial aches and pains of getting back into shape, I'm almost performing at the same level I was before I left. Even filling the role of captain is becoming more...comfortable.

On that count, Derek was right. Time has shown the guys they can trust me. Well, almost all of them. Jayce and one of the other rookies still seem to have a bone to pick with me, but I never expected to get along with all of my teammates. All that matters is that we operate as a team.

But now it's getting real. We're boarding the bus that will take us to Jacksonville to play against the Icemen. I keep telling myself it's only a preseason game—simply a warmup for the season...like practice. The coaches have already seen me on the ice, and my performance during scrimmages has gone well—almost as if I never left the game.

Yet, I can't seem to bring myself to do the simple act of climbing those steps. I started to, then made the excuse that

I needed to use the restroom, which wasn't a lie. Splashing some cold water on my face helped.

But this is no scrimmage against my teammates. These games set the tone for the rest of the season and help our coaches strategize and make crucial roster decisions.

I don't want Gabe to regret his decision to bring me on the team. And as captain, I don't want to let the guys down either.

My phone sits on the counter like a ticking time bomb. Somehow, I have to pull myself together in five minutes to board that bus. I'm tempted to call Kinsley, but I know her. She's already worried about asking me for too much help as it is. If I share this with her, she'll quit school and give up on her dream. And I can't let her do that.

My hands shake as I dry my face with a wad of coarse paper towels. I practice the breathing technique I found online. Inhale for four, hold for seven, exhale for eight. Inhale...hold...exhale. And repeat.

Seems easy enough. My heart slows, and the pressure in my chest lifts. It's working. Now, if I can drag myself onto the bus and keep breathing...

I pocket my phone, intending to leave the restroom, but the restroom door flies open, and Jayce walks in appearing as anxious as I just felt.

He swallows, then bypasses me to one of the stalls and slams the door shut. Next thing I hear is retching.

For a brief moment, I consider leaving to give him some privacy. But something in my gut says I should stay. I wait for Jayce to emerge, which he finally does, looking less green.

He doesn't meet my gaze. Just heads to the sink to rinse his mouth and splash water on his face.

"You okay, man?"

He lifts his eyes and looks at my reflection in the mirror. "Yeah, I'm great."

I allow a tight grin in reaction to his sarcasm. "You'll be fine. The first game is always the hardest."

Mostly true. I'll spare him the rest, as I don't think he needs more pressure than he's already feeling.

Indecision scatters across his expression as he dries his face with those course brown paper towels. "Did you puke before your first game?"

I nod. "And the next three. It gets easier."

He's thoughtful at first, but then his facial features relax. "Thanks."

"No problem." I pause, considering what I'm about to say. "If it happens again, come find me. I'll, uh, talk you through it." I hold the door open.

"Yeah, okay." He tucks his chin and rushes out.

I take a moment to consider the irony of the situation—me trying to pull myself together and then winding up giving Jayce a pep talk. Or is that hypocrisy? Because I'm feeling like a hypocrite at this point. If I can't get my act together, what message will I send to Jayce and the other rookies?

As I walk down the hallway, Sophie exits the women's room. Seeing her shifts something in me for the better. I can't describe it—I only know I need it desperately right now, as if she's some kind of lifeline for me.

The pull to her lengthens my strides until I catch up with her at the exit. I reach my arm out ahead of her to open the door, but my sudden movement startles her, and she jumps back.

"Sorry. I thought you heard me come up behind you."

She holds a hand over her chest. "It's okay. Guess I was just lost in my thoughts."

A breeze wafts through the open door, lifting her floral scent to my nose. I instinctively inhale and find the effect settling. Her presence seems to calm the raging battle in me despite seeming somewhat unsettled herself.

Is that because I startled her or because of something else? "Ready to tackle that interview?"

Her eyes widen for a second, which is impressive since I didn't think they could get any bigger than they already are. "Are you?"

I'm so distracted by the way the sunlight hits her irises, bringing out the nuances of rich browns and a touch of gold around her pupils, that I have to remind myself to speak. I clear my throat. "I read over your questions last night."

One brow lifts to match the tilt of her mouth on that side. "Color me surprised."

If pink is the color of her surprise, she's wearing a ton of it today. I didn't know there was such a thing as pink jeans, with tiny yellow flowers and green leaves dotted all over them. At first glance, her top appears white, but compared to the white doorframe, the fabric has a slight blush. Her slip-ons are dark pink canvas, and her small suitcase is hot pink—the kind that makes finding your bag at the airport a lot easier than the usual black, blue, or gray.

The only thing she's wearing, or rather carrying that's not pink, is that bag of hers. All brown leather except for the pink tassel. I'm guessing she added that herself.

And let's not forget the adorable pink blush rising up her cheeks as I study her.

I clear my throat. "Sorry. I've never met anyone who seems to love pink as much as you do."

She grins. "Guess I never lost my childhood crush on the color."

The bus horn sounds. Gabe waves at us from the door. My heart starts to race again, and my chest tightens. The back of my neck feels hot, and I feel sweat trickle down my back.

Sophie touches my arm. "Hey, are you okay?"

I snap my gaze to hers. If I tell her the truth, will she include that detail in her article about me? I can see the headline now...

Sun Kings Captain About to Sink Ship

"Yeah, I'm good. Just in a rush. We better get on the bus."

Once she clears the door, I measure my strides so she can board first. Part of me hopes Gabe forgot about the interview or that there are no more seats together, sparing me the need to conceal my anxiety over this game. I hope that's all this is and doesn't become a pattern. The other part of me wants to sit with her because of the relaxing effect she has on me, which is odd considering how much I dislike reporters.

But Sophie says she's a photojournalist. I'm still fuzzy on the difference.

She hands her suitcase to Derek, who loads it into the storage areas of the bus.

Gabe points to the seats behind the driver. "Saved those for you two."

Great. Guess I get to see how good of an actor I can be.

Sophie takes the window seat and sets her bag down by her feet. Grateful for the leg room, I take the one next to the aisle.

Neither of us says a word until the bus merges onto the interstate. My nerves are still on edge, but the warmth of Sophie's shoulder against my bicep has given me something to focus on.

She reaches into her bag. "I'm sure you're anxious to take your nap, so I'll get my notes, and we can start."

Not as anxious as I was, thanks to her. I nod, then glance across the aisle. Gabe grins and gives me two thumbs-up. He may be a friend, but right now, he's my coach, so I'll do my best to behave.

Sophie flips her notebook open to the page she showed me in her makeshift office. "Okay, we covered the first three or four questions…"

I point to the fifth one. "Start there."

She lifts those big browns of her to stare at me. "Are you trying to commandeer my interview?"

"Not at all. That's where we left off. Like I said, I read over your questions last night, so I'd be prepared as you suggested. And that's where we left off. Just being helpful."

"You like being helpful, don't you?" She tilts her head, waiting for my answer.

The intensity of her gaze makes it hard to breathe. I guess it could be from the anxiety I'm battling, but this feels different. "I suppose. Yeah. Sometimes, it seems necessary."

"I assumed you deemed these interviews *unnecessary*."

Is she teasing me? "Did you just admit to *assuming*?"

"Yes, I did. Care to comment?" She looks down at her notebook as she flips to a blank page, pen poised to write.

I try to suppress my smile as I shake my head. "Not at all."

"All right then. Let's get started.

She starts with my stats while playing with the Barracudas, then transitions to joining the Sun Kings. No questions about my mother's accident or leaving hockey to take care of my sister. It's strictly about the game, the team, and my expectations for the season. The more I talk, the more relaxed I feel, as if talking things out helps relieve whatever's causing me to feel anxious.

Thirty minutes later, she snaps shut her notebook, drops it into her bag, and plucks out another book.

"What's that?"

"A book. Ever read one?"

My chuckle comes naturally. "Yes, many, in fact. I just wasn't sure if it was something to do with your interview."

"Nope, we're all done. You can go to sleep now." She flips it open to her bookmark and starts reading.

Well, okay, then. Guess that's my cue to leave her alone. I hunker down in my seat, crossing my arms over my chest and my ankles in the aisle. And I may have intentionally nudged her arm as I did this—perhaps my way of settling the score between us.

And she may have pushed back, biting her bottom lip as she did and appearing more impish than my senses can take, so I close my eyes.

But it's the warmth of her arm against mine that sends me over the edge into a peaceful sleep.

The lurch of the bus stopping and the sounds of shuffling feet bring me to the first level of awareness. Next comes Coach's instructions about taking the evening to relax, curfew, and pregame practice in the morning.

Then, I notice a warm pressure against my left arm. I glance over to see Sophie's book lying open in her lap and her head snuggled against me. And she's still asleep.

I should shift so she knows we're here, but I can't stop studying how her dark lashes rest on her cheek and the way the sunlight streaming through the window makes her hair glossy all over like black silk.

The guys are ready to file off the bus, so I slide my ankles in and bend my knees, careful not to disturb her. Ethan stops next to me and places a hand on my shoulder.

I look up and raise my brows in question.

He points to Sophie and raises his.

Not entirely sure what he's asking, I gesture with my right hand to point out the obvious more so—she's asleep against me, and I'm trying not to wake her yet.

My movement stirs her, but instead of sitting up, she snuggles in more, rubbing her face against my sleeve. I try not to smile, but I think I'm failing.

Ethan snorts and keeps going. I bite down on my bottom lip to stop the laugh building in my gut. Not at her, per se, but more like delight in how adorable she looks.

And how nice she feels against me.

I may need to do those breathing exercises again.

Her eyelashes flutter just before she jerks away from me. "What…" She grabs her book before it tumbles to the floor of the bus. "Are we there yet?"

I slide upright in my seat, still taking in every bit of her as she tries to wake up and fighting my wandering thoughts. Is this what she looks like in the morning? And why does that question ignite a longing inside of me to see this every single day?

I stand up so she can get out of the aisle. "Just arrived."

She blinks up at me and points to my arm. "Sorry about that."

I track where she's pointing and find two black smudges on my sleeve. Mascara, I'm guessing.

"It's an old shirt." One of my favorites, too, but I secretly hope the stains don't wash out.

"That's good, I guess." Still sleepy, she stuffs her book into her bag and slings it over her shoulder. I continue to block the aisle so she can get out, ignoring Jayce's impatient sigh coming from behind us.

We spend the next few minutes grabbing our bags and duffels as they're unloaded from the bus while Gabe and Derek check us all in.

Once inside, the coaches reiterate their instructions and hand out our room key cards. Judging by the way Ethan and Payton stepped back from the group with their heads tipped toward each other and their voices at whisper level, they're definitely up to something.

They stare at me and grin.

Time to make a run for it. I head toward the elevators just as the doors close on several of my teammates and Sophie. She really did look like an imp standing among a bunch of giants. My impatience for the next elevator doubles. I have no intention of starting anything with her, but the idea of one of them hitting on her makes me see a red that has nothing to do with our jerseys.

Unfortunately, my distraction with Sophie leaves me wide open for Ethan and Payton's antics. They push in behind me, along with Wade and Elias.

Ethan holds his room key out to me. "Swap rooms with me."

I narrow my eyes as I study first him, then Payton, who's standing next to him with a suspicious grin on his face. "Why?"

"Because it's by the elevator. You want me well rested for tomorrow, right, Cap?"

I snort. "What about me? I need my rest, too."

Payton opens his mouth to say something, but Ethan cuts him off. "You slept on the bus most of the ride up. You didn't even move when we stopped for gas and snacks. Nothing wakes you once you're out."

I grunt, then hold out my key card. "Fine."

Payton leans in to see the room number on the envelope. "Added bonus. Now our rooms are next door."

Ethan rolls his eyes at him. "What are you, like eight? This isn't a sleepover, man."

Payton clutches his chest and sighs like a girl. "And here I thought you loved me."

I can't get out of this elevator fast enough. Those two resemble a pair of mischievous sea otters on the loose.

When we file off, I check the signs to see which direction to go. Turns out my newly assigned room is down a long hallway and nowhere near the elevators.

"Hey Ethan, you said—"

They've already disappeared down the opposite side. I shake my head and continue toward my room. As I reach my door, Sophie comes out from the one beside mine.

If we didn't have a game tomorrow, I'd teach Ethan and Payton a serious lesson tonight that may or may not involve a hockey stick.

Her expression shifts from surprise to irony. "Imagine meeting you here."

"That would be Ethan and Payton's doing."

She frowns in confusion.

I shake my head and hold my key card over the lock. "Never mind. Have a nice evening." I push open the door, fully intent on crashing for the evening. Right now, room service is about my speed. I may even give my sister a call and see how her week went.

"Aren't you going to dinner?" Sophie's perky voice turns me around in the doorway.

"Did I say I wasn't going to eat?" I'm trying my

damnedest not to smile because teasing her is becoming way too much fun.

She presses those gorgeous pink lips of hers together.

I wait in my doorway as she strides down the hallway with that large bag swinging on one side. Then she turns around and marches back.

"Why do you do that?"

"Do what?"

"Throw my words back at me."

I chuckle. "Didn't you just throw my words back at me? I told you to have a good evening first."

"You know what I mean. It's like every conversation has to be competition with you. Why?"

I hold my hands out. "I'm a hockey player?"

Her lips twitch. She's trying hard not to smile. And right now, I want nothing more than to see her face make that transformation so I can watch how her eyes sparkle with delight, how the corners of her delicate pink lips lift, and how her cheeks warm with a soft blush.

"Hey, I told you what I do for a living this time." I quirk a grin, waiting for my reward.

And there it is. That smile's fast becoming one of my favorite things. I wonder what it would look and feel like to make her laugh?

The twist in my gut is either warning me to back off or trying to tell me something I'm not ready to hear.

"There's a little place about a block from here that has the best pizza of your life. I highly recommend it." I push my door open more, intending to put my bag inside and scrap my plans for room service and a dumb movie. That is if she'll even want to go with me...

"Wait." She's staring at me again with those big browns.

"You must be hungry since you didn't get a snack when the bus stopped."

I'm a six-foot-three hockey player. I'm always hungry. And I think she's about to beat me to the punch. "I am."

"Pizza sounds great. Care to tag along?"

"Sure." I toss my bag inside the room and shut the door.

We head back toward the elevators in companionable silence, only glancing at each other as the bell chimes and the doors slide open. I make a casual gesture for her to enter first, keeping my gentlemanly stance in place. I even clasp my hands in front of me as we ride down to the bottom floor.

I may appear calm on the outside, but my insides are buzzing as if I just scored a goal.

Chapter Twelve

LUKE

I should have realized I wouldn't be the only one to think of this place. Their pizza is legendary in my book. But I'd hoped to have the chance to spend some one-on-one time with Sophie.

Why? That's a good question. One I'm not sure how to answer right now. Let's just say I'm drawn to her, especially after seeing her asleep against my arm, snuggling in closer when I moved. The rest of her interview questions were curious yet respectful. I thought for sure she would have probed further at times, but she didn't. So, yeah, maybe I'm rethinking my take on reporters—journalists.

As soon as we walk in, several of the guys whistle or call us over. Ethan gives me a bro hug, then orders Payton and Wade to move down a seat, leaving the two chairs at the end of the extended table for Sophie and me.

I glare at Ethan to make sure he gets the message to stop orchestrating things to put Sophie and me together. He shrugs as if he's totally innocent. I send the same warning to Payton, who pretends innocence as well. Wade must be in

109

on it, too, because he's trying his hardest not to look at me. They better use gloves with their phones later because I intend to burn them good in our group text.

Sophie slides into the chair at the end of the table, while I sit on the side next to Ethan.

My knees bump into hers when I sit down. "Sorry."

"It's okay." She scoots farther from me, presumably to create more space. But that puts her closer to Jayce, who, unfortunately, is sitting across from me.

Great. I get to stare at his mug for the evening instead of Sophie's beautiful face. Doesn't help that she's angled toward him now.

Perhaps for the best. Just because she happened to be there when I was about to have a meltdown doesn't mean she's attached to me.

The guys had already ordered several pies and enough salad to feed a herd of cows, as well as four large orders of spaghetti and meatballs so we could eat family-style. Plenty of carbs and veggies to load up on for tomorrow.

Sophie takes her first bite and hums in appreciation. She turns those eyes of hers my way. "You weren't kidding about the pizza."

"I never kid about pizza." I've already inhaled the one piece I'm allowing myself so I can work on the rest. Too much cheese makes me sluggish, and I need every bit of speed I have for tomorrow.

Jayce shrugs. "I've had better."

I choose to ignore his remark, recognizing it for what it is. Jayce makes everything to do with me a competition. Remembering that Sophie accused me of the same thing hits me square in the face. Guess my brain gets something to gnaw on as well.

Doesn't take long for a team of hockey players to inhale

our meal. As they finish, they trickle out, planning to return to the hotel or do some sightseeing. Ethan, Payton, and Wade stand up at the same time to leave.

"Where you guys headed?" I'm not ready to go back to my room, so I'm curious about what they're up to next.

Wade yawns, but I can tell it's fake. "Back to the hotel to get some rest. Big day tomorrow."

After a glance at Payton, Ethan pats me on the shoulder. "Same here, man. It's almost my bedtime anyway."

I check my watch. "It's barely six."

He shrugs. "I need time to unwind."

Payton's sly grin tells me he's in on whatever this is, too. I blast him with a glare worthy of my nickname. He opens his mouth to say something, but Ethan grabs him by the collar and drags him toward the door.

Sophie and I are the only ones left at a table that looks like a food Armageddon.

Once we pay our bills—she flat-out refused again when I tried to pay for hers—she rises from her chair and slings her bag over her shoulder. "The light's amazing this time of day. I think I'll go take some exterior photos of the arena to help with my article."

I beat her to the door again, earning me a smile that makes me forget my concerns. All I know is I'm not ready for our time together to end.

A light breeze welcomes us as we walk outside. The sun has lowered, softening its light in preparation for the impending sunset. A sudden sense of ease overcomes me as if time slowed to allow us space at this moment.

The stretch of sidewalk is clear, so I zip ahead of her and turn around, walking backward. "I can show you how to get there. I know the area."

An amused expression crosses her face. "What makes

you think I don't?" She pretends to be shocked. "You're not making an assumption, are you?"

I feel myself smiling, and I can't stop it. "Busted."

This time, her surprise is genuine. "You didn't..."

The soft tone in her voice stops me, and that itch I felt in my chest earlier floods back stronger than ever. "Didn't what?"

She shakes her head, brushes past me, and then calls over her shoulder. "Doesn't matter. Feel free to tag along."

By the time we reach the arena, the first glimmers of the sunset streak the sky, casting abstract shapes of blues, purples, and pinks across the glass panels of the building. Sophie's right. The lighting is perfect.

With a soft gasp, she stands in front of the arena like a kid on Christmas morning, floating her gaze from one side of the arena to the other.

"It's gorgeous." She pulls her camera out and shoves her bag against me without even looking at me. "Hold this."

Camera stuck to her face, she moves in a fluid motion I find intriguing. And as mesmerized as she appears to be with the color display dancing across the architecture, I'm equally captivated by her.

Oblivious to anything else going on around her, she snaps shot after shot, changing direction and angles like a pro. Her focus reminds me of how I feel during a break-away, intent on getting to the opposing team's net before they can steal the puck. In those moments, the noise of the crowd ceases to exist. It's just me, the puck, and the sound of my blades cutting through the ice.

Finally, she lowers her camera and does a sweeping scan

of the arena from one side to the other. More purple than pink streaks the darkening blue sky now.

She walks over to where I'm leaning against a light pole right as it flickers on, casting a warm glow over her. "I think that's enough. I can get more in the morning if I need it."

I sling her bag over my shoulder and take the camera from her. "Stand under the light."

"Why?" She makes a grab for it, but I lift my arm out of her reach.

"The light's amazing right now," I tease.

She lifts a brow, her expression sardonic, but does as I ask. "You're ridiculous sometimes, you know that?"

I frame her face in the camera viewer. The lighting isn't just good, it's perfect. The lamppost back-lights her hair, making her look like an angel.

Click. She shakes her head and rolls her eyes.

"Stop." She waves me off and turns away, showing me her profile. Her nose has a slight curve and tilts up above the swell of her lips.

Click. Click.

"Okay, that's enough, don't you think?" She puts her hands on her hips and faces me, eyes wide, which about does me in.

I'm a sucker for them every time. *Click. Click. Click.*

"I think you've filled my data card enough, thank you very much." She holds her hand out, wiggling her fingers for the camera.

"Sorry, not sorry?" I chuckle and hand it back to her. "How often do you get to be on the other side of the lens?"

"Never. And I prefer it that way."

"Huh. Sounds familiar, doesn't it?"

She takes her bag back and crouches down to pack the

camera in its special case. "I have no idea what you're talking about."

I squat down in front of her, which puts my head above hers and close enough to take in her sweet scent. Her ponytail slides over her shoulder, impeding what she's doing. I didn't plan to do it. Just made sense to move her hair out of the way. But my callused fingers linger on the soft, silky strands.

"What are you doing?" Her voice sounds hushed. Almost husky.

She lifts her face, studying me. Of their own volition, my eyes drop to her lips for a brief second. "Your hair was in the way. I was trying to be helpful."

And totally worth it.

Her gaze drops, yet seems to linger on my mouth. "You have chiseled lips."

That's unexpected.

"Chiseled?" I touch my fingers to my mouth as I stand.

She rises. "Yeah. You know, well defined. I took a couple of art classes in college to feed my creativity, but I found it super helpful for my photography. Lips kind of fascinate me."

"That's…interesting." I'd love nothing more than to press my *chiseled* lips to hers right now and find out if they're as soft as they look.

Even in the lamplight, I note the crimson color tinging her cheeks when she glances at me. "It's getting dark. We should go back to the hotel."

"Sure. No problem." I take her bag to carry it for her.

"Bags, too?"

"What?"

"You always open my door, and now you're carrying my bag."

I offer her a slight smile. "My mother made it a point to teach me good manners." Something I wish I could thank her for now that I've met Sophie. Mom would have loved her.

We share a taxi back to the hotel and then an elevator up to our floor. I hand over her bag when we reach our doors.

Her fingers brush my hand as she takes the straps. "Thanks."

Affected by her touch, my voice rasps out, "No problem."

She unlocks her door but pauses before going in. "Aren't you going into your room?"

I lean against the wall between our rooms. "I will once I know you're safely inside."

Her eye roll reminds me of Kinsley. She steps inside but peeks out. "See? All safe and sound."

Seeing her eyes framed like that sends my pulse into high speed and brings a smile to my face. "Good night, Sophie."

She lingers before shutting the door. Did I imagine we had a moment there?

Once inside my room, I fall back onto the bed. My phone buzzes in my pocket. I debate whether to look, but what if it's my sister?

I groan and roll my eyes as I read the text.

ETHAN: How was your date?

LUKE: Wasn't a date. She wanted to take some photos of the arena, so I helped her out.

MATTÉO: Is that what kids are calling it these days? Helping?

> LUKE: Shut your trap, Barbie Man. Nothing here to see.

MATTÉO: Ew, he gets even grumpier when you pin him down.

> LUKE: Since when is Mathéo part of this chat?

ETHAN: I added him.

PAYTON: We've been back for hours, and you just got back to your room.

> LUKE: It was barely an hour and how do you know I just got back?

ETHAN: We were sitting in the lobby. You walked right by us.

WADE: That's 'cuz he couldn't stop looking at Sophie.

MATTÉO: …

> LUKE: Enough with the matchmaker antics, or I'll make sure your dentist gets extra business.

PAYTON: You're right, Mathéo. He does get quite irritable.

ETHAN: That's just his nature.

> LUKE: Isn't it past your bedtime?

ETHAN: Headed there now.

WADE: Big day tomorrow!

PAYTON: Stop saying that! You're giving us a complex.

ETHAN: Relax, Pay. You're going to do great tomorrow. We all are. The Icemen will melt in the blaze of the Sun Kings!

MATTÉO: …

WADE: Nice segue!

LUKE: I think I may have puked a little.

PAYTON: I found it rather clever.

LUKE: Of course you would. Get some sleep.

ETHAN: Sure thing, Cap. 'Night.

PAYTON: Sweet dreams.

WADE: What happened to Mathéo?

LUKE: Probably asleep like you should be.

WADE: Fine. Good night.

MATTÉO: …

Chapter Thirteen

SOPHIE

Thirty minutes until show time. Gabe thought it would be a good idea if I took some pictures of the players before they head out to the ice. Derek ushered me in with the reassurance that the guys were presentable. Still, I entered with caution and eyes averted to be sure. And I held my breath, just in case.

Except for gloves and helmets, they're geared up and gathered around as the coaches give them some final instructions and a healthy dose of encouragement. Coach Gabe may be on the younger side as far as coaches go, but he has an age and wisdom about him that I've watched influence these guys for the better. They're looking more like a team than just a bunch of hockey players.

And I'm pretty sure Luke deserves some, if not most, of the credit. I've caught moments of him talking to the players during practices, watching through my photo lens. I couldn't always hear what he was saying, but I know how to read body language enough to understand the guys respond well to him. Even Jayce seems more open to his input of late.

Almost makes me reconsider my opinion of him.

I move to the other side of the locker room to take more shots of the players as they listen to the coaches' last words.

Coach Markelson takes a few steps forward until he's standing on the Icemen logo in the middle of the floor. "And remember—a team above all. Above all, a team, right?"

"Yes, Coach!" The guys agree in unison.

Luke's intense expression makes me pause when I snap a shot of him. He looks like he's ready to kick butts and take names, but the strain around his lips is the same as yesterday before he got on the bus. I could sense his anxiety then, and I suspect it's back.

First game jitters, maybe? I wanted to ask him about it after we finished his interview, but by then, he appeared more relaxed and settled, so I didn't want to poke the bear.

The players head toward the tunnel to start warm-ups on the ice.

I catch Luke near the end of the line. With his skates on, he towers over me. "You okay?"

"Are you asking for my benefit or yours?" He stops and stares down at me, mild suspicion sitting in his eyes.

If he wasn't wearing all that gear, I think I'd gut-punch him. I lower my voice to a harsh whisper. "Yours, of course. You look like you're about to murder anything that gets in your way."

The entire terrain of his face changes. I can only describe it as somewhere between surprise and curiosity, as if he's caught off guard by my concern.

One side of his mouth twitches, and his glare warms to something almost flirtatious. "Are you worried about me?"

"You're delusional." I shove his arm, which doesn't affect him at all. The man is a wall of muscle wound tight for the game. Now I kind of wish I'd caught him with his shirt off so I could see what's under his jersey.

The realization hits me that he's not saying anything. His eyes, on the other hand, are telling me an entire story. He's looking at me, but I don't think he's really seeing me, if you know what I mean. Could be pregame jitters, but this seems like more than that.

I tug the bottom of his jersey. "You've got this, Captain."

His gaze clears as he takes a deep breath. His exhale is shaky at first, then smooths out. "Thanks."

The appreciative smile he leaves me with sends an unexpected warmth through me. But before I can even consider what it means, a woman with blonde curls dressed in a staff uniform catches my eye. I don't recall seeing her at practices, but I heard they hired a new massage therapist for the team. No better time than the present to get the story.

I follow her into the treatment room where she sits down, watching the game on the provided screen. "Are you the new massage therapist?"

Her subtle frown reminds me she probably has no idea who I am.

"Sorry. I'm Sophie Adams. I'm the journalist assigned to the team for the season."

Her expression shifts to a smile. "No, I'm just filling in for Angela tonight since she's sick. I usually handle their physical therapy treatments. I'm Hannah, by the way. Hannah Lawless."

"Oh, I was hoping I'd get a chance to interview you as part of the series. You treat animals, too, right?"

Her curls bob around her face when she nods. "Yes, I do."

"Mind if I ask you some questions?"

"Not at all. I'm not going anywhere."

I drag a chair over to sit near her. "So, what animal would you compare to treating hockey players?"

She does a snort-slash-laugh combo. "I didn't see that question coming."

I shrug. "Just thought it would add a little humor to the interview."

"Nice. I like it." She rolls her lips in as she thinks. "Let's see. I would compare treating a hockey player to..." Her studious expression transforms into delight, "a turtle!"

Now it's my turn to laugh. "I'm guessing Nick inspired that one."

"How do you know Nick?" A mix of curiosity and suspicion tinges her tone.

I give her a sheepish look. "I did the article about the mysterious philanthropist who funded the Turtle Patrol program."

Hannah lets out a soft gasp. "Oh, I loved that article. Nick really appreciated you keeping his identity out of it."

"I totally understood. So, back to the turtle analogy, please. I can't wait to hear this one." I sit with my pen poised, ready to capture the meaning behind her intriguing comparison.

She giggles, then lifts a shoulder. "Yeah, they wear all that gear for protection, but underneath, they're as squishy as the rest of us."

"But with muscles." I laugh.

"I'm speaking metaphorically. They're tough on the ice, but in life, they're some of the sweetest guys I've ever met."

Of course, my thoughts flit to Luke. Anytime I've

managed to get past his protective walls, I've caught glimpses of a guy willing to make great sacrifices for those he loves, like leaving hockey to take care of his sister.

I hold up my camera. "Do you mind?"

"No, not at all." She pushes a rogue curl out of her face.

After taking a few shots of Hannah, I pull out my notebook again to jot down her answers as I question her about her return to Sarabella and starting her own practice. "When I get done with this assignment, I'd love to write a follow-up piece on you and Nick for a column I'm hoping to write for the paper. Would you be interested?"

She tugs a card holder out of her pocket and pulls out a card. "Sure. Give me a call when you're ready."

I slip her business card into my bag, then slip it over my shoulder with the intent to go out to the game. "Thank you. I really appreciate it."

Before Hannah can reply, she's on her feet, studying the screen as the ref extends a fisted hand out to his side to signal roughing.

I step closer to get a better look. One of the players is down on the ice, holding his knee. My heart thumps to my feet when I recognize the jersey number...twenty-four.

The ref and several teammates surround him until the team doctor comes on the scene with his team. Hannah and I continue to watch as they help him up and lead him off the ice.

Hannah turns to me. "Time to get to work."

I clutch my bag closer. "Mind if I stay? What goes on behind the scenes is just as important."

She pauses as if in thought. "I don't see why not. Just stay out of the way."

"Sure thing." I pick a spot in the back corner as the doctor and one of the trainers help Luke to a treatment table. His glance skims across the room but stops when he notices me. And I think he might have smiled. Or maybe that's wishful thinking on my part, and he's just grimacing because of his knee.

Hannah elevates the head of the table so Luke's sitting up while the doctor removes his sock and shin guard. "Could be a sprained MCL, but let's get some ice on it and give it a few minutes."

While Hannah retrieves an ice pack and lays it over Luke's knee, Payton waddles in next with a bloody cheek and perches on the second treatment table.

Luke frowns at him. "What did you do, Pay?"

Payton shrugs. "Got into a bit of a scrum with the idiot that roughed you up."

With a smirk, Luke fist-bumps him. "Thanks, man."

I move closer to stand near his head. "You okay?"

He stares at me for a good five seconds, then faces Hannah. "What do you think, Doc?"

She snorts. "Not a doc, and you'll live. Second period ends in three minutes. That should give you a good twenty to ice, and the doctor can reassess whether you can play the last one."

"Thanks." Luke gives her a tentative smile, then lays his head back.

Now that there's room, I creep away from my corner and stand at his side. "Okay if I stay?"

He grins, bringing that dimple of his out to play. Maybe he's happy to see me after all.

"That depends? Are you here as the press?" Luke raises a single brow with his question, but his tone turns soft... teasing.

I push my bag behind me. "As a friend."

"A friend, huh?"

Is he flirting with me, or did they give him something for the pain? And is it weird that I'm drawn to a simple dent in his face? I squelch the temptation to touch it. "What? I'm not here to interview you, so that seems the logical choice."

"So, we're friends now?" He lifts his head, his gaze challenging me to explain further while the guttural tone of his voice sends waves of heat through me. There's no mistaking the shift in the mood between us, like a static charge about to ignite. And the question in his eyes has nothing to do with friendship.

Maybe because we're in an unfamiliar place or because he seems vulnerable, I'm tempted to throw caution to the wind and explore his unspoken invitation. But what if I do, and it turns into another heartbreak?

I glance away. "Sure, why not?"

He grunts, then lays back down on the table. "Guess one can never have too many friends."

I manage a tight smile while I mentally kick myself for being a coward—more like my own personal civil war raging between my heart and my mind. My heart's clamoring that Luke isn't like the other goons I dated while my head says I probably dodged another disastrous romance bullet.

But I'm not sure which side I want to win.

I returned to my corner of the room while the medic finished cleaning up Payton's cheek—he didn't seem to mind when the doctor said he'd likely wind up with a scar marring his pretty face—and did another assessment of Luke's knee. Most of the team straggled in to check on Luke at the end of the second period, which seemed to surprise him that his fellow teammates wanted to make sure he was okay.

The moment felt significant like one of those times a journalist knows will be remembered as the start of something bigger—something stronger and unexpected. I stayed inconspicuous as I took some shots of the guys surrounding Luke, capturing their concern, smiles, and jovial reassurances that they would not let their captain down since he'd be sitting out the rest of the game—doctor's orders.

That and their win tonight by one point will make this article more than just a report on the events of a hockey game. And I suspect it will go a long way in overcoming the lingering controversy shrouding the team from last season.

My fingers are itching to get back to my hotel room and hammer out a first draft of the article formulating in my head—and my heart—about what I see and sense happening with this team. I may have started this assignment with reservations, but I'm getting sucked into this unfolding story I get to share with the rest of the fans out there.

I laugh to myself—guess that makes me a fan, too.

When I get back to my hotel room, I set up my laptop on the desk, connect my camera to upload the images, and start writing. I told Marty I'd finish and upload the piece tonight so it could run in tomorrow's edition.

Judging by the shouts and laughter coming from next door, the guys must be celebrating with Luke. I'm so tempted to knock and see what that looks like, but this article won't write itself.

Just as I'm hitting my rhythm and the words are flowing, a loud bang on the connecting door makes me jump in my seat. I shake my hands out and pick up where I left off, but another knock stops my progress.

A muffled voice comes through the adjoining door. "Open up, Sophie."

Sounds like Wade, but I'm not sure. I unlock my side and yank it open. "What?"

He does a pretend tip of a nonexistent cowboy hat. "Come join the celebration, pretty lady."

I do a scan of the situation. The guys must have come straight from the bus to Luke's room because they're still in their suits, though most have shed their jackets. I feel like I just opened the door on a GQ spread featuring hunky athletes at their finest, with their shirts unbuttoned at the top and their sleeves rolled up. If I inhale any more testosterone, I might pass out.

But I'll play along for now. Leaning against the doorway, I cross my arms. "I don't think there's room for one more."

I'm teasing, of course, but not by much. I've never seen a hotel room appear so inadequate and small. Six of them are sitting on the empty bed, two have claimed the armchair and footstool, another is in the desk chair, and the rest are either standing around in whatever space is left or out in the hall. All of them are holding either a beer or soda bottle.

Clearly, the party has started.

Luke's on the other bed with pillows behind him against the headboard and one under his injured leg. Ethan walks over with a bag of ice, which he places on the towel draped over Luke's knee.

When he notices me, I lift my chin as a gesture toward his leg. "How's the knee?"

Ethan answers for him. "He's fine. Just needs to rest it for a few days."

I pin him with a mild glare. "Thank you, Luke."

The rest of the guys let out hoots and groans at my comment.

Mathéo says something in French, and when we look at him for the translation, he shrugs. "Translated simply, she burned him."

That brings more laughter and ribbing around the room.

I bring my fingers to my mouth and reveal my one trick —I can whistle with the best of them. All of them stare at me with eyes as big as that puck they like to swat around. "Listen, guys, I have a deadline to meet. Enjoy your celebration, but leave my door out of it." I finish with a short laugh so they know there are no hard feelings.

The rest of my article flows easily, and I manage to complete the rough draft about the same time I hear the guys leaving Luke's room. I'm in need of a good stretch and a soda from down the hall, so I open the connecting door to check on Luke's ice situation.

Ethan and Payton are sitting on the bed opposite Luke, but the rest of the guys are already gone. Ethan dons a smirk. "I swear I was being quiet."

Payton's expression turns sheepish. "Did you make your deadline?"

"Almost." I shift my gaze to Luke. "I'm headed to the soda machine. Need anything?"

For some reason, this causes Ethan and Payton to glance at each other in silent communication. They jump up and express hurried goodbyes to Luke.

I wait until they leave. "What was that about?"

Luke smirks. "Just ignore them."

"No, seriously, what are they up to?" I take a step closer to his bed.

He rubs a hand over his mouth. "Nothing you need to know."

And here I thought we were making progress in the trust

department, especially after yesterday. He did let me fall asleep against his arm on the bus ride up. And the way he took my camera and took pictures of me felt like more than just two people hanging out.

Okay, maybe not. I lift my hands from my sides, then drop them. "Fine. Forget I asked. Do you need ice or a soda or something?"

He pins me with that penetrating stare of his again. "Ice would be appreciated." He lifts the bag of ice that's now melted off his leg and holds it out to me.

"No problem." I step into the bathroom to empty the bag in the sink, stopping to notice his toiletries arranged around the sink. His spicy sandalwood scent lingers in the air. Before I'm tempted to do something stupid like touch the strands of hair in his brush or sniff his towel hanging over the shower, I grab the ice bucket and head back to my room to grab my key.

When I return, Luke appears to have dozed off. I can only imagine how exhausted these guys are after a game. I leave the bucket holding the bag of ice on his nightstand.

Sleep has relaxed his features, giving him a peaceful appearance. I follow the line of his jaw to his chin and up to those beautiful lips of his. Then up the sweep of his nose to the smooth arch of his dark brows.

He's on top of the covers, so I tug the comforter off the neighboring bed and drape it over him. As I'm about to turn off the nightstand light, he reaches up and grabs my wrist. The warmth of his hand on my skin sends a thrill through me that's exciting and comforting all at once.

His eyes open a crack, and his voice sounds sleepy. "Thanks."

"No problem," I whisper.

His hold loosens, and his hand slides down to rest on his

stomach. I wait a moment to see if he says anything else, but his breathing continues to slow. I turn out the light and head back to my room.

But I can't bring myself to close the connecting doors and decide to leave them cracked in case Luke needs help during the night.

Once I complete a read-through and edit of the article for Marty, I drag the document and the accompanying images into the folder on the newspaper database.

Before I crawl into bed, I shoot Marty a text to let him know the article is ready for him so he can take a look and let me know if I need to tweak anything. About five minutes later, he replies.

> MARTY: Great job, kiddo! I think this is one of your best pieces.

> SOPHIE: Thanks. It was an epic game.

> MARTY: I knew you'd score on this piece (pun intended).

I let out a soft laugh and shoot back a barfing emoji, then turn out my light. However, my last thoughts are not of the spread in tomorrow's paper, featuring the Sun Kings and their first victory.

Instead, it's a sleepy pair of eyes and the lingering sensation of his touch that make me smile as I drift off to sleep.

Chapter Fourteen

LUKE

The doc cleared me for practice after a few more days of rest, and now I'm back on the ice, prepping for our next game. For the most part, the team is gelling well. As much as I might not want to admit it, Derek was right. Time definitely helped.

But Jayce is still a bit of a wild card. I haven't figured out how to get through to him about functioning as a team. The kid is in need of a little humility.

I skate over to the boards where Ethan's chugging water and snow him. Ice shoots almost to his waist—my best to date.

Ethan shakes his head. "Gee, thanks, Jammer."

I smirk. "I'm pretty sure I owed you one."

He gestures toward my leg. "How's the knee?"

"Good as new." Which was a relief. When I went down, my first concern landed on what the end of my hockey career would mean for Kinsley's college tuition. But then my thoughts drifted to the idea of not playing again, and that tightened the fist in my gut even tighter.

"And you and Sophie?"

I shake my head. "Give it a rest, man. We're not together." I gave her an opening, and she declared us friends.

But the mention of her draws my attention upward to where she's sitting with Ethan's fiancée, Mia, a few seats above the net. Sophie aims her camera at the second line, taking slapshots in rapid succession. Wade's getting his goalie workout times two today because the next team we play is known for their aggression and speed.

She lowers the camera and darts a glance my way that doesn't stick. I haven't seen her much since Jacksonville, and I'm beginning to think she's avoiding me now that my interview is finished. Probably for the best. Right now, I need my head completely in the game for what's ahead.

Ethan nudges my arm. "Did something happen between you two after we left your room?"

I swivel toward him so fast a muscle spasms in my neck. "What? No, of course not."

He holds his hands up in surrender. "Hey, I didn't mean it that way. Just seems like you two connected on the ride up. We figured you might have had a chance to *talk*."

I don't miss his emphasis on the talking part. "She was finishing her interview with me. That's it. So you and your cohorts can quit playing matchmaker."

Although I'll admit, I keep revisiting how she pulled the comforter from the other bed and kind of tucked me in before she left. And I may have been a little more awake than she thought. Can I help it if my curiosity got the better of me?

I almost wound up like the proverbial cat—killed by the compassion I glimpsed in her eyes. Then she left the connecting doors open, which I assume she did in case I needed help during the night. That right there made something in my chest tighten and grow warm all at once. Her thoughtfulness reminded me of how my mother would leave Kinsley's door cracked so the hallway night light would stream into her bedroom.

I'm finding Sophie's compassion even harder to resist than those eyes of hers. By the time I woke in the morning, the doors were closed. I thought about knocking but figured I'd see her on the bus, but she wound up sitting with Hannah.

"Nope, I fell asleep right after you guys left."

Ethan lifts his attention to where Mia sits. She smiles and waves at him, and he grins like a lovesick puppy. "Don't fight it, Jammer. Could wind up being the best thing that ever happened to you."

"It's not that. I just—never mind." I shake my head with my words and pull my gloves off to grab some water. How can I attempt to explain when I'm not sure about what I'm feeling toward Sophie? Every encounter with her tears down my self-protective measures. Up to this point, I've seen nothing in her articles that's concerning. I want to trust her, but that niggling doubt never completely goes away.

He puffs out a small chuckle. "See? You're fighting it."

I decide to get real with him—as real as I can without giving him the full sob story. "I have enough on my plate at the moment." Which is true. I have to stay focused. Distractions won't help, and there's a lot more than just the team succeeding riding on my shoulders.

As Derek blows his whistle to end practice and signal it's time to go to the workout room, Payton joins us. His gaze bounces between us, then settles on Ethan. "What did I miss? Did they...you know?"

I want to swat his lifted brow right off his face. "Will you two give it a rest?"

Ethan shakes his head at Payton. But I'm still not sure they believe me. "Time for workouts. Get moving."

We're shedding our gear in the locker room when I hear a familiar voice coming from the coaches' office. I tug on a dry shirt, ready to head in that direction.

Gabe's command stops me. "Everyone, get decent."

He scopes the locker room, then waves someone in—my sister, Kinsley. She hesitates at first, then walks past Gabe. She crosses her arms and lifts her chin as if to challenge me.

A cat-call whistle comes from the lockers to my left. "She's a—"

Without taking my eyes off my sister, I shoot my hand out and pin Jayce's head to the cabinet door above his cubby. Like I said, I've got three inches and a good thirty pounds on the kid. He isn't going anywhere until I let go.

"Kinsley, what are you doing here?"

Coach walks up behind her with a concerned expression and shrugs.

She drops her arms. "I'm quitting school."

I drop Jayce like the hot potato he is. "You're what?!"

Like the spoiled brat she's NOT, Kinsley puts her hands on her hips, tilts her head, and enunciates every syllable, making me feel more like a parent than her brother.

What has New York done to my sister?

"I said. I'm. Quitting. School."

First, I'm grateful that Gabe made sure the team was presentable before he brought my sister into the locker room. Second, Kinsley met Gabe during my Barracuda days and always liked him, so I'm glad he had first contact. He said we can use his office to talk, but I don't want interruptions. And I especially don't want Jayce anywhere near my kid sister.

The conference room is occupied at the moment, so the only place I can think to go is the end of the hallway near Sophie's office. I don't recall seeing her today, so maybe she's not there. Even if she is, I'm sure she'd give us a few minutes if she's not in the middle of an interview.

When I see that Sophie's not there, I bob my head toward the open door. "Let's go."

Her over-dramatic eye roll precedes her exaggerated clomp into the room—classics Kins.

I'm doing my best not to lose it with her—that's the last thing this situation needs, but when it comes to my sister, I'm not great at controlling my emotions either. The main reason I returned to hockey was so I could cover the rest of Kinsley's tuition. I can't let her give up on her dream this easily.

My mother told me once that I feel things deeply, yet lack a release valve, which results in an eventual angry blowout. I'm thinking she may have been right. I wish she were here now to help my sister because this feels way out of my skill set. What if I say the wrong thing and she digs her feet deeper into this decision?

I take in a deep, calming breath as I shut the door.

"Who's office is this?" She sits on the gray bench and tugs that pink pillow onto her lap—a good reminder for me to remember how my mother used to handle situations like this. I vaguely recall Kinsley having a similar moment at age ten when she joined a soccer league. She wanted to quit after the first week, but Mom talked her into giving it more time. Kinsley wound up playing all the way through high school.

I sit against the edge of the desk and cross my arms.

"Sophie Adams. She's the repor—journalist assigned to the team. Now, explain to me why you're here?"

She takes on a curious expression. "Assigned to the team?"

"Yeah, to do profiles on us. Answer my question, please."

"Is she covering the games too?"

"Yes." I drop my hands to my hips. "Cut the crap, Kins. What are you doing here?"

First, her chin trembles, then one fat tear slides down her cheek, only to be followed by several more in rapid succession.

My chest clenches about as hard as my jaw. It takes a lot to bring my sister to tears—like losing our mother. Something major must have happened at school to make her want to quit, and my brain resembles a drop-down menu, imagining a list of worst-case scenarios with very specific and succinct responses. In other words, no one messes with my sister and gets away with it.

I rein in my gut reaction and crouch down in front of her, putting my hands on her knees. "Hey, it's okay. Just tell me what happened."

She wipes her eyes and sniffles. "I don't think I'm good enough."

I yank my head back in disbelief. "What are you talking about? Of course, you are. You got a partial scholarship to Columbia. If that's not confirmation, then I don't know what is."

She shrugs and lifts her hands. "Then they made a mistake!"

I tuck my chin and take a breath, trying to keep my expression neutral. "Start at the beginning and tell me what happened."

The door opens, and Sophie walks in. Her eyes widen at the site of us. "Oh, sorry." She looks behind her as if to make sure she's in the right place. "I didn't know anyone was in here. Of course, how would I, since it's my office. Do other people use it when I'm not here?" She lets out a soft giggle and holds her hands out. "That's fine if they do. I was just curious. I mean, why not, right? It's totally understandable—"

Fighting a grin at how cute she looks, I rise, holding my hand up to stop her verbal vomit. "Sorry we invaded your space. We just needed a quiet place to talk."

She bounces those gorgeous brown eyes between Kins and me. "Is this your sister?"

I nod. "Kins, this is Sophie Adams, the journalist I told you about."

Sophie blinks at me and smiles. "How about I go grab a cup of coffee and come back later?"

Kinsley stands as well. "Wait. Maybe you can help."

"Oh?"

Totally caught off guard, I glance between them to gauge the situation. "Kins, I don't think she has time—"

"Why not ask me first and find out?" The slight upward twitch of her brows feels like a challenge.

My sister smirks at me. "She probably would know better than a jock."

I grunt.

Sophie lets out a soft giggle. "What is it you need help with?"

"One of my assignments. Write about someone who's had the most impact on your life."

"What are you studying?"

"Journalism."

"Journalism?" Sophie snorts first, then laughs before shooting a scathing look at me. "Really, now?"

I must seem like a walking, talking hypocrite at the moment, but part of the reason Kinsley decided to use her love of writing this way was to offset the damage that rag reporter did to us. My sister is a modern-day Joan of Arc and always has been. Give the girl a cause, and she runs with it until she either wins or falls flat on her face—hard. That's when I usually step in and pick up the pieces, which have been literal at times.

Let's just say I'm glad her weapon of choice is a keyboard and not a sword.

Kinsley swings her attention between us with a confused expression. "Am I missing something here?"

Realizing I've lost control of this conversation, I run a hand across the back of my neck, trying to figure out what to say or do next.

Sophie approaches my sister. "No, not at all. What's your question?"

I pause in mild shock. Sophie had a clean opportunity to expose me for being a hypocrite because my sister's studying journalism, yet she didn't.

Kinsley rummages in her backpack until she pulls out a paper and holds it out to Sophie. "He gave me a C minus, but I know this is some of my best work." She hedges her hand back, seeming hesitant to share after all. "I thought I was good enough, but now I'm not so sure."

Sophie extends her hand. "May I?"

I can't stop staring at her. Her voice is warm and compassionate toward Kins, as is her expression.

Kins hands over the paper this time. "You sure you don't mind?"

"Not at all. Happy to help." Sophie sits in the chair at

her desk and then scans the pages, flipping from one red-marked page to the next until she finishes the last one. "This is really good."

"My professor clearly didn't think so."

Sophie tilts her head. "His comments aren't saying that at all, Kinsley."

My heart warms at how she says my sister's name like a caring friend.

She rises from her chair and hands the paper back. "He's trying to push you to expand your thoughts and bring more emotion into your writing. That's one of the biggest challenges we have as writers—to tap into that emotional place so we can inspire, uplift, educate, or captivate the reader. Emotions are a big part of a piece like this."

Kinsley nods, but she still appears as if she's on the verge of tears. "I'm not sure I'm cut out for that."

Sophie shakes her head. "I disagree. I think you're more than capable. You're just afraid. I hope that's not too blunt." She casts a hesitant look my way as if to check and see if she's out of bounds.

I give her a curt nod, encouraging her to continue.

"Part of writing is accepting criticism. For some people, that's not too hard. For others, like you and me, it's more challenging because it feels like a knife to the heart at times."

Kinsley's eyes widen, and she bounces on her feet. "Yes! Exactly."

Sophie points to the paper. "And this is about your mother, who you tragically lost. Those are big emotions. It's understandable that you'd be afraid of them. Can you ask your professor if you can revise it or maybe explain your situation? He might let you submit something new...something a little less painful."

Kins nods vigorously. "He said I could talk to him about it."

Her face lit with excitement, Sophie holds her hands out. "See? He's trying to help you."

My sister tucks her chin and stares at the paper. "So… you think I'm good enough?" She lifts hopeful eyes to Sophie. "To be a journalist…"

"Definitely. And that's the point of a critique—to teach us what we did well and what we can improve upon. It's an ongoing process of growth and improvement." She shifts her focus to me. "Kind of like your brother learning to play hockey. He wasn't pro-worthy from the get-go, right?"

Kinsley smirks. "Not. At. All."

"Hey!" I growl and give her a light shove.

Sophie smiles at us. "Don't give up before you become good at what you love, Kinsley. You'll get there."

Kinsley does something I've rarely seen my kid sister do with anyone other than me or our mother. She rushes over and throws her arms around Sophie, thanking her. And I think Sophie's eyes are a tad glassy.

Once Kinsley let go, Sophie grabs a business card from her desk and hands it to her. "If you ever need input with a project or just want to talk about being a journalist, call me. I'm happy to help."

Kins beams at her. "I will. Thank you."

I'm still staring at Sophie when my sister jabs her elbow into my side.

I let out an *oof* and rub my side. "Right. Thanks."

Sophie gives me a pointed stare that promises a revisit to my sister studying journalism. And I'm actually looking forward to it. Because even when I'm not talking to Sophie, I'm thinking about her.

All the time.

Chapter Fifteen

LUKE

"I like her. She's really nice." Kinsley bites into her slice of pepperoni pizza with gusto. After talking to Sophie, I let Gabe know I was taking Kinsley back to our house in Clearwater for the weekend and would commute for practice and our game on Sunday. Maybe being back home will help her gain some perspective.

If I'd given up on hockey the first time I hit the proverbial boards, I wouldn't have lasted a week. Somehow, I need to convince Kinsley to stick with it and give this journalism thing a chance. I read her paper after we left Sophie's office, and she was right. My sister is a great writer, and I firmly believe she could impact the field for the better.

"Yeah, she is." I keep my eyes diverted to my own slice, hoping she'll move on to something else, like this new pizza joint that just opened nearby. We could have a long discussion about all the sports pictures on the walls. I'm pretty sure there's an autographed picture of Wayne Gretzky on the back wall—right next to a picture of Jason Sedakis as Ted Lasso, one of our favorite TV shows. The pizza's good too. Not quite as memorable as the joint in Jacksonville, but close.

Sophie loved the pizza there. Maybe she'd like this place too. Bet she'd love my mother's pink roses also...

That thought stops me in my thinking tracks. Time to switch rails, or whatever you call it, because that's a dangerous path to tread. After I checked out the first run of articles Sophie did on the team—especially the spread about Gabe—my determination not to trust her diminished.

She did a great job painting the team in a positive light and focusing on who we are and where we're headed—an underdog king of spin, overcoming the odds without dredging up the drama that went down last season.

I liked that a lot.

Kins studies me as she chews. "You like her."

I cough as I swallow. Did she crawl into my head and sift through my thoughts? Time for a diversion. "How did you get here, by the way?"

"Avoidance tactic. I'll allow it."

I chuckle. Spoken like a ref.

She wipes her hands. "Brandon was driving down for the long weekend, so I hitched a ride."

I'm not smiling anymore. This better be someone she knows and not some random stranger she rode a thousand-plus miles with. "Who's Brandon?"

"Just a friend from school. Relax. Besides, I'm not his type."

"Good to know." I may be happy about that, but I'm unconvinced she is. Could she have a crush on this Brandon dude? I may have to pay her a visit in New York in the very near future.

We eat in silence for a couple more minutes, but I'm certain there's more brewing in my sister's head.

She takes a sip of her soda, then sits back in her chair with half of her pizza sitting there, getting cold.

"Done already?"

She shrugs. "Just not super hungry."

I sigh. "Kins, Sophie's right, you know. We have a saying in hockey. 'Winners train. Losers complain.' And I know, for a fact, that my sister isn't a loser."

The smile I love seeing returns. "Not bad, Lukinator. You got game."

I almost blow soda out of my nose when I laugh, then shake my head. "There is no way in H E double hockey sticks that you're not good with words, Kins. You could write satire if you wanted to."

Her face lights up. "That's what I plan to do in my next life after I take over the world. Something to do in my downtime."

I grin, loving the ease between us. Reminds me of how things used to be. "We don't stand a chance."

After we finish eating, we head back to the house. Mom's roses are fading, and so are the orchids with the onset of fall. But the subtle shift of coolness in the air fills me with a contentment I haven't felt in a long time.

Kinsley stops by one of the bushes and inhales the scent of a lingering pink rose. "I missed these."

The pink pillow in Sophie's office comes to mind. As does her smile and the way she helped my sister. "I know. I miss her, too." Oddly, it's not my mother's face I picture as I say that. "Remember when Mom found that nursery an hour away that had a half-price sale on rose bushes that turned out to be in some guy's backyard?"

Kins appears genuinely surprised.

"What?"

Her expression warms. "I think that's the first time you've talked about her."

My turn for an epic eye roll. "I talk about her all the time."

She snorts. "No, you don't. You listen to me talk about her and grunt in agreement."

She's right. It's been too hard until now. I'm not sure what shifted, but now I want to talk about her. And remember.

I divert my gaze down the row of rose bushes displaying their last bursts of color, waiting for dormancy to prepare for a new season. Maybe that's where Kins and I are finally at—leaving the weariness of grief to step into a new season of life and living.

I unclench my jaw. "Guess I just needed time."

"Yeah…"

We climb the steps to the front door. Might as well say what I've been holding back and get it over with. "You're not quitting school."

She lets out a long sigh. "I know. Brandon's picking me up Sunday after your game."

"You had that planned all along, didn't you?"

The soft shadows on the porch dance across Kinsley's features as she turns around, and I'm struck by how much she resembles our mother.

Then she dons a satisfied smirk and shrugs. "Just in case."

I grin. "Brat."

I asked Sophie if my sister could sit with her during the game. That way, I know she's not getting into trouble or running into Jayce. I still haven't figured out how to reach that kid to help him understand the dynamics and importance of working as a team.

Most guys get this pretty quick. Usually, a few slams against the boards help reinforce Coach's instructions do the trick. But so far, nothing's getting through.

We head down the tunnel to the ice for the first line to be introduced by the announcer. Judging by the cheers and shouts, the place is over half full. I guess we have Sophie's profiles to thank for that. Mine is due to print next week, and I'm not dreading it as much as I was after seeing what she's done so far.

After the singing of the national anthem, we get into position for the puck drop. Things move fast after that—too fast for me to scope out where Kins and Sophie are sitting. When I take a turn on the bench, I search for them, but still can't locate them.

At the end of the first period, we're tied. Coach gathers us for some strategizing during intermission. First line starts again, and I score a goal within the first two minutes with an assist from Ethan. I feel like I could stay on the ice longer but rotate so I don't wear myself out. My blood is pumping hard, and I'm revved up to get back out there.

I don't know if my sister being here with Sophie is fueling me, but this is the best I've felt on the ice so far. More like things used to be before...

Nearing the end of the second period, I break away and fly toward our opponent's net. I've got their goalie in my sites as I estimate when to make a slapshot. I know the other team's defensemen are coming for me, but I also know Mathéo and Payton have my back.

I take the shot and score another goal as one of the other team's players and Mathéo go down in a tangle of legs and sticks. The ref blows his whistle, signaling the end of play.

But Mathéo isn't getting up. I immediately skate over to see what's going on. His grimace is my first indicator that he's hurt, so I track his arms to where he's holding his left ankle. Once we help him up, it's obvious he can't finish the period and needs medical attention.

The doc and his team lead him off the ice, leaving the rest of us to hope it's just a sprain. If we have a chance at the Kelly Cup, we'll need Barbie Man to help get us there. He's one of our best. But more importantly, we'd rather not see him struggle with a career-changing—or ending—injury.

We finish the period holding the score in our favor. I pat each player on the back as they leave the ice, giving them reassurance that Mathéo will be all right and so will we. Do I know this for sure? No, but I want to believe it with everything in me.

Just as I'm about to follow the last one in, a waving motion catches my attention. Kinsley and Sophie are standing by the plexiglass. I lift my hand to wave but then notice they're both wearing Sun King jerseys.

I skate over and smile at them. Kins nudges Sophie, then turns around. At first, Sophie hesitates, her cheeks a deep shade of pink. Kins points her thumbs over her shoulders while Sophie pulls her ponytail over her shoulder.

My name blazes across both shirts.

Sophie does a slow turn, giving me a hesitant smile. Our eyes lock, and something thrums between us.

She's wearing my name…

I've seen other guys' girlfriends and wives do this and figured one day it might be me too. Never in a million years did I expect it would be Sophie, considering we didn't exactly hit it off in the beginning.

Coach yells for me to get moving, so I wave and skate back to the tunnel. Kinsley said I like Sophie, and I do. But I suspect what I'm feeling for her goes beyond like. Could Sophie have caught feelings for me, too? Something's definitely sparking between us, but I'm still not sure if it's anything more than animosity and grudging attraction.

Knowing my sister as I do, I wouldn't be surprised if she manipulated Sophie into wearing my jersey. Just what I need —another matchmaker trying to make us a couple. Guess I'll have to apologize for my sister's antics as well.

Again, Coach walks us through some strategy ideas because the team we're playing is known for amping up their speed in the last period.

Coach pulls me aside. "Mathéo's not going to finish the game."

"Is he okay?"

He nods. "Probably just a sprain, but he can't skate. I'm replacing him with Jayce."

I huff out a humorless laugh. "Jayce? You sure about that?"

"He's one of our fastest. And we're going to need it. Keep an eye on him, okay?"

I want to argue, but we're due back on the ice. "Sure thing."

Once we're out there, Jayce is full of himself, but he manages to steal the puck during a breakaway, which is impressive. Then he shoots back down the ice so fast I'm worried the play will wind up offside.

I race to catch up with him and match my pace when he slows, waiting for Ethan to get out of the offensive zone. Good to see he's using his head.

Unfortunately, that margin of delay gives the other team time to go after him. Jayce barrels down like he's going to make a play, but he can't see what I do. They'll slam him into the boards before he gets a chance.

I'm about to look for Payton for backup when Jayce sends the puck my way.

Shock slices through me. He did it. He made the pass.

No time to think more about it. I take the puck down toward the net. About ten feet in front of the crease, I spin to my left and make the shot.

And score.

The fans go nuts, loving that I did a hat trick. I can't believe it myself, especially considering it happened with an assist from Jayce. We skate by the bench, fist-bumping our teammates, then leave the ice as the second line flows over the wall.

Jayce sits between Payton and me. I spit out my mouth guard. "Good pass, Jay-man."

He snickers, then shrugs. "I did it for the team."

Payton shoots me a slanted grin, marking the moment as a success.

Maybe I'm getting through to this kid after all.

Chapter Sixteen

SOPHIE

I hadn't planned to wait for the guys to come out after the game. Just like I hadn't planned to wear a Sun Kings jersey. But Kinsley had insisted both times. She's tough to resist. I don't think I've ever met someone with so much wit at such a young age. And sarcasm. The girl has it down to a science, and I find it incredibly amusing. I can already tell she will make an amazing journalist.

The first of the players walks out, freshly showered and back in his suit. His girlfriend rushes at him and throws herself into his arms. It's heartwarming...a real picture of what goes on after a game. I yank my camera out as fast as possible and take a couple of shots of them embracing, then walking down the hallway hand-in-hand.

I hadn't planned this either, but I've no doubt a glimpse of these guys dressed so voguish with their sweethearts will go a long way in connecting the fans to the players. A peek into the real side of the hockey persona that comes with the job. And then it hits me—it's kind of romantic, too.

That's a spin I can easily add. If the fans go nutty not

just over the sport but also the romance of it, what better way to transition my coverage of the team into a regular column?

I'm so giddy over the idea that I have to bite my lip to keep from squealing. More of the players file out, so I continue snapping shots of them either reuniting with a loved one or bro hugging each other in celebration of their win.

Finally, Luke walks out. His damp hair curls over the collar of his white button-down, and he's neatly shaven. I want the Sun Kings to make the playoffs so I can see what he looks like with a beard.

And that suit… I think my face just turned fifty shades of pink. The jacket emphasizes his broad shoulders, then narrows down to his waist. I've always loved a man in a suit. There's simply something about it…

"Great game, big bro. Loved the hat trick." Kinsley wraps her arms around him, her head barely reaching his shoulder.

The tenderness in Luke's expression as he kisses the top of her head about does me in at this point. I snap a few shots to capture the moment, grateful the camera acts as camouflage, hiding most of my raging blush.

Kinsley's grin is epic, making her eyes squint. Pure delight covers her face. The bond between these two is something to behold, and I can't help but feel a twinge of bittersweet that their mother isn't here to see it. I know family can come in all shapes and sizes—having Marty and Clara in my life is proof of that. But knowing what Luke and Kinsley have gone through and seeing their closeness now sends an ache through me. My mom died when I was so little, and my dad never remarried, so no siblings for me.

He lifts his head and does a full body scan of me. "Wearing my jersey, I see."

My breath catches at the flair of heat riding his gaze. He likes that I'm wearing his name,

When Kinsley insisted we match, I wasn't sure it was a good idea. I get what it can mean to these guys to see their girlfriends and wives in their jerseys. But I'm neither to Luke.

Yet there's no mistaking his reaction to me wearing it. With a nervous laugh, I shift my camera to one hand and pull out the bottom of the jersey with my other. "Kinsley's idea. She wanted to make sure you were well represented."

"Doesn't it suit her?" Kinsley's upturned face turns into pure mischief, and there's a subtle coo to her voice, telling me this girl is definitely up to something.

Luke grunts yet says nothing. But one side of his mouth lifts in a partial grin as his eyes rove over me again, sending a shiver through me. Reminds me of that warm feeling you experience when you leave the chill of air conditioning and walk outside on a hot summer day.

Kinsley lets go of Luke and reaches for my camera. "Stand by my brother so I can take a picture of the two of you together."

Together... Why does that bring something in my heart to life in a big way?

"Sure." I set my bag down and show Kinsley how to operate my camera.

I attempt to gauge Luke's reaction to his sister's request as I stand next to him, but his stoic expression tells me nothing.

Kinsley lowers the camera and frowns at us. "Try to look more natural."

Luke glances at me, then lands his gaze on his sister. "What do you mean by more natural?"

She shrugs. "I don't know. You both look so stiff. Maybe put your arm across her shoulders."

I suspect Kinsley has the wrong idea about Luke and me, but before I can say anything, Luke's hand slides onto my hip and tugs me against him, causing me to squeak like a timid mouse.

He must still be overheated from the game because the heat radiating from him envelopes me like a warm blanket on a chilly day. I don't think I've experienced anything like it before—an intense attraction intermingled with a sense of peace as if returning home after a long trip.

Kinsley totally gets into the role of photographer and snaps a stream of pictures, giving us instructions on how to pose. At one point, she instructs Luke to hug me, which he does. A kind of sideways hug that presses me against him. The deep rumble of his chuckle ripples through me in waves, making me hyper-aware of his spicy clean scent and the firmness of his chest. He's like a wall of muscle.

"How about you two turn and look into each other's eyes?" Kinsley bounces expectant eyes between us.

I step away from Luke and take the camera from her. As much as I'd like to think Luke is enjoying our close proximity, I know he'd do anything to make his sister happy. "I think we have enough pictures now."

While I'm crouched down, finishing packing my camera, Luke reaches down and takes the handles of the bag.

"Let me help you with that." He's leaning over me, his face close as I stare up at him.

The man seems to make helping people his mission in

life—something I'm finding as attractive as those sculpted lips, which are a mere breath away from mine, by the way.

"Okay. Thanks." My voice comes out breathy.

As I rise, he leans in closer. His lips brush my ear as he speaks, sending a wave of heightened anticipation through me.

"I wouldn't have minded another picture or two with you."

His words snatch every bit of oxygen out of my lungs. Before I react, let alone say anything, he stands next to Kinsley, whose smug expression compliments Luke's cocky grin.

His gaze challenges me as if he's asking what I'm waiting for. I resist the urge to close my eyes and relive that brief brush of his lips on my ear so I can brand it into my memory because I know my track record, and I don't want Kinsley to suffer more disappointment than she already has.

I inflate my lungs as full as possible so I don't faint or wobble as we leave the arena. Once outside, I take my bag from Luke. "Thanks."

"Anytime."

One simple word, yet the tone of his voice wraps around me like an invitation for more. And I so want to accept. Thankfully, my common sense overrides the silly romantic in me before I do something foolish.

A young man walks toward us, a friendly smile on his face as he approaches Kinsley. Her grin, however, tells me she sees him as more than just a friend. Her entire demeanor changes from a confident yet sarcastic young adult to a shy and somewhat awkward teenager. "Brandon's here."

Luke's easy expression shifts to a scowl as he studies first his sister, then Brandon. I may not have any siblings, but I recognize an overprotective brother when I see one.

Kinsley gestures to her friend. Or should I say boyfriend? "This is Brandon."

Luke reaches his large hand out to shake his hand as Kinsley introduces him.

"Good to meet you, sir." Brandon's voice holds exactly the right amount of respect and fear.

Luke grunts, then clears his throat. "Good to meet you, Brandon." He pronounces both syllables of his name succinctly with an underlying threat, which makes Brandon's eyes widen.

Voice dripping with sarcasm, Kinsley pats Luke's arm. "He's just being friendly."

Luke crosses his arms, but he's wearing his suit jacket, so it makes his biceps and chest appear larger. I'm pretty sure that was intentional.

He lifts his chin. "What's the plan?"

Brandon darts a panicked look at Kinsley. "Plan?"

Luke takes a menacing step closer. "Driving straight through or stopping for the night?"

"Straight through, sir. We plan to take shifts driving and sleeping. I have snacks and drinks in a cooler already, and our route mapped out. We should arrive back in New York by dinner time tomorrow," he rattles off like a soldier under the gun.

I'm kind of impressed by this guy. He's obviously a planner and seems trustworthy so far.

The muscle in Luke's jaw ticks as he considers Brandon's answer. "Good."

I give Kinsley a hug. "I guess this is goodbye. Call me if you need help with anything, okay?"

She smiles and nods.

Luke's eyes are like twin lasers as he stares at his sister. "I want a phone call at every stop."

"But we'll be driving all night."

"I don't care. Call," Luke growls.

She rolls her eyes. "And there's the Lukinator. Yes, I will call you at every stop and give a full report when we arrive."

Luke hugs his sister, then gives Brandon a menacing look that makes him trip.

I cover my mouth to hide my smile.

Kinsley gets about ten feet away when she turns and points at us. "You two should go out and celebrate."

Luke lowers his chin, looking rather fierce, and growls, "Call me."

His sister rolls her eyes again before spinning back around. Brandon has his hands in his pants pockets and keeps his distance as they stride across the parking lot. I think Luke accomplished putting the fear of annihilation in him if he does anything out of line.

We stand there, saying nothing as they drive away like two parents watching their kid leave for college or something. I find the feeling rather surreal.

"Hungry?"

The sudden break in the silence makes me jump. I tilt my face toward Luke, who's still staring out over the emptying parking lot. I think I saw a couple of fans pointing at him, but I'm guessing his fierce stance scared them off.

"I rode up on the bus."

He leans toward me, sending a rush of excitement through me at his nearness. "I'm driving back to Sarabella tonight. I can drive you back."

The wise thing to do here would be to go back with the team, but I'm not feeling much wisdom at the moment. I can't shake the sensation of Luke's mouth brushing my ear, which has me wondering what those chiseled lips of his would feel like on mine.

Going out to dinner with him could be asking for trouble. Not in a dangerous way. I feel safe with Luke. My heart, on the other hand, is cautious, of course. I know me. I'm not good at romance. So maybe I can figure out a way to keep this to friendship.

That's doable, right? "Sure, why not? I'll text Coach and let him know I'm heading back with you."

"Great." He takes my bag from my shoulder. "I'm parked over there."

When we reach his SUV, he puts his hand on the small of my back as he opens the door for me. I lift the hem of the jersey, intending to take it off so I don't look quite so casual next to Luke in his suit.

He pushes my hands down. "Maybe you should leave it on. It's getting cooler in the evenings."

The heart in his eyes reveals the real reason he wants me to leave it on. I remember full well how the hockey players in college loved seeing the puck bunnies wearing their names. But I only wore Luke's jersey to make Kinsley happy. Mostly.

I confess I did think of how Ethan reacted to Mia wearing his jersey. You'd have thought the guy had won the Stanley Cup. "But I'm underdressed next to that swaggy suit of yours."

"Not a problem." He slips his jacket off and tosses it onto the backseat without a care, then rolls up his sleeves despite the coolness of the evening air. "There."

I think Luke's sexy factor just doubled. "Now *you* might get cold."

"I live on the ice. I'll be fine." He stows my bag behind my seat as I get in, then closes my door and jogs around the car to the driver's side.

After he starts the engine, he twists to face me. "What kind of food are you in the mood for?"

I try not to stare at him like he's the sustenance for this hunger ripping through me that has nothing to do with my stomach. He's a beautiful man—sexy as all get out, strong... caring...always helpful. And I'm getting the feeling this dinner celebration is turning into something...more.

I blurt out the first thing that comes to me. "Pizza?"

His grin is slow...easy, making me feel all wobbly inside again. "Perfect."

He settles into his seat, shifting the car into drive.

Remembering a remark Kinsley made earlier makes me giggle.

He glances over at me. "What's so funny?"

"Lukinator?"

He grunts. "Long story."

———

"You still haven't explained your sister's nickname. Should I be worried for my safety?" I take a large bite of my pizza, savoring the gooey cheese and mushroom combination. Luke said this new place was almost as good as the one in Jacksonville, and I'm inclined to agree. Plus, I'm digging the sports bar vibe. Takes me back to my college days.

Luke indulged in four slices of pepperoni pizza—his way of celebrating his hat trick—before moving on to his large salad with chicken. He wipes his mouth. "When Kinsley hit her teens, she was hell on wheels. Mom needed some help with her." He sighs. "That's when the nickname started."

"She's quite the dynamo."

"You have no idea. And thank you, by the way."

I sit up straighter in my chair. "For what?"

"Helping her see she's a good writer." He stares at me while he chews, and I'm fascinated again with how his lips move.

I have to drag my eyes away because my thoughts are hopping down a bunny trail that's getting harder to resist exploring. "She wasn't going to quit. She just needed a little encouragement."

He grunts as he shifts in his seat. "Sounds familiar."

I jerk my head up at the vulnerability in his voice and lock eyes with him, wanting to ask him to expand on his comment. But I recognize this as a tenuous moment—one where silence is the better invitation for him to continue.

The focus of his gaze shifts to the brick wall behind the booth where we're sitting. "I didn't plan to return to hockey."

His confession pushes my question to a whisper. "Why did you then?"

His shoulders relax, and those delicious lips of his turn upward in a warm smile that reaches his eyes. "Kinsley. She deserves to go after her dream. And college isn't cheap."

"No, it isn't." Seeing the love swimming in his gaze while he speaks about his sister causes a knot of emotion in my throat. And a longing for someone to look like that when they talk about me makes breathing difficult.

Another bunny trail trying to run off with my thoughts? I fold my second slice in half and take a bite, then do a sweep of the pictures on the wall above us.

"Is that Wayne Gretzky?" I point to a picture of a hockey player in motion, bent over his stick and skating with the puck.

One side of Luke's mouth tips up as if he's pleased I knew who it was. "Yep."

"Good ole 99," I say with a swagger.

He raises his brows in a mix of surprise and humor. "I think I'm impressed."

I set down my pizza to take a drink of my soda. "I was a sports editor for my college newspaper. And we had a hockey team."

"Really?" Sarcasm drips from his voice.

My defensive nature rises with the challenge. "Yes, really. And I enjoyed it. Except for the smell. No one enjoys that."

He grunts again. "You'd be surprised."

But then his smile slides into something more serious. Exactly what? I'm not sure because his chin is tucked, shielding his expression from me. "But you weren't thrilled about being assigned to cover the Sun Kings."

That earlier knot of emotion settles back into my chest as I recall our first conversation in the locker room, and a need to explain overwhelms me. Not to justify myself but because I care very much about what he thinks of me. I don't know when that happened—maybe in Jacksonville when he commandeered my camera and took pictures of me.

I still haven't uploaded the images to my computer and looked at them. I'm tempted to just delete them, but I'm also curious to see what he captured. When I'm behind the camera, it's not just the imagery that guides me but the emotions the imagery evokes. I guess that's what makes me afraid to see what he saw.

As if preparing to give my confession, I wipe my hands and mouth. "You're right. I wasn't at first. It felt like a step backward and away from what I really wanted."

"Your own column?" His intense stare stops my inhale midway down to my lungs as if what I say next could either tip the scale in my favor or against.

"Yes. I have this vision of writing about romance in Sarabella."

His confused expression borders on a sneer. "A dating column?"

I shake my head. "No. More about the best places to plan a romantic dinner or take a sunset walk or propose marriage." I rush into more of an explanation as my cheeks heat. "The idea started while helping my best friend plan her wedding. But now I'm realizing there's so much more that this column can be."

He's not saying anything, so I stumble on.

"My original idea was to focus on romance *in* Sarabella. But now I see it more as Sarabella *is* the romance." I feel the passion and parameters of my idea expanding as I speak it out loud and lift my hands to gesticulate. "Sarabella may be a small, albeit growing, beach town, but there's so much more to it than just the gorgeous beaches and sunsets. There's a creative and entrepreneurial spirit that's erupting in quaint businesses, a growing movement in the arts, and now a hockey team that's adding to an emerging sense of community."

I stop to catch my breath, but the admiration in Luke's expression snatches it away again. His Adam's apple bobs with his effort to swallow before he tucks his chin. "We should get going before I'm too tired to drive us back."

Something in me sinks. Does he think my idea's ridiculous? I thought for sure he'd be pleased to hear how I consider the Sun Kings part of the romantic appeal in Sarabella. It certainly would go a long way in bringing up the team's reputation.

Or does he still lump me in with those reporters who dig up dirt on anything and everyone just to gain notoriety?

Unfortunately, I can't blame him. I finally had a chance to read the article Marty gave me, and it's not pretty. The reporter glossed over his mother's accident and revealed some very disparaging things about Luke's father. Arrested and sent to prison for drug dealing not long after he walked out on his family—I did the math.

The gossip rag that broke the story is known for inflammatory reporting and gets sued regularly. I'm guessing that explains the short life of the piece, but obviously not before the damage was done to Luke and his sister. I can only imagine how exposed that made Luke and Kinsley feel.

I want to ask him more about it, but I won't because he'll think I'm just digging for a story, which is as far from the truth as the sun is from the moon. I'd never include anything about it in my profile on him or the team.

But in light of his confession about returning to hockey, I can't help wondering about his decision to walk away from the sport he clearly loves and is extremely good at. Couldn't he have figured out a way to keep playing?

Maybe Kinsley needed him more than he's let on, but my instincts tell me his choice wasn't just about his sister.

Chapter Seventeen

LUKE

I intentionally kept our conversation light on the car ride back to Sarabella. Otherwise, I'm afraid I'd spill my guts to this woman who's taking up a lot of real estate in my head these days. Seeing her in my jersey decimated the last of my resistance. I didn't plan to catch feelings for her, but I did.

And I am. More so with each minute I spend with her.

Which scares me, because I'm not sure I could deal with losing someone close to me again. Every time I see Kinsley's name on my phone, fear spirals up from the pit of my stomach and deadlocks into my chest. I keep thinking this will improve with time, and it is. But it's still my gut reaction.

It took all the strength I had left over from the game not to yank Sophie out of her chair and kiss her at the restaurant after she explained her expanding vision for that column she covets so much. The passion in her voice…how her eyes widened with excitement…makes me want to jump in and experience life the way she does.

To live my life out of passion and not fear. And yeah, I wanted to kiss her right there, greasy lips and all.

I park the car in front of the building she directs me to. "I'll get your door."

She starts to argue with me, but I stop her. Here I am again, trying to be the man my mother raised me to be. Every day, I try to make her proud, as if that will erase the truth that she's gone.

Sophie takes my offered hand when she gets out. "Thanks for the ride."

"My pleasure." I follow her up the sidewalk.

She stops and turns around. "What are you doing?"

I skim the night sky above us, noting the heat lightning crawling silently through the clouds. "Making sure you get to your door safely."

She shakes her head, then crosses her arms and tilts her smile. "First the hotel room. Now my apartment. You make this sound like we're on a date or something."

Moonlight reflects off her bangs, and a cool breeze rustles the palm fronds overhead, lifting a tendril of hair across her face. Standing with her in the shadows of the night somehow emboldens me.

Drawn to move closer, I tuck the wayward strand behind her ear, brushing the soft swell of her cheek with the back of my fingers. My voice roughs out, "And what if it was? A date, that is."

She blinks several times, her pink lips parting with surprise as she drops her arms. "Oh...yes. I mean, I was actually joking. Well, kind of...but I think that would be okay. But no pressure! I wouldn't want you to think—"

I dip my head, my mouth hovering over hers. So close yet not touching. "And what if I kissed you good night? Would that be okay too?"

Her lashes flutter as her eyes drop to my mouth. "Yes."

Slow and soft, I brush my lips over hers, figuring that would be a good first kiss. But then Sophie leans into me, sliding her hands up the front of my shirt as she parts her lips with a sigh that blows my mind.

Our kiss intensifies and deepens, then slows, giving me time to memorize the taste and feel of her. She's soft in my arms, so I press her closer. I want to explore everything about her, but I also don't want to rush this. That's what my mind tells me, but then I remember she's wearing my jersey and every part of me ignites on a whole new level.

For the record, drawing away from her is one of the hardest things I've done to date. I rest my hands on the curve of her hips and lighten the kiss back to where we started, softly sweeping my lips over hers before lifting my head.

Her smile is tentative as she lifts her hand to my face and traces the outline of my lips with her finger, which somehow affects me even more than her sigh did. "The shape of your lips is so fascinating."

Laughter rumbles in my chest. I hope that's a compliment because I definitely want a repeat. "Yes, you mentioned that before. I assume that's still a good thing."

Giggling, she bites her bottom lip, making me want to kiss her again.

Her breath fans my face as she lets out a breathy exhale. "Very good. Who wants to kiss someone with lizard lips?"

"Another lizard?" I quip.

She blurts out a laugh. "There is that."

Expecting her to turn around and go inside her apartment, I let her go, but instead, she tugs my head down for another kiss, running her fingers into the back of my hair. I lose track of time and don't care, to be honest. For once,

I'm letting myself just be in the moment—with her. I'm tired of worrying about the future—mine and my sister's. And I'm realizing I want more moments like this…with Sophie.

Maybe even a lifetime of them.

She rests her cheek against my chest as she wraps her arms around me. "Is this okay, too?"

I hum and kiss the top of her head, relishing the way she fits against me. And how easy this is. It's as if we're meant to be together. Right here, right now. "More than okay."

She looks up at me. "Are you sure?"

Seems like a simple question, but I'm almost certain she's asking if I trust her. And I do. She's not at all what I first assumed her to be—she's so much more. I don't think I've ever been more sure of anything.

"Why do you ask?"

At first, she shrugs, then glances to the side as if she's embarrassed.

I lift her chin and wait for her eyes to meet mine. "Tell me."

"I'm not good at this."

"At what?"

"Romantic relationships." Even in the dim light, I can tell her cheeks are darkening with that adorable blush of hers.

"I find that hard to believe, considering what you want to write about in that column of yours."

"It's not mine yet."

I trace her lips this time. "Just a matter of time, I'm sure."

"Thank you, but you need to know that when it comes to relationships—the romantic kind—I'm jinxed." Her eyes widen as if she hadn't meant to say that. "Or rather, I've been told I'm a bit much at times."

Again I brush away the silky strands the breeze teases across her face. "And who told you that? An old boyfriend?"

She tips her head down. "A few, actually."

"Hey." I lean to the side until she looks at me. "Those guys were idiots."

The smile she brandishes settles the urge in my gut to find those jerks and ask them what their problem was. Sophie is the brightest, most caring and compassionate person in this sometimes dark world.

She tugs one side of her bottom lip between her teeth.

I study the fascinating display of emotions running across her face.

"You really think so? I mean, I do tend to spew words like a can of snakes. Especially when I get nervous, in case you didn't notice."

Soft laughter rumbles up from my chest. "Oh, I noticed."

She cringes.

I rush in to reassure her. "I like it when you do that. It's your tell."

"You sure about that?" Her eyes dart back and forth as she searches my face, as if she wants to believe me.

I kiss the tip of her nose. "Surer than sure."

I think I've searched for Sophie in the bleachers at least a dozen times during practice. She said she'd be here today, so maybe she's just running late. I'm sure she's fine, right? Probably had to check in with her editor or feed her cat—does she have a cat?

She'll be here any minute—that's what I keep saying to myself to stave off the panic. But the pressure building in my chest tells me another story. What if something happened to her? Memories of the night of my mother's accident flood back in a torrent that makes breathing difficult. I thought…hoped that fear was limited to my sister, but my head and heart are more wrapped up with Sophie than I realized.

Jayce skates up next to me. "Your shot, old man."

I grunt at his dig at my age, which I find hilarious. I'm not the oldest player on the team. Plus, I'm only twenty-six, but I noticed Jayce grins when he says it. So I'm taking it as a sign that he's accepting my leadership as captain.

Moving the puck back and forth, I skate toward the crease, do my signature turn to make a slapshot, and miss. Several of the guys snicker.

Ethan and Payton glide up alongside me as I circle behind the net.

Payton hands me a water bottle. "Drink up. You need a boost."

Hot and frustrated, I yank my helmet off and douse my head while I try to figure out how to get my figurative one back into the game. Losing focus now would be a definite setback.

Ethan narrows his eyes at me. "Anything you want to share with the rest of the class?"

I glare at him. They've thrown comments at me all day, trying to finagle details about what happened after the game last night because they know I drove Sophie home. By the time I got back to Gabe's place, the string of texts waiting for me was nearing almost fifty. I ignored all of them and went to bed.

Derek blows his whistle, giving us the signal to transition from drills to scrimmages.

Wade skates over and pulls his helmet off as he stops. "Well?"

Ethan and Payton shake their heads in unison.

Wade's thick brows dive together over his nose. "Ah, come on, man. Give us something to hang our hats on."

Payton flatlines his mouth. "He's an absolute vault."

While taking a long slug from what's left of my water, I catch a glimpse of movement up in the seats behind the net. Sophie's perched on the back of a seat with her camera trained on us. The tightness in my chest loosens, allowing me to fill my lungs with air again.

I stare right at her, knowing she can see me way better with that telephoto lens than I can see her. She lowers her camera and smiles at me.

Unfortunately, I forgot I'm surrounded by a bunch of nitwits who have followed the direction of my attention and are now ribbing me with light shoves and comments.

Any concern I have over my teammates' witnessing our flirtation flies away faster than a puck on an icing call, and I can't help the grin that spreads across my face. I've fought the distracting memory of her tracing my lips, calling them sculpted, and the way she felt in my arms all day. But now, I let them have free rein in my head.

One of the guys makes kissing sounds—real mature. Good thing I didn't see which one because he'd be making out with the plexiglass right about now. Wade waves at Sophie, then points to me, shaking his head. Then he gestures to himself and gives her a thumbs-up. I smack him in the breadbasket with my mitt.

He smirks at me. "Someone's testy today."

Sometimes this guy has the rizz of a rhino. "Give it a rest, Wade," I growl.

Ethan leans in and whispers, "Glad to see you quit fighting it."

I appreciate his discretion, but that doesn't stop me from giving him a hard shove, propelling him backward toward the center of the ice.

He laughs as he glides away. "You know I was right."

When I glance up to where Sophie was taking pictures, only empty seats greet me. Now I'm paranoid she's upset about the way the guys were ribbing me about her. I wouldn't blame her either. They were being total goofballs.

Before I shove my helmet back on, Gabe waves me over to the players' bench.

He doesn't say anything at first. That's when I realize he's waiting for the rest of the guys to join Derek by the net, putting them out of earshot.

"What's up, Coach?" That tightness is back in my chest. This feels way too similar to how things went down that night when my last coach waved me over during the game to tell me about my mother's accident.

He grins, sending a wave of relief through me. "I'm going to tell the rest of the guys after practice that it's official—we're a farm team for Tampa Bay Lightning. I wanted you to know first."

"Because I'm the captain?"

He shakes his head. "No, because they're looking at you."

"Seriously?" This could be huge for Kinsley and me. We're getting by on my ECHL salary, but just barely.

He pats me on the shoulder. "Keep pulling hat tricks, and you'll get bumped up by the end of the season."

Caution slides in, tempering my first reaction. "Is that definite?"

"No, but I believe in you, Luke. You've always had what it takes."

I swallow and give him a curt nod. "Thanks."

After practice, I get cleaned up, then head toward Sophie's office to see if she might be free for dinner. Or something. I just want to see her. Get a feel of where we stand in the daylight. That kind of thing, you know?

But she's not there, and when I asked a couple of the trainers, they said they hadn't seen her.

I pull out my phone to text her but find she beat me to the punch.

Sophie: I'm heading to the beach to take some pictures. Want to tag along?

LUKE: Where are you now?

SOPHIE: Parking lot.

Pocketing my phone, I head out the exit. She's leaning against her car, eyes closed with her face tilted up toward the sun. Her jean-clad legs are crossed at the ankles, and she's wearing a light pink T-shirt.

Because I want to memorize every detail about her, I slow my steps, but the crunch of my shoes on the asphalt alerts her to my presence.

She smiles at me. "Does this mean you're coming along?"

I hold my hands out from my sides. "That's why I'm here."

She smirks. "Think you can take a little heat, Iceman?"

No one's ever called me that, and I think I like it... coming from her, that is. "It's not that hot out."

"Then let's go."

Once we're in the car, my phone pings with multiple texts. My first thought is what Gabe told me during practice. Maybe he has an update already? Or it could be Kinsley. When I check, I find several messages from the guys.

> PAYTON: Did I just see Jammer with Sophie?
>
> WADE: Yes. I'm here to say I was a witness.
>
> ETHAN: Way to go, bro!
>
> MATHÉO: What did I miss?
>
> WADE: Luke's got it bad for the camera girl!
>
> MATHÉO: You mean Sophie? Really?
>
> WADE: Yeah, man. Get your head out of your bucket. Practice is over.
>
> ETHAN: Take it easy, guys. Let's not ruin the glow of his hatty.
>
> PAYTON: ...

At least Ethan's trying to control that Gongshow.

Sophie glances at me. "What's all that about?"

I turn off my phone and shove it into my pocket. They can find their entertainment somewhere else. "Nothing. Nothing at all."

Chapter Eighteen

SOPHIE

The arena isn't far from the beach, so we arrive within minutes. The sun peaked several hours ago and will soon descend into sunset, with the days getting shorter. And that's what I'm waiting for—the magical display of colors that streak the evening sky over Mango Key Beach.

I know sunsets can be a little cliché, but I can't help myself. It's my own personal challenge—to take THE BEST one yet. And sunsets tend to be more intense after a thunderstorm, but they are always spectacular on Mango Key Beach.

Romantic too. Opening up to Luke last night about my pitiful track record wound up relieving this pressure I didn't realize was there. I feel like I've been justified in a way. Almost as if Luke defended me against the ghosts of my past boyfriends.

More importantly, he doesn't think I'm an emotional spew bag. Maybe those other guys were all wrong for me. Does that mean Luke's the right one?

Once we're on the beach, I hold out my bag handles to

Luke. He's here, so I might as well take advantage of his helpfulness. "Do you mind?"

He holds his hands out. "Not at all."

I pull out my camera and swap lenses.

Luke studies my every move, making me feel self-conscious. "Can I ask you something?"

I pause what I'm doing at his serious tone. "Sure."

"Why isn't your bag pink?"

I bark out a laugh mixed with a little relief. "I didn't expect that question. Why do you ask?"

"It's obvious you love pink. Just makes sense that you'd have a pink bag."

He noticed my love for pink…I mean, it's pretty obvious, since I intentionally wear something pink on my person every day. Kind of a joke that started between my dad and me. Almost a game.

I keep my focus on adjusting to my camera because talking about my dad sometimes brings out my emotional side. Guess I'm still nervous about showing him the full Sophie effect. "My father bought it for me as a graduation present."

I dare a glance to gauge his reaction, too, because I know he's still dealing with the loss of his mother.

His expression warms. "Sorry."

"For what?"

"Bringing up a painful subject."

"It's okay. I love talking about him." I gesture with my camera toward the shoreline to let him know where I'm heading. "My dad loved to tease me about my love of everything and anything pink. So it became a game. I would wear something pink every day, just to see him shake his head or laugh. He would buy me things that weren't pink, saying he had to balance me out."

He lifts the bag up. "So he bought you a brown bag."

I giggle. "Yes, he did. And it reminds me of him every day." I sigh. "We'd planned to take a trip to Japan one day to see the cherry blossoms in bloom—my ultimate pink dream."

"He sounds like he was a lot of fun."

"Yes, and a bit of a prankster, but I knew how to get even." I incline my head toward the bag. "Look inside."

Luke peeks in. One side of his mouth kicks up as soft laughter rumbles up from his chest, making my pulse go haywire. "Everything in here is pink."

"Sometimes revenge is pink," I muse as I lift my chin.

He whistles through his teeth. "Wow, you really *are* good with words."

If I could, I'd preen like one of those wild green parrots that flutter about the palm trees. As it is, I'm sure my cheeks resemble the bright pink starting to streak the sky. "Why, thank you."

"I mean that." He dips his chin with an uncharacteristic shyness. "I read the articles you've written so far and was genuinely impressed. And your photos are some of the best I've seen."

This lightness overcomes me, making me realize how much tension I'd held in anticipation of his reaction to my work. I think I could walk on the waves riding up onto the shore right now.

I smile at him. "Does that mean you don't think I'm some dirt-digging reporter anymore?" I regret the words the minute they leave my mouth, even if I meant it as a joke. "Sorry. Forget I said that."

He stops me from walking away. "You're an amazing *journalist*, Sophie. I'm sorry I was so quick to judge."

I shield my eyes from the glow of the dipping sun. "It's understandable."

His head tilts to the side in a micro movement as his brows draw down.

"I read the article that came out after your mother's death. You know that paper was just a gossip rag, right? They get sued at least once a month."

"That doesn't justify what they did." A fierceness flashes in his eyes, then recedes like the waves from the shore. He tips his head back with a long exhale. "Sorry. Just when I think I'm past it, I get angry all over again."

I press my lips together and nod. "It made me angry too."

His eyes flash as he impales me with that molten gaze of his. "Thank you for saying that."

"I meant it." We both seem to be saying things we mean right now.

One side of his mouth tilts up. "I believe you."

We continue our trek toward the water as the growing sounds of ocean waves dance up the shore in a steady rhythm. Just above the shoreline, I stop and take a few shots of a boat that has a pelican perched on the bow, voraciously gobbling down chunks of fish left out for him.

Luke draws in a deep breath next to me, then releases it with a sigh. I had a feeling this would be good for him, to decompress from the pressures of the new season starting... and looking out for his sister.

He doesn't know that Kinsley texted me that her professor allowed her to resubmit her paper. She wound up changing her mind about the entire thing and wrote about Luke instead. I wish I could be a fly on the wall to see his face when she tells him.

"This was a great idea." He sounds calm...peaceful.

"I had a feeling you'd like this."

He swivels his head toward me. "Thank you. Again."

I tilt my smile and lift one shoulder. "Don't mention it, Iceman."

But there's something I would dearly like to mention myself. Not to be nosy, but to prove to him that I'm not some reporter digging for dirt. I care about Luke—maybe more than care, but I'm not ready to examine that yet—and I want to know everything about him.

I take another shot of the pelican flapping his wings at the boat owner, demanding more fish. "Can I ask you a question?"

"Shoot." He ticks up one side of those gorgeous lips of his into a lopsided grin. "Pun intended."

I resist the urge to roll my eyes at his almost dad-level joke. But speaking of dads… "Do you remember anything about your father?"

His smile slips as he looks away, but not completely. He stares out at the water in a pause long enough to make me think he won't answer. Maybe I overstepped, and now he's rethinking his opinion of my work. Or me. Maybe I am a nosy reporter who should have kept her mouth shut. Before I can take my question back, he starts talking.

"Not really. He wasn't around much. He would go on these business trips and be gone for weeks at a time." He puts air quotes around 'business trips.'

The article I read said he was arrested for drug trafficking, so I assume that's what he's referencing. "That must have been hard on your mom."

"Not really. Funny thing is, our house was peaceful when he was away." He clears his throat. "I didn't find out until later that he was dealing drugs."

His honesty ignites not only my curiosity but this desire

to listen and hear his heart. I suspect Luke hasn't had that in his life since his mother died. "Your mom told you?"

He shakes his head. "She just said he walked out on us. I found out the truth after her death."

The pieces click into place. "From that article."

He grunts.

"And Kinsley knows too?"

"She read it too," he grumbles.

"That must have been so difficult for you both." I rest my hand on his chest. My eyes are burning with tears for him and his sister. I wish I could go back in time and either deck that reporter or be there for them both as they grieved.

And they're still grieving...

He lifts my fingers to his mouth first, then kisses the inside of my wrist, making me feel wanted...chosen. But his lips are like a branding iron, sending heat all the way up my arm. And I can't stop staring at those delicious lips when he lowers my hand in a motion that draws me to him.

Our lips finally meet in a kiss that's tender and sweet, a soft whisper of gratitude dancing between us, as if he's thanking me for every moment of care that's woven us together thus far. The sun bathes my back in golden warmth but pales in comparison to the heat radiating from Luke's body pressed against mine, igniting every nerve in my being.

He cradles my hand against his heart, its steady rhythm pulsing beneath my palm—a powerful, comforting beat that echoes the stirring in my own heart. As he deepens the kiss, the world around us dissolves and fades into nothingness. All I know is the intoxicating connection between us and this amazing, mind-blowing, never-want-it-to-end kiss—hashtag neverbeenkissedlikethis.

When he places his other hand on the small of my back,

the bag he's so patiently held swings into the back of my knees, making them bend. I jerk away in reaction to the sensation of falling, but Luke catches me.

"I've got you." That slow, easy smile of his makes a path across his face like the sun arcing through the sky. Sunlight glints off his irises, revealing tiny amber streaks that I didn't notice before. If I could touch those like I did his lips, I would. They resemble the first glimmers of a sunrise and are filled with the promise of something I want more than anything but am afraid to hope for.

I'm like that greedy pelican, hungry for more of the fisherman's catch. And I shudder in the reality that not only did Luke catch me, but he's caught my heart as well.

Hook, line, and sinker.

After I dropped Luke off at his car, I'd intended to go home, but Marty sent a text asking if I could come see him at the office. I don't think he ever leaves work before seven most evenings.

When I arrive, the place is empty and dark, except for the glow of light streaming out of Marty's doorway. I stride in, plop my bag in a chair in front of his desk, and drop into the other one, folding my hands over my abdomen. "What's up, Marty?"

He pushes his reading glasses to the top of his head as he looks up from the piece he's editing, which he taps with his forefinger. "This piece on Luke Jameson is some of your best work, kiddo."

I didn't think this day could get any better. My smile's so broad it makes my cheeks hurt. "Thank you. I'm pretty proud of it myself."

"I can't wait to see the reaction to this one tomorrow. Are the photos for it already uploaded?"

"Yep. My best shots are in the folder."

He studies me for a moment. "You put a lot more emotion in this one."

His cautious tone puts me on alert. "Yeah, I guess so. This assignment's really turning into something more than I originally thought."

"Do you mean Luke is turning into something more than you expected?" He smiles in a fatherly way.

I straighten in my chair, attempting to appear as oblivious as possible. "What are you talking about?"

He tilts his head at me as if I'm being evasive, which I am. "I know you and your work well enough to read between the lines, Soph. You're invested."

"So I care about what I'm writing. What's the big deal?"

"I think this is more than care, kiddo."

I stare down at my hands. "And what if it is?"

He clears his throat, which is his way of telling me to look at him. "Does he have feelings for you too?"

I pinch my lips together and nod.

"Then I'm happy for you, but a word of caution." The subtle lift of his brows signals his request for permission.

"Yes?" I hope he speaks fast because I'm not sure how long I can hold my breath.

"Be careful. The season has barely started, and you'll be with the team for several months. I'd hate to see you navigating that with a broken heart."

"What makes you think that's going to happen?" I fist my hands in my lap.

"He's a hockey player? And a damn good one from what I'm reading here."

"So? What's that got to do with it?"

He hesitates. "Rebecca Piedmont called to rave about your work."

Okay, still not sure where he's going with this, but I'm feeling that need to preen a little. "That's great! But what's that got to do with Luke potentially breaking my heart? Which, for the record, I disagree."

He leaves his chair to perch on the edge of his desk in front of me. "She thinks our coverage helped boost the image of the Sun Kings, which made a difference in their negotiations to become a farm team for Tampa Bay Lightning. And she may have mentioned they have their eye on Luke already. I have a feeling your article about him will help make it official."

"That's fantastic!" But in light of what Luke shared with me today, I'm not convinced he would want that. More exposure and publicity, for sure, which he seems to avoid like the plague.

Marty holds his hand out for mine, then pats it with his other one. "Fame and fortune change people. An NHL player is on the road a lot more too, and you and I both know ice bunnies are a real thing. I just want you to be cautious."

"Luke's not like that." My words come out harsher than I intended. "I mean, he's honest and real with me. Besides, he's not interested in that level of exposure. I'm pretty sure he'd find that kind of attention...off-putting."

What I'd really like to say is he'd see right through those chickas and tell them to get lost. At least I hope he would...

"Then just accept my concern as an overly cautious funcle, who doesn't want to see his favorite person get hurt."

I giggle at his use of my nickname for him. "Don't worry. I'll be fine. I have no intentions of doing anything drastic."

Mostly the truth. What I won't tell him is that my heart is already at risk—big time.

"Good." He releases my hand. "Glad we got that over with. This is why Clara and I never had kids. Too stressful."

I try not to giggle but fail because I've watched the man juggle more challenging situations than a love-sick teenager. Which I'm not...definitely not a teenager, anyway. "Anything else you'd like to impart to me, Funcle?"

His grin returns at the use of his nickname. "No, that's enough for the rest of this year. Just keep doing what you're doing, kiddo. This could turn into something big."

A ripple of excitement surges through me. I'm finally beginning to see the fruits of my labor, and it's even sweeter than I ever imagined.

Chapter Nineteen

SOPHIE

"This is total sour grapes." I sweep my gaze across the quaint chapel that was supposed to be the perfect setting for my best friend's wedding. Water stains cover the walls where the brocade wallpaper peeled off in patches. The parts that hadn't come off—yet—bulge in places where rain from a recent tropical storm invaded their leaky roof in a mass exodus. The once creamy carpet in the aisle looks more like a pack of muddy dogs ran through, and the dank smell will choke me soon if I don't get out of there.

The plan for today was to decide where we wanted to place the flowers in the chapel, determine where the caterer would position the food in the reception area, and let the venue coordinator know how many tables to assemble and drape. Obviously, none of this is happening.

Or in time for Mia's wedding.

She sniffles next to me. "They said the reception area is even worse. I can't bring myself to look at it." She lets out a sob. "And they said remediation alone will take at least a week and repairs several months. What are we going to do, Soph? The wedding's in two weeks?"

My shoulders and my spirit sag. "We could reschedule."

She shakes her head. "Ethan's entire family went through a lot of trouble to secure flights and lodging. His brother is flying in from California and had to fight for time off from his company, which they only agreed to when they found out he's the best man."

"Those bastards." I lace my voice with humor so she knows I'm joking.

She snorts and *almost* laughs. "Seriously…what are we going to do?"

One way or another, I will get a giggle out of her because I know it will help defuse the stress of the situation. "Elope?"

Mia groans. "My mother would never speak to me again."

"I was joking." I give her a sidelong glance. "Then we find another venue. There has to be some way to make this work."

She lets out a shuddering breath. "Got anything in mind?"

"Not yet, but I will." I check the time on my phone. "I have to go to the game, but afterward, I'll do some brainstorming and research."

More tears leak out of her eyes, making a path down her already tear-stained cheeks. "I hope this doesn't throw Ethan off his game tonight."

"Does he know yet?"

The subtle shake of her head is minuscule.

"Then don't tell him."

She makes a circular gesture with her hand in front of her face. "He'll read this like a book, Soph."

"Then tell him we have a backup plan."

"I don't want to lie."

"You won't be. I'm going to figure something out tonight, and tomorrow we'll implement it, okay?"

The battle of emotions roving Mia's face shifts from outright despair to doubt and then to hope as she lifts her brows. "If anyone can figure out how to keep this wedding on schedule, it will be you."

I hug her. "Don't worry. Sometimes, the worst situation can turn into an even better outcome than you originally planned."

She draws back from me. "I don't think I'm capable of thinking like that."

"But you trust me, right?"

"Of course." She rolls her eyes as she tilts her head— quite the feat.

I squeeze her arms for reassurance. "I promise your wedding is going to be everything you wanted it to be, if not more."

She nods with a watery smile. "Thank you. You're the best, Soph."

"No, just scrappy. And determined to see my best friend's wedding become the event of a lifetime."

"At this point, I'll be ecstatic if we don't have to cancel."

"We won't. I promise."

Arriving late to the game cost me seeing the introduction of the starting line-ups. I'm kind of bummed because I didn't get to see Luke geared up and standing proud on the ice, representing the Sun Kings. In college, I would roll my eyes at that part—and the gaggle of girlfriends swooning over their hockey boyfriends.

But now I get it. Luke is hecka sexy all on his own. Put the man in a suit pregame and then his Sun Kings gear… my heart never stood a chance. Now I get how Mia fell so hard and fast for Ethan, who turned out to be a great guy. I was so glad he disproved my initial skepticism because I really didn't want to have THAT conversation with my BFF.

I make my way to the press area in the newly renovated and expanded luxury box to find the team owner, Rebecca Piedmont, chatting with a guy wearing a USA Hockey Magazine badge. She's all business with her gray and black tailored suit and heels.

Hmmm, maybe Rebecca is schmoozing the press on a bigger scale to benefit the team's profile. Makes sense. If Marty hadn't told me she'd called, raving about the pieces I've written so far, I'd be totally paranoid seeing her here.

The first time I met her, I was so intimidated by her strong persona and business acumen that I stumbled over my first few questions. But her insistence that I call her by her first name and her gracious nature settled my initial anxiety, and we hit it off.

I muster my courage and take a position in her sight line, hoping she'll see I'm there. And I'm hoping the more points I can win with the team owner, thereby growing my reputation, the better my chances of landing that column. Marty seemed truly impressed that she called.

To my delight, she glances my way and smiles with a double take as she waves me over.

I put on my best game face (pun intended) and join her. "Good to see you, Rebecca."

"Sophie, I was hoping I'd run into you tonight." She

gestures to the man standing with her. "This is Peter Orion with USA Hockey Magazine. I was just bragging about the pieces you've been writing about the team."

"Rebecca gave me a copy. I'm looking forward to reading it." Peter tugs a folded paper from under his arm and opens it—the sports and leisure section of the Sarabella Herald Tribune.

A journalist from a national magazine intends to read my work? I think I'm about to float over the ice and become a human drone, covering the game.

"I'm excited for you to read it. Thank you." I smile my thanks at Rebecca, who gives me a subtle wink.

But then I notice the picture of Luke on the front page. Not the one of him in his gear with his head tilted down and to the side to show only a smidgen of his face. No, this is the full-on larger-than-life headshot of him facing the camera with a smirk on his face that says, 'I'm fierce, hot, and I know it.'

Luke asked me to keep his face shielded, so I specifically chose images to keep Luke's face mostly hidden. The picture staring at me showed everything and was intended for my eyes only. It wasn't supposed to get uploaded with the others. I thought I removed it from the folder I planned to upload to the paper. I could have sworn—

Oh, no…that's the day Payton walked in, and then Luke showed up. I must have forgotten to remove it from the upload…

This was bad…so, so bad. Did they turn the heat on in this room because I feel like I'm about to pass out from heat stroke?

Rebecca says something to Peter about the piece I did on her when she bought the team. Her smile shifts to concern when she looks at me. "Are you okay, Sophie?"

I try to swallow, but all moisture has left my mouth. "I just need some water," I croak out, then dart over to a large bucket filled with ice and water bottles sitting on the end of the snack table. I press one to my neck before chugging down half the contents.

A touch on my shoulder spins me around.

Mia walks into the press lounge and stops next to me. "Are you okay? I hope you're not coming down with something. It's chilly in here."

Funny...feels like it's getting hotter by the second. Almost as if I've plunged into my own personal inferno. I want to spill the details of my gaff, but I'm still reeling. "Just a little sunburned, I think. I'm fine."

Her stare says she's not buying it. "Take it easy tonight."

I give her as reassuring a smile as I can fake at the moment. Once she wanders over to a seat and sits down, I turn around and pretend to rifle through a basket holding every kind of candy bar imaginable while I try to breathe normally.

I totally blew it. Luke will think I disregarded his request and never trust me again. He'll go back to thinking I'm one of those reporters who likes to create drama just for the extra exposure. This will change everything between us.

And just when I thought our situationship was moving in the right direction. Somehow, I have to talk to Luke and explain...and hope he believes me.

After reassuring Rebecca that I'm just a little dehydrated, I leave the luxury box and make my way down toward the rink to use one of the camera holes in the plexiglass to take some action shots.

Luke breaks away with the puck just as I'm getting into position, shooting ahead of Jayce and Ethan as the other team scrambles to catch up. I'm on the offensive side to the left of the net, so I have a clear shot of Luke in all his glory. And mine—this is going to be the picture of a lifetime. I can feel it in my gut.

Right as he takes the shot, so do I. The opposing goalie blocks it, but Ethan flies in after Luke and swings his stick in a blur of tangled movement with an opposing player. A double snap rings out as Ethan's stick snaps in half, and the puck shoots up, smacking the top bar of the net. But then it bounces off the goalie's shoulder into the net.

A deafening roar fills the place as the crowd cheers and stomps over the Sun Kings, scoring the first goal—also evidence of the team's growing popularity. But I'm too focused on Luke, who's skating toward me instead of making a pass by the rest of the team on the players' bench.

He whips off his helmet and wipes his mouth on his sleeve before lowering his face to the camera hole.

He's waiting for a kiss…

He wants to kiss me through the camera hole…

As if he's announcing to the world that I'm his girlfriend and he's proud to be with me.

My heart does a happy dance in my chest before sinking into the pit of worry in my stomach. Once he finds out about my flub up, he may not want anything to do with me, which would just prove I was right to begin with—I'm a disaster when it comes to boyfriends.

I guess my hesitation was enough to get the crowd involved. Their chant clarifies as it grows louder.

Kiss him! Kiss him! Kiss him!

Even Mia's jumping up and down in the front of the luxury box above the stands.

If I kiss him, he might wind up madder at me later when he finds out about the picture in the article. But if I don't, he might think I don't want something serious with him. And I do, more than anything, I'm realizing. I also don't want to embarrass him or put a dent in the team's growing popularity. A kiss can mean a lot these days, it seems.

I shut down my brain, my worries, my overanalyzing, and lean in, offering my puckered lips to this man, who's not only showing his presence on the ice but in my heart as well.

His kiss is salty with residual sweat but still warm and sweet with his gentle touch. When I start to draw away, he lingers, his eyes demanding more. And I oblige. How can I not?

The crowd goes nuts again, eclipsing their celebratory clamor over the first goal of the game. Luke smiles and winks before skating off to join his teammates, who take turns patting him on the shoulder and juggling him around while I stand in shock.

My father used to say that a moment can either be a crossroads or a defining factor in a person's life.

This feels like one of those, but as to which one…?

I have no idea.

Chapter Twenty

LUKE

"That game was epic, y'all!" A bare-chested Wade struts around the locker room, high-fiving anyone willing to smack his sweaty hand.

And so was that kiss with Sophie. I'm not normally a PDA kind of guy, but the rush of scoring like we did—as a team in sync—fueled something in me. So I went for it.

But when she hesitated, everything surrounding us faded —the chanting of the crowd, the faces of the fans lit with expectation, the sounds of skates and sticks on the ice behind me. Nothing existed but her, me, and a moment that would define the trajectory of whatever was growing between us.

I literally held my breath until she leaned down and met my lips with hers.

Wade stops where I'm sitting on the bench in front of my locker. "You, my friend, were a force to be reckoned with tonight. And I'm not just talking about scoring the first goal." He holds his hand up, waiting for my slap as he wags his eyebrows in a comical fashion.

Seeing as how I have plenty of sweat of my own, I use the bottom of my water bottle to smack his waiting hand. "Ethan brought it home."

Ethan pulls a skate off and grins. "Team effort."

My chest must be expanding with the surge of pride filling it—Wade's right. Tonight's game felt like the Sun Kings stepped up a level. We're gelling as a team, and it shows on the ice. Jayce may have scored the winning point tonight, but he also set a new personal record for assists.

Blows my mind to think I've gone from wanting to drop-kick the guy to another team to valuing him not only as a teammate but also as an integral part of what we're turning into. I tried to get out of captaining the team that first week, and now, weeks later, I've found my groove, and it feels... almost natural. I certainly don't miss that pregame anxiety that plagued me in the beginning.

Maybe this means—

No. I *know* it means the past is finally staying where it belongs. Even Kinsley is thriving better than ever. She always texts me before a game to wish me luck, but this time, she mentioned she had a date—with Brandon. I'm guessing their road trip proved she was more his type than she thought.

I may have to plan a surprise visit to make sure this guy is worthy of my kid sister. She deserves the best. Mom would want that, and I intend to make certain of it.

Jayce tosses his sweaty towel at me, but I swat it away with a grunt. "Where's your head, old man? You look like you left us for the clouds."

I give him as evil a grin as I can muster. "A place you can only dream about."

He dons a cocky expression in reaction to my ribbing.

"That's my reality. Welcome to the club. And that sweet sna—"

"Don't push it, Jayce," I growl at him.

His Adam's apple bobs as he swallows. "Sorry, Cap. Just happy for ya."

I reward him with a tight grin. "Thanks."

With a brief nod, he walks off to chat with some of the guys at the other end of the room.

At record speed, I get cleaned up and back into my suit. I sent Sophie a text, asking her to be there when I walk out. I want—need to see her because she needs to know that wasn't a show for the crowd. That was me asking for something more. Something lasting. And I need to know if she feels the same.

My gut tightens as I reach for the door leading to the back hallway where wives, girlfriends, and sometimes family will wait for us. I can only compare this feeling to the time I was in the presence of the Stanley Cup, but you don't touch the cup until you're a winner.

I stored that moment away as a promise to myself—one I thought was lost after I left hockey. But whatever this is with Sophie feels bigger. More promising.

The thing is, I already feel like a winner when it comes to Sophie. Even though we've only been involved a short time, she's helped me believe in myself again. But I need to know she didn't just kiss me through that camera hole because she felt she had to.

Takes me a moment to find her, and then our eyes lock. The rose-colored shirt she's wearing reveals the soft skin of her shoulders to perfection, and all I want to do is put my hands on them.

She smiles—that's a good sign—and takes a step toward me as I rush to close the gap between us. And then she's in my arms, with her head lifted and those gorgeous eyes of hers swallowing me whole.

I don't think. At all. And I don't care who's watching. As if what happened on the ice wasn't enough, my teammates are about to get solid proof that Sophie and I are officially more than friends.

But the moment my lips touch hers, I forget all about that. I cup her beautiful face as her arms wrap around my waist underneath my jacket. The warmth of her hands seeps through my shirt and sends an ache through me that makes me realize she's my missing piece.

I lift my head and stare down into her eyes, trying to convey some of what I'm feeling right now. The guys whistling and making catcalls as they walk by isn't helping, though. This would be a lot easier if we were alone.

"Thank you."

"For what?" She leans her head back to look up at me with those big eyes that envelop my soul.

"For being here. For kissing me through the camera hole." I chuckle, and…I think I may be the one blushing this time because heat is rising up my neck, making its way to my face. "I didn't do that for the crowd."

She blinks twice, and those sweet lips I want to kiss again part to say something. Doubt flashes in her eyes.

Uh oh… Did I misread her? Maybe she did just kiss me out there because she didn't think she had a choice. The thought makes me sick inside.

"Luke, I need to tell you something." Her gaze darts back and forth as she searches mine.

I glance at the mix of players, girlfriends, and a couple of wives milling around us. Ethan and Mia are lip-locked, as per usual. I gesture down the hall toward the exit. "Let's go outside."

As soon as we step out of the door, a small crowd surges toward us. All young women, and they're heading toward me.

"Luke!" Several female voices call out, but one rushes forward. She holds out something to me and lowers her voice to a sultry tone. "Sign it to Ella...with love...please?"

An image of me fills the front page of the paper. Other smaller pictures of me with the team intermingle with the article. But the main image is just me. No gear. Full detail. Sitting in Sophie's office on that bench with the pink rose pillow.

I dart my gaze to Sophie.

"That's what I needed to tell you." Her voice shakes with her whisper.

Something primal surges up in me that makes me want to either run or beat the crap out of that newspaper. But I know that won't fix what just happened. I force a grin and take the woman's pen.

"Sure. To Ella." But I finish it with 'thank you for your support' because love has nothing to do with what's going down here, and I think that's what's wrecking me right now. I trusted Sophie to keep my full face out of this.

After a few more signatures and passing glances of curiosity from some of the guys walking out, I grab Sophie's hand and stride toward the parking area. At the sound of her frantic steps to keep up, I slow down.

When we reach my car, I drop her hand, pinching the bridge of my nose with my other one, and pace back and forth. I'm not even sure what to say at this point. I asked her not to show my face like that for a reason.

Just before Gabe reached out and asked me to join the team, I received a notice that my father was released from prison on good behavior. I requested that I not be contacted again. I don't want to see him. I don't want him to know anything about me. Or Kinsley, for that matter. We've dealt with enough, and our lives are *finally* getting back on track.

Rather, they were…until now.

Sophie's panicked voice breaks into my internal rant. "I'm sorry, Luke. I didn't intend for that picture to be used in the article. I didn't realize I'd uploaded it to the paper until I saw it tonight. I'm so sorry."

I stop pacing and stare at her. Do I believe her? I want to, but I'm struggling. I know how much she wants her own column. And that image of me is powerful—even I can see that, regardless of how uncomfortable it makes me to be so exposed.

Amazing how one pivotal moment can shift into another in a blink. A moment ago, I thought my life was finally turning into something good again. And now, I'm not so sure.

I run my hands through my damp hair. "What's the reach of this article?"

Confusion flashes across her face. "Less than thirty thousand. Why?"

"And only Florida?" The notification I received about my father mentioned he would be in a halfway house up north somewhere.

"Southwest Florida." She looks like a terrified kitten ready to bolt for cover.

And I feel awful for making her feel that way. It was an honest mistake. And she even said she needed to tell me something when I first walked out. It wasn't her fault that a fan beat her to the punch.

I exhale with a noisy breath and hold out my arms. "Come here."

She walks into my arms, pressing her face against my

chest between my suit lapels, mumbling against the fabric of my shirt.

A low chuckle rumbles through me. "I didn't catch anything you just said."

Her head falls back, but her eyes are closed as if she's trying to hide her deepest self. But what she doesn't realize is she's given me full access to her neck, and I'd like nothing more than to nuzzle the area behind her ear down to the gentle curve of her collarbone. Then I'd brush my lips over the soft skin of her shoulders, left bare by that enchanting rose-pink shirt she's wearing.

I take a deep breath to clear my head and wait for her to speak first.

"I can't believe I screwed that up, Luke. I mean, how could I do something so stupid? I promised you I wouldn't let your full face be shown, and I blew it." Her eyes pop open. "And why aren't you mad? I thought you'd be livid, but instead, you're being so...so..."

I can't contain the grin spreading on my face. "So...?"

She looks down, her voice barely a whisper. "Nice."

I hook my finger under her chin so she'll lift her face. "It's okay. Crisis averted."

That's what I'm choosing to believe, anyway. As long as those photos stay in Florida, I don't have to think about the possibility of my father deciding to make contact. He made the choice to leave his family for a life of crime a long time ago, and we did just fine without him, thanks to my mother. Kinsley and I don't need him in our lives.

"Aren't you going to beat me up about it? Just a little bit?"

I grunt. "I think you've done a good job doing that all on your own."

Her eyes turn watery, her voice a husky whisper. "I really am sorry."

I nod. "I know. It's okay. Now let it go."

"Are you sure?"

A slow smile spreads across my face because I've never been more sure about anyone like I am about her. "Surer than sure."

Chapter Twenty-One

SOPHIE

"So, what do you think?" I'm holding my breath as I wait for Mia's reaction.

The idea hit me this morning during a much-needed walk on the beach at sunrise to contemplate my situationship with Luke, which is fast turning into a relationship. I know I should be over the moon, especially after that very public kiss at the game. And the way he handled the mess up with his photo—thinking it through rationally—felt like he was fighting for us.

But I'm afraid to get my hopes up, considering how well I've done so far in the romance department in the past.

Yep. Sophie + romance = disaster.

However, whatever this is between Luke and me feels different. More natural and surprisingly easy at times. With the other guys I dated, I tried so hard to make the relationships work. Maybe too hard. Like trying to fit two pieces of a puzzle that didn't belong together.

But when I'm with Luke, I can be myself—something

that seemed to work against me with my previous boyfriends.

Mia faces me, arms crossed. "We're standing in a parking lot staring at the Turtle Tide and the Sandpiper Inn. What exactly am I supposed to see, Sophie?"

Just before dawn, I headed to the beach with my camera to capture the sherbet colors painting the sky and reflecting in the water. Behind the lens, I can connect with nature and myself, which allows my brain to process whatever I'm struggling with. I figured that would help declutter the Luke-chaos lingering in my head. That's when I saw two of Sarabella's most favored places in a whole different light—literally and figuratively.

Standing behind her, I turn her toward the restaurant and the inn. "Two years ago, the owners built that breezeway so that guests could go back and forth without getting soaked during the rainy season."

She sighs. "Goody for them."

"But they also used it for their Christmas wedding, which I heard was an event to remember. Just picture it, Mia. You in your Madam Tulard original gown, walking down the breezeway to where Ethan is standing, looking gorgeous in his tux, waiting to make you his wife." I add a dramatic flourish to my voice.

"But where will the guests sit?"

One of those whining trumpet sounds, signaling an epic fail, would work right about now.

I take a deep breath of salty ocean air. "On either side. The breezeway will be the center aisle, with a big canopy covering both sides. There's a place in town that rents temporary flooring for beach events and chairs too. Here, Madison sent me some pictures." I pull out my phone and scroll through them, giving her the full effect of Dominic and Madison's wedding.

She hums. "I never considered doing an outdoor wedding. Just seemed too risky."

"Right, but the weather this time of year is nice, and if it does rain, which I'm believing it won't, you're still covered. Literally!" I laugh. "And we can wrap the posts in those fairy lights you wanted, but the other venue wouldn't let you use. See? It's perfect!"

Mia lets out a sob, then wraps me in a tight hug. "You did it, Soph. And you're right. It's even better than the original plan."

I exhale my relief. "I already talked to Madison and Dominic, and they're happy to help with whatever we need. And this will make things so much easier for Ethan's family since most of them are staying at the inn."

Mia shakes her head. "It's brilliant. Absolutely brilliant. But what about the caterer? Will that be an issue?"

"No. When I explained to Dominic that we already had a contract for the food, he made a call to the owner. Turns out they're friends. He's not only giving them use of the kitchen during your wedding but also offered to help. I let Amanda know the change of venue so she can reconfigure the floral arrangements as needed. She did the flowers for Madison and Dominic's wedding, too, so she's already familiar with the layout."

She shakes her head with an incredulous expression. "I can't believe how well this is working out."

I grin. "I call it the magic of Sarabella."

"More like the magic of Sophie Adams, if you ask me. Don't cut yourself short, girlfriend." She shoots me a wicked grin. "Speaking of girlfriends. Are you?"

"Am I what?"

She rolls her eyes. "Do I really have to spell it out? Are you and Luke together now?"

I tug one side of my bottom lip between my teeth. "Maybe? Yes. I mean, no. I mean, I don't know!"

"How can you not be after what happened at the game?!"

"I know, I know!" I pat my chest with my palms. "But you know my track record. I'm a disaster at relationships."

"Just because those didn't work out doesn't mean you're a disaster, Soph."

"I'm zero for three, Mia. What else could it mean?"

She touches a finger to her mouth. Seems I'm not the only one pulling out the drama today.

"Hmm, let's see. How about those guys were total jerks?"

I bite my lip. "When I told Luke about them, he said the same thing."

She claps her hands in excitement. "Oh, I knew I liked him for a reason. He's right, Sophie. And I think he's right *for* you."

My turn to cross my arms. "Maybe. Or am I just doing what I did before? Even after it was painfully obvious that the relationships were doomed to fail, I continue to try and make things work."

She waves me off. "That just means you're loyal."

"Or stupid. See? Terrible at romance." I drop my hands to my sides and pout. "I really do want to believe things are different this time."

"Then let's make a list of what's different from those other relationships."

I groan. "What if I'm grasping at straws?"

"Then I'll tell you."

I consider for a moment. "I don't even know where to begin."

"Fine. I will. Let's start with your first kiss through the camera hole."

"That wasn't our first kiss," I blurt out.

She swats my arm. "Why didn't you tell me he kissed you before that?"

I shrug. "I forgot?"

She rolls her eyes at me again but adds a dramatic sigh to the mix. I think I'll call her the queen of eye-roll drama from now on. "Okay, then, who initiated the first kiss?"

"Luke did."

"Have there been any other kisses?"

"Last night, after the game."

She swats me again.

"Hey! I'm telling you now!" I whine.

"Fine. Who initiated that one?"

"Um…we both did." Heat rises up my cheeks at the memory.

She looks off into the distance. "Oh, interesting."

"What? What does that mean? Is that bad?"

She pats my arm as if to undo her earlier slaps. "No, that's good. I was beginning to think Luke was doing all the work."

Just as I'm about to get offended, she giggles.

"You're a rat, you know that."

She huffs out a laugh. "Soph, it sounds like he's pursuing you like crazy. This is nothing like those three losers you dated. If you ask me, they did you a favor by bailing before things got too serious."

She's right. I think I initiated the first kiss in all three of those relationships. And none of them were out in public for the whole world to see. Luke said he didn't do that for the crowd. I assumed he meant he did it for him. But what if he did it for me, too? Like staking his claim.

Despite my love for everything romance, I never imagined myself wanting a guy to say she was his, but I'm kind of finding the idea…hot. No one's ever made me feel as desired or special as Luke does.

And after seeing all those women waiting for him after the game, I'm beginning to think I need to stake my claim on a very sweet, *helpful*, sexy, and sometimes grumpy hockey player.

I wonder what Luke would think of me then?

Practice is long underway by the time I arrive at the arena, so I head to my office to get prepped for Wade's interview. As the goalie, he's the last one I have left to interview, so I won't need to be here as often. I've snapped more than enough shots of all the players for their individual articles.

That means I'll only see Luke at games…unless we start officially dating. Maybe I should quit holding back and do a little pursuing myself.

The scent of roses alerts me to their presence first. A tall, pale pink vase filled with dusty pink roses dwarfs my small makeshift desk. I pluck out a folded piece of paper nestled between a few of the stems.

Sophie,
I decided to catch a last-minute flight to
spend a couple of days with my sister for her

birthday. When I get back, I'd like to take you on a date, if that's okay. I'll pick you up on Tuesday evening at 7 p.m., if that's okay.

Can't wait to see you...

I hope that's okay too,

Luke

I smile at his references to how I asked him if it was okay when I hugged him. He's poking fun at me while sounding flirty and affectionate. And I love him for it.

I look up from the note as goose bumps cover me in waves.

Love him for it...

Do I love him?

Ever since that day on the beach, he's taken constant residence in my thoughts, my dreams, and even my work. I suspected then I was headed here. I might as well just admit it to myself.

I lean over the bouquet and inhale the sweet scent of the roses, then finish reading his note.

P.S. These roses are from my mother's garden. This one in particular was her favorite, because I bought it for her several years ago. I think she loved pink almost as much as you do.

I take a couple of steps back until I feel the bench behind my calves, then drop down on the seat. The man drove all the way from Clearwater to Sarabella to leave me a pink vase of pink roses from his mother's treasured rose garden before flying to New York to help Kinsley.

He did all of that...for me.

If I hadn't already fallen for the man, I most definitely would now.

Chapter Twenty-Two

LUKE

"How many books do you need, Kins?" I manage to sound sarcastic while lugging a box containing an unassembled bookshelf to her dorm room—her birthday present that I'm about to spend the next two hours assembling. I've yet to meet one of these that didn't take twice as long as it should.

"Need and want are two very different things. This is a want, thus why I *wanted* a bookshelf for my birthday."

I lower one end of the box to the floor and hold the top. "Then consider me assembling it your Christmas present."

She mocks a gasp. "Low blow, big bro."

Kinsley holds the door open for me as I drag the box into her room. I squat over the carton, cutting open the taped flap with a pair of scissors I swiped from a pencil cup. Books fill the two built-in shelves above her desk, and more are stacked on top. Additional piles of books stand in clusters by the corner.

"I'm not sure this will be enough, Kins." I chuckle.

"What can I say? Words are my life." She drops with a bounce on the twin-sized bed, sitting against the opposite wall along with a small dresser nearby. Seeing the quilt Mom made her draped over the mattress brings a smile to my face.

But no pang of grief…interesting.

I gesture to the book stacks. "I assume you want this there."

"Yes, please. Then I can take you to this really cool ramen place I found around the corner." She jumps to her feet and starts shifting the books onto her bed.

I lean back on my feet, hands out. "Seriously? I'm in New York, and you want me to eat noodles?"

"Ramen," she groans. "You can have pizza tomorrow. I'm sure there's a spot close to your hotel."

Light streams in through a window that overlooks a sea of windows on the opposite building. The room is small, but Kinsley did a great job of making it feel cozy with some throw pillows and pictures from home.

Once I get her shelf assembled, she relegates me to the handing her books so she can arrange them in the order she prefers, which she goes into great detail explaining her system. I pretend to listen while my brain drifts to Sophie.

She should have found the flowers I left on her desk by now. I glance at my phone in case she texted me, but there's nothing there. Maybe she hasn't made it to her office yet. I think she finished interviewing the rest of the team, and we don't have a game until Thursday this week, which was why I decided to hop a plane and see my sister. And maybe check out this new boyfriend of hers a little more.

"Will Brandon be joining us for ramen?" The only ramen I've ever had were those little cheap packages you cook yourself. I hope this place does a better job than that.

"No, he's probably on a date with Ashley."

"Who's Ashley?"

"His new flavor of the week." Instead of placing one at a time, she slams a small stack of books onto a shelf, making the whole thing shudder.

"Hey, take it easy with that. I did build it, after all." I'm trying to lighten the mood, but inside, I'm seething at this guy.

"Sorry." Her voice sounds uncharacteristically quiet. And she's staring at her hands.

Rising from her bed, I drag her resistant body into a hug. "Do I need to have a talk with Brandon?"

She's stiff at first, then softens.

"No," she mumbles against my shirt.

I take a deep breath, drawing courage to ask what I feel I have to know. "Did he do anything to hurt you?"

She sighs, then looks up at me. "Maybe just my pride? I thought he really liked me. Guess I wasn't interesting enough."

I snort. "Not likely. You probably intimidated the hell out of him."

She throws a pillow at me, which I catch.

"Kins, I meant that as a compliment. You deserve a guy who appreciates what a strong person you are. Brandon didn't strike me as having the guts for it."

She blurts out a laugh. "No guts, no glory?"

"Sounds about right." I hand her more books.

She cradles the stack against her chest. "Thanks, big bro. That helps."

"Good. Now, get me some food before I faint dead away."

She pushes me with a gentle shove. "You got that from the back of one of my books, didn't you?"

I flash her a mischievous grin. "Maybe."

"You're the worst." She grabs her jacket and keys.

As we walk out, the door across the hall opens, and a girl around my sister's age smiles at us. "Hi, Kinsley."

My sister points at me. "Sarah, this is my obnoxious brother, Luke. The hockey player I told you about."

I side elbow Kins, evoking a satisfying grunt as I shake Sarah's hand. But as her brother, I'm feeling kind of proud that Kins talked about me. "Nice to meet you, Sarah."

She pauses our shake as she leans in to study me, then her eyes widen. "Wait here a minute. Don't go anywhere!" She dashes into her room, leaving her door cracked, but not enough to see what she's doing.

I shoot a questioning glance at Kinsley. But she shrugs and holds her hands up, indicating she hasn't a clue.

Sarah rushes back out, holding a magazine to her chest. "My brother just got drafted by the Rangers, so of course, I had to get a copy of USA Hockey Today to clip the article."

She flips open the magazine to a two-page spread, then hands it to me. I'm expecting to see a resemblance between the guy in the picture and Sarah, but then I realize the full headshot is me. And I recognize the other pictures, too. My eyes drift to the byline.

Sophie's name sits right there under the headline. And it's in a national magazine.

Sarah holds a pen out with a shy smile. "Do you mind signing it?"

Everything inside me locks up. Like a robot, I scribble a loose signature on the main photo and hand her pen back.

"Thanks! Can we get an us-ie?" She stares at me with expectant eyes and a wide grin.

Kinsley snorts, then laughs at the Ted Lasso reference.

"Sure." I sound about as deadpan as I can get. Doesn't matter now, does it? If Sarah figured out who I was, anyone can. Am I foolish to hope my father has no interest in hockey and won't ever see it?

Sarah whips around to stand next to me while my sister scans the article.

"Sophie wrote this?"

I grunt while fake-smiling for Sarah's picture.

"She's a really great writer." She hands the magazine back to Sarah. "I even made it in there."

I snag the magazine before Sarah can take it back. "Where?"

Kinsley leans in and points to a paragraph on the second page. "There. I thought you would have seen it already."

Sure enough, Sophie mentions that I have a younger sister, who I "raised after our mother's death," making me sound so noble. Or something.

But right now, I'm feeling anything but noble. I'd tear the magazine to smithereens if it would make it go away permanently. The article even states that Kins is a student at Columbia.

"No, I didn't want to read about myself."

Kins does her eye roll thing again. "So humble."

I hand the magazine to Sarah and drag Kins along by the elbow. "Let's go get ramen."

Kinsley gives Sarah an awkward wave over her shoulder. "Don't mind him. He's always this way."

I grunt at her comment but keep us moving toward the stairs. I need air. I need to think this through. I need to know why Sophie would do something like this.

Yet, I already know, don't I? This is even better than a column in the local paper, isn't it? National exposure will go a long way in getting her that and more, I'd imagine.

As much as I'd love to see her realize her dream, I just wish it didn't come at my and my sister's expense.

Now, I have to tell Kinsley about our father's release from prison. Because if he sees the article, he'll know where to find her. And that makes the already sinking feeling in my gut plunge a lot deeper.

Once we get our orders and sit down, I lean back in the hard plastic booth, close my eyes, and try to center myself. The anger I've kept buried is like a pot of pasta about to boil over. I can't lose control. Not now.

When I open my eyes, Kinsley's staring at me. "What's going on?"

I consider my words as she slurps up ramen noodles. "I got a notification that our father was released from prison to a halfway house several weeks ago."

She wiggles in her seat and glances around. "Okaaaay. So?"

"If he sees that article, he'll recognize me and know where you are."

She drops her gaze to the bowl in front of her, running her chopsticks in a circle through the noodles. "Is that a bad thing?"

"Yes!" I run a hand over my mouth, schooling my temper. The woman at the table next to us darts a glance my way and frowns.

I lower my voice to a whisper. "Yes, that's a bad thing. I don't want him back in our lives."

She drops her chopsticks into the bowl. "Why not? He's the only parent we have now, Luke."

I grunt. "We don't need him."

She presses her lips into a line and knits her brows together, which tells me the wheels of her brain are working overtime.

"But what if I *want* to meet him?"

I almost choke on a bite of noodles. "That's a bad idea too. I may have been young, but I remember how much better things were for us after he left. Mom became happy."

Doubt clouds her eyes, but she nods. "Okay."

My phone vibrates in my pocket, so I tug it out.

> SOPHIE: The roses are gorgeous! Thank you, Luke. And yes, it's all okay. I'm looking forward to our date!

The mix of emotions rising in me brings a growl deep in my throat.

Kinsley snatches the phone right out of my hand.

"Hey, that's private." I make a grab for her wrist but her other hand swoops in for a switch.

"Not if it makes you react like that." She holds my phone behind her as she twists around in the booth to read it, then meets my gaze. "Roses? Couldn't you be more original? And one would think this would make you happy. She's clearly into you. Are you two official?"

I just realized my sister does a similar kind of word spew as Sophie, only hers is cute whereas Kins' is confrontational and makes my head spin.

"The roses are from one of Mom's bushes. And no, we are most definitely not official. Nor will we be." I busy myself with another bite of my meal that's turning out to be much better than those cheap ramen packages at the store. Maybe Kins will get the hint that I don't want to talk about it.

She hands my phone back. "Okay, let me get this straight. You went to the trouble to give Sophie roses from Mom's bushes—nice touch, by the way—and asked her out on a date, but you have no intention of making things serious. That sounds like a bone-headed hockey move to me."

My appetite walks out the door with the hipster who has no business wearing pants that tight. I toss my chopsticks into my bowl. "I told Sophie at the start of this to not use any shots of my full face because I didn't want to risk our father finding us. She told me when that first went to print in Sarabella that it was an accident. She didn't mean to upload that picture to the paper, which, fortunately, has a limited reach in Florida."

"Okay. If it was an accident, why are you still mad at her?"

"She knew how I felt, yet she goes and lands a feature in a national magazine with the same article and photo. She's no better than that reporter who dug up the dirt on our father after Mom's accident. All she ever wanted was her own column, and now she has a byline in a national magazine."

Her mouth makes a circle with her silent 'oh.' "Are you sure she did it on purpose?"

I lean back in my seat and snort. "How else would that happen? And why are you defending her?"

She lifts her shoulders. "It just doesn't sound like her."

"You hardly even know her."

"And you do? Are you sure this is something she'd do? Because I didn't get that vibe from her."

A weariness I'm accustomed to feeling after a game settles over me, but without the satisfaction of knowing I played my best. "You always look for the good in people, Kins. But it's not always there."

"Then talk to her. Listen to her side of the story."

"I did that once. Gave her the benefit of the doubt. You know the saying, fool me once..."

"But what if it's not what you think, and you miss out on something great?"

"I can't trust her, Kins. And without that, there can't be anything between us." My words settle into my gut, making the contents of my stomach turn sour. Speaking the truth out loud doesn't make the situation any more palatable, but it does clarify what I need to do.

And I'm not sure what hurts more—feeling betrayed by Sophie or knowing this connection we have can't go anywhere. It's not fixable in my playbook. I took a risk that might bring trouble from the past. Best to cut my losses now and be done with it.

Besides, I need to focus on what's in front of me— getting promoted to an NHL team. That will go a long way in securing mine and Kinsley's future.

I pick up my phone and shoot Sophie a reply that shreds my soul.

> LUKE: Consider the roses a congratulations for your article going national. I have to cancel our date, though. I'm sure you understand why.

My appetite flies away, along with the message I just sent. Now it's my turn to aimlessly swirl ramen noodles around the bowl with my chopsticks.

Kinsley is quiet again...until she isn't. "You sure this isn't about something else?"

Her unexpected question lands somewhere dead center in my heart, but that's a place I stopped visiting a long time ago. I frown at her. "What are you talking about? What else would it be?"

She lifts one shoulder. "I don't know. I'm just asking a question."

I lean against the back of the booth. "Okay, besides the fact that I can't trust her, I don't have time for a relationship. Gabe told me I may get promoted. That means more traveling."

Kins smile brings some comfort to the ache in my chest. "Congrats, big bro. That's amazing!" Her expression turns deadpan. "But no, that's not it."

I blurt out a short laugh. More like a snort. "Then you tell me, because you clearly think you know the answer."

"Maybe."

"But you're not going to tell me."

She shakes her head. "That would defeat the purpose."

I'm beginning to think Kinsley missed her true calling in psychology. The thing is, she's dangerously close to a truth I barely acknowledge myself these days. Necessity required I bury that part of me so I could return to hockey.

"Think whatever you want, Kins, but there's no other reason."

She points at me with her chopsticks. "Now I know I'm right."

Chapter Twenty-Three

SOPHIE

I think I've read Luke's text at least a dozen times. First, to make sure I didn't misread it, then out of confusion. I told him the article's reach was limited to Southwest Florida, so I don't understand what he's talking about.

Did he change his mind, deciding he's mad at me after all? Or did this just become a convenient excuse for him to end whatever this is between us before it turns into something serious?

The worst part? I'm right back in that place again, wondering what it is about me that makes every romantic relationship in my life fail. And each time I try to compose a reply to his message, my fingers freeze and my heart aches.

I'm glad the team isn't practicing today, so I can finish loading the few items from my temporary office into my car without questions about the tears running down my cheeks. Now that I've finished the interviews and have plenty of shots from practices, I don't need an office space anymore. I only have to come for games and special events.

I should be happy about that, but instead, I'm crumbling inside. Marty tried to warn me, but I convinced myself things would be different this time. But I should have known this thing with Luke wouldn't last. Like I said, romance and I don't mix. Here's yet another failed relationship to prove it. If it ever was a relationship...

When will I learn my lesson and stop trying or believing I can have something wonderful, like what Mia and Ethan share? We didn't have an official first date. More like a couple of happenstance meals together.

But those times with Luke were unlike any of my other first dates. We connected on a deep level faster than I thought possible for two people who started off at odds with each other. I went from dreading interacting with him to wanting to be with him all the time.

And I'd hoped he felt the same.

I need to make sense of this because something doesn't fit. Once I finish loading my car, I drive to the office. Maybe Marty can help me figure out what Luke's talking about. When I walk through past the sea of cubicles, Charlene waves me over. I hold up my a finger to let her know I'd be there in a minute and walk into Marty's office.

His grin widens as he stands. "There she is! I have a surprise for you, kiddo. I was waiting for you to get here so I could show you."

As I reach his desk, he spins a copy of USA Hockey Magazine to face me, then flips it open. Luke's handsome face stares at me from an image that fills most of the left page. At the top of the right, under the title, my name sits in the byline.

The memory of the team's owner introducing me to Peter Orion from the magazine flashes front and center. "Oh, no...no, no, no...this can't be happening."

Marty's grin crashes into a frown. "I thought you'd be

ecstatic." He taps the article with his finger. "Soph, this is even better than your own column. This could lead to something much bigger."

A full understanding of Luke's words hits me in the face, and I can tell you, I have no helmet strong enough to shield me from the impact. He most likely assumes I saw an opportunity to vault my journalism to a national level. He must think I'm no better than that reporter who shredded his family after his mother's death.

And I don't have a clue of how I can fix this. If I put myself in Luke's shoes—or rather, skates—I'm not sure I'd believe me either.

I lift tear-filled eyes to the man who's been like a substitute father to me for five years, who stood by me as I grieved my father's death while he mourned the loss of his best friend, and who I know only wants to see me succeed. And now I'm going to disappoint him too.

"I made a promise to keep Luke's full face out of the article, and I blew it, Marty. That photo of Luke wasn't supposed to be in there. I uploaded it by mistake. He forgave me when I explained the limited reach of our paper, but I never imagined the piece would get picked up."

Marty lowers himself back into his seat at a snail's pace. "I'm sorry, Soph. I thought you'd want this. When their editor called about it, I gave them the go ahead."

I wipe my cheeks dry. "It's not your fault. I didn't think telling you mattered since the article was already out there. I just never imagined—"

"You should, kiddo. You're that good." His tone is emphatic and warms me to the core.

As much as I'd love to tell him thank you, I can't. I'm still too caught up in what this means for Luke and me. If there's even any hope of an 'and.'

Marty leans forward and clasps his hands on his blotter. "Why did Luke ask you to keep his face out of it? That's kind of hard to do for a profile."

"It has to do with his father. I had a picture picked out with his helmet on with his head turned more to the side, but I forgot to remove the other one from the upload folder."

"You didn't do it on purpose, kiddo. Tell him I'm the one to blame."

I shake my head. "It was my mistake. I'm just not sure there's a way to fix this. I broke his trust."

He studies me and hums. "You're in love with him, aren't you?"

A knot forms so fast in my throat that I can't speak, so I nod.

"Then don't give up fighting for him. And if he doesn't forgive you, then maybe he's not the right guy for you after all."

Marty may be right. And that would add a fourth strike on my romance record. I truly thought Luke was different than the first three boneheads I dated.

Perhaps I was wrong about him after all.

As soon as I filled Charlene in, she grabbed her purse, then dragged me across the street to get our favorite coffees at the Last Bean coffee shop. She even treated me to a double-sized portion of the local bakery's stellar banana bread, which has become a known entity throughout Sarabella.

Char pushes her empty cup to the side. "Listen, I get how this looks, but I still think you should text him back and explain what happened."

I shake my head. "What's the point?"

"Um, hello! True love, maybe…possibly. Come on, Sophie. You have to at least try."

"You know my track record. I suck at relationships. But I'll think about it, okay?"

She lifts her eyes in a half roll. "Fine. I guess that's better than a flat-out 'no.'"

My phone buzzes on the table and my heart jumps when I see 'Jameson' crawl across the top of the screen. But it's the first name that gives me pause—Kinsley.

I'm sure Luke has filled her in with his version of what happened, so there's a good chance she's mad at me too. However, I told her to call me if she ever needed help, so it could be that—only one way to find out.

I swipe to answer the call. "Hi, Kinsley. Everything okay?"

"That depends. Define okay."

Definitely an edge to her voice, but that's almost Kinsley's norm, from what I seen so far. I cringe, mentally preparing myself for the onslaught about to be unleashed. "I'm guessing Luke told you about the article."

"Actually, we found out at the same time. My neighbor across the hall recognized Luke from the picture. Really nice photo, by the way."

"Um, thank you?" I do a mental double-take. Maybe she's not as angry as I thought. "Kinsley, I had no idea my article would get picked up like that. My editor gave approval without asking me." Realizing how that sounds, I rush in with an explanation. "But only because he believed that's what I would want. Really and truly, it wasn't intentional."

Her breathy sigh filters over the connection. "I figured."

"You did?"

"Yeah, just didn't seem like something you would do."

I hold a hand to my chest. "Thank you."

"So, are you going to tell my boneheaded brother?"

"I don't think he'll believe me."

"Then convince him."

Fresh tears burn my eyes. "Kinsley, I appreciate what you're doing, but maybe this is working out for the best." I want to believe that, but even I heard the way my voice broke when I said it.

"Wow, you two are so much alike." She snickers.

"What do you mean?"

"Luke likes you a lot, Sophie, but he's scared."

"Scared of being in a relationship with me?"

"No, scared of losing you."

A teeny tiny spark of hope flickers to life in my chest. "Did he tell you that?"

Char raises her brows in question at me. I shrug and hold up my hand so I don't miss what Kinsley's saying.

"You know that our mother was killed in a car accident, right?"

I get a mild case of whiplash with her subject change, but I'll roll with it. Maybe all this has stirred up some old emotions for her, which makes me feel even worse to think about. "Yes, I do. I hate that you two went through that."

"It happened on her way to Luke's game."

"I remember reading that." I massage the spot between my brows. The article Marty found mentioned it briefly, so I didn't pay much attention to it.

"Luke blames himself."

I jerk my head up. "For what?"

She lets out an exasperated sigh. "Wow, for being older, you two sure act a lot dumber. For her death. That's why he left hockey."

"I thought he left to take care of you."

"That's what he wants to believe. Did he tell you the significance behind his jersey number?"

My mind is jumbled by trying to follow Kinsley down this rabbit hole, so I close my eyes as I recall what I wrote about that. "He said it was his mother's favorite number."

"No, he wore that number because she predicted Luke would make the NHL by the time he was twenty-four."

I mentally flip through my notes—Luke turned twenty-four early the same year of his mother's death. "But he left before that could happen."

"Exactly. I think my brother thought if he failed, it would make her death seem even more pointless."

A blinding light switches on in my head. "Because she died on the way to his game."

The pain I felt earlier over Luke's rejection pales in the presence of the ache I feel for him now. And he's carried this burden alone, among all the other responsibilities he had to take on.

"Yes." Her voice takes on a soft yet sad quality. "And he's pushing you away out of fear too."

A surreal calmness settles over me as a determination replaces my self pity. If Kinsley is correct, then I need to have a conversation with Luke. I have to at least try, right?

The only thing that eclipses my gratitude for Kinsley's call is how blown away I am by her ability to not only tell a story but to lead me full circle back to the truth.

"Thank you, Kinsley. Has anyone ever tell you that you're going to make a fantastic journalist?"

Her snort pierces my ear. "No comment."

Chapter Twenty-Four

LUKE

I'm playing angry, and I know it.

Instead of going out with Sophie like I'd hoped, I spent Tuesday evening moving into Payton's apartment. With Gabe's wife so close to her due date now, they need to start setting up the nursery. Turns out, Payton needed a room-mate, so it made sense.

Unlike anything else in my life, at the moment.

And I'm angry as hell about it. Just when things seemed to fall into place, that article—and Sophie—upended every-thing. I'm mad at myself for taking a risk with her when I should have listened to my gut from the beginning. But then I got to know the beautiful mind ticking behind those gorgeous brown eyes of hers and quit listening.

Even now, I can't stop reliving the feel of her in my arms and the soft caress of my lips against hers...the floral yet musky scent of her hair as I nuzzle the spot below her ear...the way she pressed in closer, letting me know she wanted me too.

I'm also mad at hockey—and myself—for wrecking

mine and Kinsley's lives. If my mother wasn't rushing to yet another one of my games, maybe she'd still be here now, and Kinsley wouldn't have had to grow up faster than necessary. That kid should seriously consider a minor in psychology.

And I'm mad at a father I don't even know—who walked out eighteen years ago and could wind up showing up again at some point, especially if he sees that article. The NHL means more money. The last thing I need is a dead-beat dad looking for a handout.

The chaos swirling in my head has made me lose my edge. Instead of using this break on the bench to study my opponent and strategize, I'm consumed with a dark-haired journalist with oversized soulful eyes that make my world spin on an entirely different axis. I *need* to focus on the game —not Sophie.

Yet, I keep searching the arena for her. Is she here tonight? Now that she's writing for a national magazine, maybe she considers covering a third tier team beneath her. Or could something have happened to her on the way here? I close my eyes, pinching the bridge of my nose, and focus on my breathing. I'm sure she's fine. She's just not here.

Two guys from the fourth line return to the bench as Ethan and I flow over the wall and enter the fray of what's left of the third period. With the score tied, the opposing team has defaulted to playing dirty. Happens that way sometimes, especially when we're gunning for the Kelly Cup playoffs.

I fly in and steal the puck from their captain, slamming him into the boards. Then I make a run for the offensive zone. Just as I'm getting closer, their enforcer makes a grab for me, misses, then resorts to hooking. The ref's whistle goes off, as do my gloves.

Next thing I know, I'm going after the guy, fisticuffs in full swing, which sends his helmet flying. A ref pulls me off and sends me to the sin bin to blow off some steam. Gabe will likely chew me out afterward, seeing as we're just minutes from the end, and I'm stuck in a glass cage for two of them. If we lose this game, that will be my fault too.

Just as my time's up in the penalty box, Payton makes a goal, putting us ahead and giving me some relief from my self-flagellation. When I leave the box, Gabe waves me to the bench where I watch my teammates maintain our lead, until the final whistle blows and the rest of the team takes the ice for a well-earned celly for winning.

I skate over to join them, but I'm not feeling it. However, I'm the captain, so I want to show up for my team. They carried this game when I was lacking, which I'm grateful for.

The guys line up, each waiting for their turns to touch helmets with Wade and bask in our win. I wait near the end, patting each player on the back for a job well done as they leave the ice.

Jayce pauses next to me. "Jammer came out to play tonight."

I shake my head. "Not my finest moment."

He shrugs and moves on, but I can tell he's assessing my actions and my words. I *need* to do better. This is the first time I've ever been glad my mother wasn't here because I'm sure that fight would have disappointed her. But what I'm most worried about is what Sophie thinks about me now—if she was even here.

My eyes drift up again in a casual search of the lingering fans and half empty seats surrounding us. Yet no one with bangs and eyes the size of the moon stands out.

Why am I still looking for her? I'm the one who broke

our date with no intentions of a redo. But she's all I can think about. I just can't seem to move past this feeling of betrayal. Plus, there's the whole trust issue. How can I be in a relationship with someone I can't trust?

In front of me, Payton glances over his shoulder. "Good game, Captain."

"Yeah, thanks to you."

"We're not a team of one, bruv. You know that better than most of us."

Guess I needed a reminder. Or something to punch me out of my self pity. That's a metaphorical jersey that never fits and tends to have a dingy appearance. Not to mention the stench.

No, thank you.

"Thanks...bruv."

He shoots a smile at me over his shoulder for using his British slang, then glides forward. Wade pats the back of Payton's head as they touch helmets and exchange words.

My turn. Wade holds onto me. "Let it go, man."

"Who says I'm hanging onto it?"

He tugs his helmet off. "Your face. We all lose control at some point."

I grudgingly nod. "It's complicated."

"Doesn't need to be, Jammer. Just let it roll. It all works out in the end."

I wish I could share his optimism. Never been my strong suit and after the accident, I think I quit trying. Kinsley pointed out that I don't engage when she talks about Mom, that I simply grunt. When did I turn into a grump with a hefty touch of cynicism?

And look where it got me? Somewhat humiliated and choking down a serving of humble pie.

I follow behind Wade as we leave the ice and head down

the tunnel to the locker room. When we reach the fork that branches toward the guest locker room, I catch a glimpse of the other team's captain near the entrance. I wave to grab his attention.

He waddles my direction as I approach him. I can already see a welt forming on the side of his jaw from the one punch I landed, which makes me feel lower than low.

I shift my helmet to my left hand and hold out my right one. "Sorry for the punch. I shouldn't have lost my cool."

The weight in my chest lifts some when he accepts my shake. "No worries, but I appreciate it."

We give each other nods to affirm we're good, then I turn around and find Gabe standing at the fork of the tunnel, hands in his pockets and a concerned expression on his face.

I head his way as fast as my skates will let me. "I screwed up, Coach. Sorry."

He raises his chin in the direction of the opposing team's locker room door. "You made good. That counts."

"Thanks." When I move past him, he stops me.

"Tampa's GM was here to watch you play. I didn't know until near the end. I told him it was an off night for you."

The weight of his revelation feels like a slam against the boards. And the post-game body aches have nothing on the one spreading in my chest. And Gabe's not saying anything more.

I hang my head for a moment. "Did I blow my chance?"

He rubs a hand across his mouth. "I don't think so. I'll let him know you made a point to apologize without being asked. That should hold some weight."

I give him a resigned nod. "Thanks, Coach."

He slides his hands into his pants pockets. "Wanna tell me what that fight was really about?"

I shake my head. "Doesn't matter."

But as I waddle toward the locker room, it's not jeopardizing my shot with Tampa Bay Lightning that has me twisted up inside.

I'm just going to call her.

And I should. A text is no way to tell someone you're not interested in dating them. Which, technically, isn't true. I very much want to date Sophie...and more. She's like a drug, and I'm having some serious withdrawals.

Maybe I should go to her place. Show up on her doorstep like the guys in those goofy romcoms my sister likes. Kins roped me into watching one with her when she was here last. I never imagined my kid sister to be such a romantic.

With my mind decided, I shift into high gear to get cleaned up. For once, I don't begrudge putting a suit on after a game. I want to look good for Sophie. Just thinking about seeing her goes a long way in pushing tonight's events to the back burner.

The cool night air hits my damp hair and sends a chill down my back. I'm laser focused, a man on a mission, to get to my car and drive to Sophie's. But a small crowd of fans is waiting for us as we walk out, so I do my best to accommodate a few of them without appearing like I'm in a hurry, even though I am.

Finally, I'm able to break away.

"Luke?" Sophie's voice stops me in my tracks.

I search around me until I spot her by the lamppost.

Soft light reflects off her hair but leaves her eyes shadowed, and the yellow glow makes her pink top appear more orange.

But I know it's pink because I know her.

Or, at least, I thought I did. "Sophie, what are you doing here?"

Stupid question, I know. But I'm not sure where to start.

"I'm supposed to cover the games, remember? It's my job." There's an edge to her voice that I've not heard before.

Feeling sheepish, I run a hand through my hair. "Yes, I know. I just didn't see you tonight, so I thought you were busy..."

She takes a step toward me. A soft breeze carries her sweet scent to my nose, making me want to forget everything and pull her into my arms, as if I'd ached for her for a decade. Because that's what this knot in my chest feels like.

"Busy?" As she tilts her head, moonlight illuminates her eyes, giving me a clear picture of the question she's really asking. And the hurt I've inflicted.

Might as well be honest with her. "Yeah, I assumed you'd have a bigger assignment by now."

She takes another step closer. "Because you thought I leveraged the article I did on you to get a magazine byline."

Her voice sounds flat yet laced with a hint of frustration.

I can't bring myself to admit it to her, so I let my silence speak for me.

"I didn't even know about it, Luke. And the irony is, you found out before I did. Yet you *assumed* I did it on purpose, despite seeing how mortified I was about the wrong picture being used in the first run."

I attempt some levity. "You know what they say about making assumptions."

Something raw flashes in her eyes. "I'm not one of the asses in this equation, Luke. I don't know what hurts worse —that you didn't even bother to talk to me about it, or that you could think I would do something like that to you."

"Sophie, I'm—"

"You know what's even more ironic about this. USA Hockey Magazine offered me a job because of the reaction to that article. The fans loved it. And they want more pieces like it."

Despite not wanting the exposure, I can't help but be happy for her. This is what she's wanted, to have recognition for her journalism skills. "That's great, right?"

"No!" She lifts her hands into the air with her frustration and starts pacing back and forth. "I have no desire to bounce around all over the place, dealing with smelly locker rooms and arrogant hockey players, or riding on stupid buses and sleeping in hotels. I just want to write a column about Sarabella, the town I love and want its residents to know and love too. But I thought you understood that."

I did understand that about her. But I thought...I made the mistake of assuming 'opportunistic' always applied to someone in her field, even if they defined themselves as a journalist and not a reporter. But more importantly, and profession aside, I should have known Sophie would never do something like that simply because she's not that kind of person.

I swallow down any pride I have left. "You're right, Sophie. I am an ass. And I'm so sorry."

She stops and stares at me. "That was unexpected."

"What? That I said you were right or admitted I'm an idiot for assuming."

She blinks. "Both?"

I don't miss the way she's trying not to smile, but I see it in those beautiful big brown eyes that make me want to depart my world and enter hers. "Will you forgive me?"

She crosses her arms, but her gaze is borderline flirtatious. "I'll think about it."

And she has no idea what she's doing to me. I slip my hands into my pants pockets, resisting the urge to crush her against me and use my sculpted lips to show her what I'm feeling. We have a chance to turn our rough start into something solid and lasting if she's willing.

"Okay. I'll wait." I let one side of my mouth slide up in a half grin because I can tell she's putting on a show. She wants to make me work for it, and, surprisingly, I'm okay with that. But first, I'm going to enjoy teasing her a little.

I cross my arms, mimicking her stance without breaking eye contact.

She lets out a frustrated growl and drops her arms. "Whatever."

When she whirls around to leave, I grab her wrist and yank her toward me. Our bodies collide right before my lips crash onto hers. There's no way I'm letting her walk away without showing her how much I want and need her in my life.

And she rewards me more than I could have hoped. We're like two people starved and our only sustenance is each other. The kiss is frantic and passionate, and I'm completely lost in the feel and taste of her. The blaze between us finally simmers to a low burn, making our embrace and kiss more tender and affectionate.

I'm acutely aware of how much I want more of this with her. A lifetime of fiery kisses after some playful teasing. I want her eyes to be the last thing I see at night and the first thing I see every morning as I reach out and brush long tendrils of hair out of her face. To see her smile and know it's just for me.

Ethan's whistle breaches our bubble and grabs my attention. He, along with Payton and Wade, are standing ten feet away, watching us. Mathéo walks over and joins them, flashing a wide grin.

I catch a brief glimpse of Sophie's deepening blush before she buries her face against my shirt. No doubt I'll have mascara stains there as well. But I don't care. I'll create a favorite shirts collection and rotate wearing them on days I don't get to see her.

Ethan gives me a pointed look. "Glad to see you quit fighting it, Cap."

I shake my head at them and growl, "Good night, guys."

Ethan grins, slipping his hands into his pants pockets as he steps down from the sidewalk. Wade makes a clicking sound in his mouth and points at me with a grin that reveals too many teeth. Payton dips his chin and gives me a subtle salute. And then there's Mathéo, scurrying after them as if he was late to get the message.

I kiss the top of Sophie's head. "You can come out now. They're gone."

She snuggles in closer and slides her arms underneath my jacket and around my waist. "Don't wanna. You're warm."

Wearing a suit made me oblivious to the chill in the air. I wrap my jacket flaps around her and use my arms to hold them—and her—in place. "That better?"

"Uh hmm." Her muffled reply is so cute, I can't help but smile.

"Does this mean you forgive me?"

She tilts her face up. "Look at you, asking questions and not making assumptions."

Since I have access, I tickle her side, making her squeal and wiggle against me, which ignites the spark between us again. I dip my head to devour her lips, then move on to kiss her neck in a slow and languid manner until a soft moan rises from her delicate throat.

When I lift my head, her eyes are hooded with her own desire, which does crazy things to my insides. I don't want this moment to end, but we're out in the open in front of a sports arena and though most of the team and fans have left, there are still enough people around to watch us.

I shrug off my jacket and wrap it around her, then take her hand and lead her down the sidewalk.

"Where are we going?"

"For a walk."

She crinkles her nose at me. "Around the arena?"

"Everything is closed this time of night, and I haven't gotten a date with you yet."

She glances up at me, tugging her lip between her teeth on one side and making me want to restart our make-out session. "Would you be interested in being my date for a rehearsal dinner and wedding?"

"That depends."

"On what?"

"Who's getting married?"

"Mia and Ethan."

"I'm already invited."

"But not as my date." Her voice takes on a flirty, sultry quality that I've not heard before.

There are definitely more layers to Sophie Adams than meets the eye, and I'm looking forward to peeling back each one as I get to know her better.

"Well, since I'll already be there…"

She returns the side tickle, but I grab her hands before she can get very far and pin them behind her back. We're in between pavement lights which affords us a little more privacy, so I plan to enjoy this to the fullest.

"Yes, I'll gladly sit next to you at the wedding. I'll make sure I have tissues."

"I'm the maid of honor, so I won't be sitting with you during the service. But tissues might be handy afterward."

I lean in, pressing her closer as I tease her lips with mine. "I didn't know you were in the wedding party."

"Best friend of the bride. And wait until you see my dress." She nips at my lip, spiking my pulse into overdrive.

"Can't wait," I growl against her mouth.

And then I make sure she knows it.

Chapter Twenty-Five

SOPHIE

Getting Mia's SOS text wasn't on my agenda today. But when a friend says they need you to talk them down from a ledge—a metaphorical one in this case, thank goodness—you drop everything and show up for them.

Mia hasn't stopped pacing since I arrived, and all I know so far is that Ethan's brother's company isn't playing nice. A last-minute project complication kept him from catching his flight.

I reach out and rest my hand on her arm, bringing her to a stop. "The good news is there's still time. He'd planned to come early so he and his wife could have a vacation too, right?"

She nods, then pulls away, continuing to make a discernible path in the carpet. "It seems...I mean...what if...I can't help wondering..."

"Mia, just spit it out."

Eyes wide, she faces me, hands out in front of her. "First, the venue and now this? What if the universe is trying to keep us from making a mistake?"

I was NOT expecting that. Jumping to my feet, I wrap her in a big hug I hope will settle her nerves. "You're simply experiencing some pre-wedding jitters, that's all. No wedding goes off without some kind of complication. None that I know of, anyway."

"If you say so." She sounds more like a four-year-old.

I place my hands on her shoulders and lean back. "You and Ethan are one of the most adorable couples I've ever seen. I've never once doubted whether you should be together. I'm surprised you didn't get married sooner, to be honest."

"Really?" Her expression lifts with hope.

"Yeah…really. Remember how you two connected that day at the arena? Ethan kept skating over to talk to you in between drills. He even got in trouble with the coach."

She lets out a soft giggle. "He was pretty annoying."

I snort. "You loved every minute of it."

"I did. I just didn't want him to know it." The almost devious sound in her voice is somewhat shocking and very entertaining.

"You little minx, you."

She gives me an evil grin. "A girl needs her secrets."

"If you say so." I giggle.

"Speaking of which. When are you going to share Luke with the rest of us. You two are dating now, right?"

"It's all so new. And he's out of town for a game. But I did invite him as my date to the wedding."

"Ethan already invited him."

"I know, but now he's my plus one too." I can't help the smile spreading across my face as I think about him. Our walk around the arena felt like a first date, with lots of kissing. My cheeks blaze when I remember how thoroughly Luke kissed me.

And, unfortunately, Mia notices. Her eyes widen, and she points at me. "You've already fallen for him, haven't you?"

I grin and bob my head up and down. Mia squeals, grabs my arms, and jumps up and down, taking me with her. We collapse on her couch like a couple of silly high school girls.

"How does he feel about you?"

I poke at a loose thread on the cushion. "We haven't declared our feelings, per se. But I'm pretty sure he feels the same. He seems to anyway."

Mia pulls her legs up under her and faces me. "You did it, Soph. You found the right guy."

I shrug. "I'd like to think so."

She frowns at me. "Why aren't you more excited?"

If I say it, will it make the very thing I'm afraid of happening happen? That as soon as I show Luke I'm crazy about him, he'll drop me like a hot potato? I want to find my person more than anything. Well, aside from getting my column. But what if I'm wrong again?

"I hope Luke is the..." I tip my head to the side. "You know..."

"The one," she finishes for me.

I lower my voice in case that romance curse is listening. "Yes, but I'm still not sure."

"Why? You just said you hope he's the one." Her tone tells me she's on the verge of losing patience with me.

"Technically, I didn't."

She throws herself back on the couch with a growl.

"I'm not sure how Luke feels about us. You know me, Mia. I go all in. And then I get my heart ripped out because I thought the guy was as into me as I was him. But then it turns out he's not and then it gets all weird, and he either dumps or ghosts me." I let out a noisy breath.

Mia grabs my hands. "Soph, those guys didn't deserve you. They may have tried to be worthy of you, but they totally missed the mark. And based upon what you've told so far, Luke is crazy about you, so stop doubting him."

You know you have the best-of-the-best of friends when they hear your verbal vomit and don't judge you for it. Or better yet, they wholeheartedly support you and say they're on your side.

Tears of the past sting my eyes as I throw my arms around her. "I love you, you know that?"

Now Mia is crying. "I love you too. You're the best friend a girl could ever have."

"No, you are." I sob.

"Sophie, what did you do to my bride-to-be?" Somehow, we missed hearing Ethan walk into Mia's apartment.

Wiping my face, I sit back on the couch while Mia launches herself into his arms.

"I love you, Ethan. And I always will. I will never doubt us again." She bawls into his neck.

Ethan shoots me a questioning glance, and his brows are positioned in full alarm mode.

I shake my head and wave my hand in front of me, reassuring him there's nothing to worry about.

Ethan rewards me with an appreciative smile, then kisses Mia's temple and whispers something in her ear. Next thing I know, they're making out as if they haven't seen each other in months. The sooner these two get married, the better.

I grab my purse and jump up from the couch. "Okay, I'm leaving. Mia, text me when they reschedule their flight so I can pick them up."

Without missing a beat—or kiss—she waves and gives me a thumbs up.

I make my escape before I witness anything else, but I gotta say I'm a little green at the moment.

For once, despite my miserable romance record, I'm hopeful.

Maybe Luke *is* the one for me.

It's finally here. Not the wedding, but the rehearsal dinner. So maybe instead I should say it's almost wedding time. And after the whole venue hiccup and the best man almost missing—thank goodness Ethan's brother caught a later flight—I'm ready to find a proverbial cloud to float on.

And this pink dress with tiny white rose polka dots is going a long way to get me there. When I first laid eyes on it at the Pink Hibiscus—another exceptional Sarabella shop I can't wait to feature in my future column—I knew it was perfect.

I'm excited to show it off for Luke, even though it's not technically a *date* date. So far, all of our dates have been more like happenstance. I want a real first date with Luke that's planned and just about us. No bus rides, hockey games, rehearsal dinners, or weddings. Once this weekend is over and the dust settles, we can finally focus on us because I think I may have finally broken my romance curse.

I check my bag to make sure I have all my camera equipment and then some, since I promised Mia I would take plenty of pictures of tonight. She hired a great photographer for the wedding, but tonight is my gift to her.

That's just one aspect of my duties tonight, along with

making sure the bride doesn't have a meltdown and the groom doesn't flake out. Not that Ethan would, but weddings have a way of making people do—and say—crazy things.

My fingers brush over the gift I brought for Luke. A framed picture of him hugging Kinsley after the game she attended before going back to New York. When I went through the images later that day and saw the image, I knew I had to get a print made. I think I'm more excited about giving it to him than the wedding. Definitely not going to mention that to Mia.

But the true heart squeeze came when I viewed the pictures Kinsley took of Luke and me. The look in his eyes melted me into a puddle. I revisit these often, then pinch myself to make sure it's real.

As soon as I arrive at the Turtle Tide, I get busy hanging the photo garland I created from shots I stole of them when they weren't looking and images their families provided on the sly. The series of pictures shows their love story. I can't wait to see Mia's reaction when she sees it because she loves these kinds of things.

A gasp from behind whirls me around. Mia stands there, her tear-filled eyes taking in the garland swagged over the seats where she and Ethan will sit for the dinner.

"Soph, I...I..." She waves her hands in front of her face. "Oh, mascara!"

I nab one of the drink napkins from a nearby table and hand it to her. "Do you like it?"

She holds the napkin under her eyes to catch her tears. "Are you kidding? It's so beautiful."

With a sob, she throws her arms around me, all concern about her mascara tossed aside. I pat her back, thinking about the mascara stains I left on Luke's shirt and worrying about my new pink polka dot dress. But what can I do? Something else must be happening because she's still sobbing.

I pull away enough to see her face. "Mia, what's going on?"

She dabs her eyes with what's left of the cocktail napkin. "I'm just so happy."

I lean to the side so I can get a look at her downturned face. "Are you sure that's all it is?"

She bobs her head. "Yes. No." She sniffs, then looks as if she's about to wail. "I got my period!"

"Oh, sweetie. I'm so sorry." Which I am. Not a fun way to start a honeymoon, but I'm relieved it's not cold feet or something worse, like a groom gone rogue. "Let's get you cleaned up, okay? Some cool water on those eyes will do the trick. And I brought my makeup bag, just in case."

Ethan gives me a concerned look as we walk past. Once again, I do my best using facial expressions and hand signals to reassure him everything is fine as I grab my case and lead Mia to the restroom. If this is our only hiccup for the evening, I will consider the night a win.

Once we're in the bathroom, Mia makes a beeline for the mirrors and is on the verge of another emotional breakdown when she sees raccoon eyes staring back at her. "Why do I have to be allergic to waterproof mascara?"

"It's okay." I pull her hair away from her face. "Just cup the water to your face and we'll redo your makeup."

My phone chimes, alerting me to a text message. Luke said he would meet me here after he was done with practice since the dinner was planned to be early to accommodate Mia's grandparents, who go to bed at seven every night. I know the timing's tight, so I hope his text says he's on the way.

Once Mia's face is dry, I let go of her hair and bring out my makeup case, mentally thanking my gut for the nudge to include it and check my phone.

Only it wasn't Luke, who texted me. His sister did.

KINSLEY: I need your help.

Chapter Twenty-Six

LUKE

I grab Derek's wrist and check his watch for the third time during practice. Normally, we're heading to the showers about now, but Gabe's running us extra hard today in prep for our next game. There's a lot of expectation riding on this one, for some reason, and I'm not entirely sure why.

Gabe let Ethan leave early since it's his rehearsal dinner and his bride-to-be would probably go full throttle on him for being late, but I don't think being the 'special guest' of the maid of honor will hold any clout with Coach. Not in the mood he's in today.

"Got someplace to be, hotshot?"

Derek's snarky reply isn't why I'm grinning. I have Sophie to thank for that. To think how close I came to writing her off for all the wrong reasons wipes the smile right off my face. I'm a very grateful man for her determination to correct my erroneous assumption about her.

And I plan to make that up to her for the rest of my life, if she'll have me. "Yeah, actually, I do. Kind of a date."

My teammates jump in with the usual catcalls, including

Jayce who's fast becoming one of our MVPs. I'd be surprised if he doesn't get bumped up to the NHL faster than expected. The kid may well be my competition for a chance with Tampa Bay Lightning. But I'm okay with that. I like playing for the Sun Kings. These guys feel like my family now. And Kins and I are doing okay so far. Maybe staying where I'm at is okay too.

Bigger doesn't always mean better. If I take a page from Sophie's playbook, staying put in Sarabella with the team could be exactly what I need...and want. I've known players who were content to just play the game and didn't care if they made it to the NHL. Plus, being near Sophie is a bonus.

After a couple more scrimmages, Gabe gives Derek the signal to wrap it up. I'll be late by the time I get cleaned up and dressed for this shindig tonight, but at least I'll make it. And I can't wait to see Sophie and share some of my thoughts about the future. Turns out my sister isn't the only one she inspired.

I finish showering in record speed and dress in the dressing room, so the slacks and button-up I brought won't smell like the locker room. As I'm about to leave though, Gabe calls me back.

"Luke, hold up a minute."

I stop in the doorway. "Can it wait? I'm already late."

He runs a hand down his mouth and shakes his head.

I knew something was off. First Gabe's tense mood at practice, and now this? Whatever it is must be more serious than I thought, like he's being replaced or I'm being cut loose. But the team is performing better than ever. I don't see how it could be anything like that.

What if...

I shut that fear train down faster than a flying puck. If

Kinsley needed me, she'd text. And Sophie's safe and sound at the Turtle Tide, most likely tapping her foot and wondering what happened to me.

But the pressure in my chest continues to grow as I follow him through the locker room toward his office.

I see Kinsley first. That's my first alarm. I stride over to her. "Kins, are you okay?"

"Yeah, I'm fine."

"This isn't about quitting school again, is it?"

She shakes her head, but the look in her eyes is a weird mix of concern yet hope. She slides her gaze to someone standing a few feet away. I track mine the same direction and land on an older man with a healthy sprinkle of gray in his hair and beard. I don't recognize him, but he seems familiar.

Kinsley twines one of her hands into mine—something she used to do when she was little—and gestures to the man. "Luke, he's our father."

A hush falls over the rest of the locker room, but then a rasping, robot-like breathing sound breaks the silence.

I glance over to catch Jayce with his helmet over his face as he continues his Darth Vader impersonation. "Luke, he is your father."

Muffled snickers break out, but Payton slaps Jayce's helmet down.

Jayce holds his hands out. "What? It's funny, right?"

"Or is that irony?" Wade pipes in.

Mathéo nods thoughtfully. "Could be satire."

Payton silences them with a loud whisper. "Pipe down!"

Payton and Wade round up the rest of the guys and herd them out of the locker room.

I fist my hands at my sides, unable to move or speak. I don't know what to say to, let alone think of, the man standing in front of me—the man who walked out on us, leaving our mother to handle an infant, an eight-year-old, and a mortgage all on her own.

All I can think about is what would our lives be like now if he'd chosen a different path.

And that maybe my mother would still be alive…

———

If it weren't for Gabe, I probably would have walked away. But then that would make me no better than him…

My father.

Gabe not only gave us the conference room to have some privacy, but stayed to support Kinsley and me as a friend without saying a word. I can't shake the irony of the situation, though. Here I thought my future was finally falling into place, and I wind up slammed in a different direction, like a slapshot bouncing off the goal frame.

Add to that the clock on the wall telling me I'm extremely late to the rehearsal dinner, but that's probably for the best as I'm in no condition to see Sophie, let alone interact with a bunch of people I hardly know.

After sending a text, Kinsley sets her phone on the table and divides her gaze between me and our father as if she's watching a tennis match. She frowns at me. "Luke, say something."

I snap my eyes to hers, wishing she didn't look so much like our mother at the moment because I remember that expression—the one Mom would don when she was disappointed in me.

"Like what?" I slide angry eyes across the table to…him. There's a lot I want to say right now, but I'm afraid once I start, I won't be able to stop.

He holds his hand out. "I'm so sorry, son."

I clench my jaw in an attempt to control my anger but to no avail. "No. You can't walk back into my life now and call me your son."

He withdraws his hand as if I slapped him. And in a way, I guess I did. I don't want to be angry, but that's all I can feel at the moment.

Kinsley rests her hand on my wrist. "Just hear him out, Luke."

"Why? So he can make excuses for why he left? For what he did to Mom? To us?" I shoot out of my seat, sending it crashing against the wall. "I have to be someplace."

Gabe launches toward the door, blocking me. "Don't you think this is more important?"

If my options are being here with this mess or being with Soph, the choice is obvious. I grit my teeth. "I can't do this right now."

Gabe nods, then moves away.

I glance back at Kinsley. The pull of her eyes almost convinces me to stay, but the volcano of emotions brewing within me is dangerously close to exploding. There's no way I can expose Sophie to this. I need to be alone.

"I'm sorry, Kins. I…just give me some time to think, okay?" Not the whole truth, but also not a complete lie.

She nods, but I don't miss the unshed tears in her eyes.

I storm out of the oppressive atmosphere of the arena into a flood of cool air and sunlight. The sensation is so strong it stops me in my tracks. I close my eyes and lift my face to the sun, as if begging for some kind of relief I doubt I'll find.

"Luke?" My father's voice spins me around.

I glare at him, hoping he'll get the message, and go back

inside because he's the last person I want to talk to right now.

His hand shakes as he holds out a folded piece of paper that appears to have spent a lot of time in his pocket. "I wrote this while in prison. An amends letter. I—" His voice cracks, so he clears his throat. "I never expected to give it to you, but when I saw your sister…"

I glare at the crumpled, torn paper that's more symbolic of the mess he left our lives in than the peace he's obviously seeking.

"Please." His voice grates in a horse whisper.

I swallow down the retort I'd like more than anything to sling at him and grab the letter from his hand. Then I turn around and stride away toward my SUV, making my escape.

Once I leave the parking lot, I consider finding Sophie but decide against it. The floodgates have opened, and the last thing I want is for her to see me like this.

Here I am again, failing the people I love. My sister… Sophie…

And I do love her. But now I'm not sure it's enough.

Chapter Twenty-Seven

SOPHIE

A tear falls on my phone screen as I stare at it.

I called Kinsley as soon as I knew Mia was okay to return to the festivities. Now I'm standing near the restroom again, processing what Kinsley told me happened.

And Luke's reaction.

I'm so torn. I want to go to him, but I need to be here for Mia too.

A hand touching my shoulder snaps me back to reality. I swipe away another tear and put on a smile I'm far from feeling.

Mia tilts her head toward me. "What's wrong?"

I try to keep my smile in place, but my eyes have another agenda at the moment, and it includes making my mascara run like hers did earlier. If I try to speak, I know I'll turn into a blubbering idiot and ruin the evening.

She pulls me into a hug. "Soph, what is it? Is it Luke? Did he bail on you?"

I swipe at my cheeks, still attempting to put on the show most needed right now. This is Mia's rehearsal dinner.

Tomorrow she gets married. We've worked so hard to get all the crazy pieces in place. The last thing I want is to be a low spot in her special time.

I give a vigorous shake of my head. "No. I mean, I don't know. But it's not what you think."

She leans back to look at me. "Then what is it?"

I fill her in with a brief version of what Kinsley shared.

A myriad of emotions flow over Mia's face as she processes what I said. "That's excruciating. Is he still coming to the dinner?"

Unable to speak, I press my fingers against my lips and shrug. The ache in my chest for Luke is almost unbearable.

I lower my hand and take a deep breath. "I don't know. His sister said he had someplace to be, so maybe?"

"Did you text him?"

"Not yet. But I will now."

"Good. I can ask Ethan to try texting him too."

I grab her wrist. "No. You two focus on your evening. I already feel bad about bringing you into this as it is."

Mia's eyes widen. "Soph, you've kept me from going over the deep end throughout this entire process. If it weren't for you, I'd probably be AWOL at the moment."

Our giggles echo off the bathroom walls, mine sounding more watery.

I nudge her toward the door. "Go. I'll be out in a sec."

"Okay." She squeezes my arm. "But let me know if we can help."

I nod, but have no intention of ruining their evening. Somehow, I'll figure out a way to be in two places at once. After I shoot a text to Luke, I clean up my face, again thankful I listened to that nudge to bring my make-up bag.

More guests arrive. I try not to check my phone every ten seconds, but it's getting harder the longer I don't hear from Luke. And he's obviously not coming here because dinner's halfway done and still no sign of him.

After I give my obligatory toast as the maid of honor and Ethan's brother does his as the best man, Mia pulls me aside.

"Any word yet?"

"No, nothing."

"Any idea where he might be?"

I pause, thinking about our day at the beach and how much Luke said it helped him decompress. Could that be where he is now, trying to figure things out?

"Maybe."

Mia gives me a wan smile. "He needs you, Soph. Go find him."

Tears burn my eyes again. "Are you sure?"

"Yes. I'm fine. Ethan's got me." She slides the most loving expression his way, which he replies with one of his own.

A pang hits my chest—a mix of joy that my best friend found her person, envy over that very thing, and knowing I have to let that piece of her go that used to always run to me in her time of need. She has Ethan for that now.

And I couldn't be happier for her. But a part of me still wonders if I'm meant to have that same kind of happiness. I wish I knew if Luke and I...

Could he be that person for me?

Before stepping into the sand, I slip my sandals off, letting them dangle from my fingers by the straps. I brought Luke's gift with me in the hopes it might cheer him up and give him something positive to focus on.

The beach is nearly empty except for a few stragglers and couples strolling hand-in-hand, waiting for the sunset, which reminds me of my walk with Luke around the arena. We may not have had a sunset, but it was no less romantic.

I sweep my gaze down the shoreline for any sign of his familiar form. Leaving the warm, powdery white sand to walk along the water's edge, I inhale the salty air as gulls caw in search of their evening meal.

And just as my hope to find him about gives out, I recognize his figure near one of the lifeguard towers. I quicken my step as best as I can in this dress, but as I get closer, I stop.

By the time I reach him, he's sitting on the bottom step of the tower, holding a worn sheet of paper in one hand and his head in the other.

His body language confirms the anguish I can only imagine he's feeling right now, and it breaks me. Breaks my heart. But it also gives me the courage I need to go to him and be whatever he needs.

Saying nothing, I walk over and sit on the step next to him. He lifts his gaze to mine but remains silent. The sound of gentle waves lapping the shore fills our silence. I make note of the marks on his face that show he's been crying, which makes me ache even more.

He folds the page along worn creases and clutches it. "How'd you know I'd be here?"

I manage a small smile. "You said you were glad I brought you here that day. Just made sense you might come here." I push my shoulder against his. "Kinsley filled me in."

He nods, staring at the folded paper in his hands.

I'm nervous to ask, but I want him to know I understand what's going on. "Is that the letter your father gave you?"

He nods again. "His amends letter."

I'm uncertain about what else to say as I tuck my lips between my teeth, so I press my hand on his bicep and lay my head on his shoulder so he knows I'm here for him. How ironic that, as a writer, my words seem to fail me at such a crucial moment. But actions speak louder than words, right? I can at least give him that.

"I don't know what to do, Soph." His voice grates with emotion.

I lift my head but rest my chin on his arm. "Forgive him?"

His arm stiffens, but he continues to stare out at the ocean. "How can I?" He looks down at me. "All I can think about is how different our lives might be if he never left. Maybe my mother might even still be alive today."

Hearing the anger in his voice, I straighten. "Maybe. Maybe not. We have no way of knowing. Based on what you told me, it sounds like his staying would have made things worse for you and your sister. And your mother."

I stare at the wrapped gift, unsure whether to give it to him. Perhaps it could help him see how much he has to be thankful for.

My hand trembles slightly as I hand it to him. "This is for you."

He rips the paper away, then grins with a snort. "Kinsley looks just like our mother when she smiles like that."

I touch his arm. "Nothing will bring your mother back, Luke. Believe me, I wish that were a possibility. You and your sister have an opportunity to reconnect with your father. I'd give anything to have just one more day with mine."

He says nothing, but I can feel the bristle oozing off of him. Maybe I said too much too soon. Perhaps right now, what he needs most is for me just to listen. "I'm sorry if I overstepped—"

He stands up and walks toward the water. A wave rushes up and saturates the bottom of his pants, but he doesn't seem to care.

I push off the step and wander down to join him. But when I try to slip my hand into his, he pulls away. "Things were back on track, Sophie. Finally."

His eyes glitter with a hardness that steels my breath. "I can't stop thinking how different things would be if you hadn't published that article."

His words hurt more than I'd like to admit, but I do my best not to show it because I know he's hurting. I still believe we have a chance at something special. Or is that me trying to make something work again that's not meant to be?

"Luke, you can't live life forward when you're constantly looking back."

Even in the waning light, I don't miss the way his jaw tenses. "Then go live your life forward, Sophie."

Then he walks away, leaving me in the darkness in more ways than one.

Chapter Twenty-Eight

LUKE

Put it on record. Walking away from Sophie is officially the hardest thing I've ever done. But we're clearly not on the same page, and right now, I don't have the strength to try to make sense of hers. She doesn't get what this is doing to me.

I clutch the paper in my hand, tempted to toss it into the trash receptacle I pass on the way to my car. But then I hear Kinsley's voice in my head, telling me that's a jerk move, which prevents me from following through.

Fresh anger surges through me over the thought of that man searching her out. Did he show up on her college campus unannounced and catch her off guard? And I walked out, leaving her alone with him again.

Well, not entirely alone. I'm sure Gabe looked out for her. Even so, I walked away, letting her down just like my father did with me.

Sadly, I seem to be doing a lot of that lately. Failing my team, my sister, and deep down, I know I let Sophie down too. The last words I spoke to her twist in my gut as I pull out of the parking lot and head back to...back to...

I don't know where to go. If I go to Gabe's, I'll have to talk about what went down today, and I'm not in a good place to do that right now.

Kinsley. I need to find my sister and make sure she's safe. I tap her number on the Car Play screen.

"About time you called." Her sassy tone almost makes me smile.

Almost. "Are you okay?"

"I'm fine, but I don't think you are." She's not far from the truth. My sister really should consider a minor in psychology.

"Where are you?"

"Gabe's. They invited us over for dinner while we waited to hear whether you were still alive or not." Though I find her words cringeworthy, I know I deserve it.

"Sorry."

Her sigh fills my car, and her voice softens. "Are you okay?"

I should be strong for her, but I'm feeling everything but that right now. "Not really."

"Did Sophie find you?"

"Yeah."

"And?" Her sarcasm rides in full force.

"And what? I should have listened to my gut the first time, Kins. If she hadn't fumbled that piece about me, we wouldn't be in this situation."

"What are you talking about, Luke?"

"The article. That's how he found you, right?"

"You know, for being eight years older than me, you sure can be a dumbass sometimes."

"Kins, stop with the diatribe and connect the dots for me."

She growls, sounding more like me than I'd like to

admit. "I'm the one who found him. After your visit, I looked for him."

"Why? Why would you do that?" I turn onto Gabe's street.

"Because he's the only parent we have left in this world!" she yells over the phone.

"I'm going to hang up now." I park by the curb in my usual spot in front of Gabe's house.

"Jerk."

I grunt. "I just pulled up."

"Ah, okay."

The connection ends as I climb out of the car. Kinsley walks out of the house with my father trailing out behind her.

She stops halfway down the path, glancing back and forth between us.

Kinsley fists her hands on her hips. "Seriously? Do I have to be the adult here?"

Our father descends the steps and joins her, leaving me with the choice.

Do I meet him there or walk away?

I study him, comparing his memory with the man I see now. What he wrote in his letter bounces in my head about his mistakes, regrets, and how looking back, he would have made different choices.

And then I remember the last words Sophie said to me about how you can't move forward in life if you're still looking back. Maybe it's time to put the regrets to rest and start living in the now and then go from there.

I inhale a deep breath, shove my hands into my pants pockets, and take one step, then another.

Toward my sister, my father...and my future.

Dinner was grueling. I think I felt worse for Gabe and Olivia than I did for myself, but they did their best to help us get a conversation going. The problem is my anger. I can't seem to communicate without blowing up, so I stopped talking. And now it's time to leave.

Kinsley joins me by the door, looking miffed herself. "I told Dad we'd stay at our house tonight, so you can either drive us or we'll take an Uber."

She's already calling him 'Dad.' I know she wants this, but I'm struggling. I remember what he did to our family, and I'm finding it hard to believe he could have changed, despite his in-depth explanation of how he wound up in prison after nearly overdosing and describing it as the best thing that could have happened to him.

He got sober—he got help. Specifically with a diagnosis of a bipolar disorder. Suddenly, all the pieces fell into place for him. He began to heal and make amends as much as possible from prison. He even tried to reach out to our mother, but she refused his call.

I grunt. I'm not thrilled about having him in our house again, but I'm willing to try for Kinsley. "I'll drive."

By the time we pull up to our house, it's late. All I want is to fall into bed and pass into oblivion for a while, so I don't have to think about anything, although I'm sure Sophie will invade my dreams tonight.

As we head up the path, my father stops and smells one of the remaining roses on Mom's bushes, while Kinsley unlocks the door and goes inside. Light from the lamp in the window floods the porch and leaks over onto Mom's roses. I clench my fists at my sides, resisting the urge to push him away. What right does he have to enjoy something she loved?

He lifts his head and scans the rest of the bushes. "Your mother always loved roses."

With a grunt, I climb up the steps. The sooner I get inside, the better because I don't think I have any energy left to control my chaotic emotions. Or my temper. Everything in me is numb except the anger.

"Luke."

At the sound of his voice, I stop at the front door and hang my head. "Yeah?"

"Don't make the same mistake I did."

I turn around and saunter over to the railing. "What are you talking about?"

"Kinsley told me about Sophie."

Seriously? He's going to play father now? I rub my face, wishing this day would end already. "That's none of your business."

"You're right. I have to earn that, but I never stopped loving you guys. My mistake was thinking you'd be better off without me than trying to get well so I could be with you. That's my biggest regret, so—Luke."

"So what are you saying, then?"

"If you love Sophie, fight for her. Do whatever's necessary to make things right because you have to live with your choices for the rest of your life. I'd hate to see my son live with regrets like I do." His eyes turn glassy.

Something shifts in my chest. My eyes start to burn. I grunt, then clear my throat.

I could blame weariness or the high emotions of the day, but those meticulously placed walls I've relied on to hold everything in are crashing down to dust at the moment.

"You don't think I live with regret?" A mix of sarcasm and pain coats my words.

I glance back at the window out of concern for Kinsley because I'm not ready for her to hear this, then bypass the steps in a jump that lands me in front of my father.

"You want to hear the truth?" I stab my chest with my thumb. "I'm the reason Mom's not here. I was on the starting line that night for the first time, and she didn't want to miss it. So she rushed out of a last-minute meeting to get there."

I turn away as a flood of tears accompany my confession.

My father rests a hand on my shoulder. I want to shrug him off, but I'm too tired and maybe a little desperate for someone to tell me a different story about that night. But I can't change the past.

Sophie's words slam into my head like a lifeline.

You can't live life forward when you're constantly looking back.

He nudges me to face him. "Life doesn't work that way, son. Things happen in this life that we have no control over, no matter what you tell yourself. Your mother's death wasn't your fault. She wanted to be there because she loved you. Hold on to that—same thing regarding Sophie. Make the right choice out of your love for her. Not your fear."

My gaze locks with his and for the first time, the weight of the guilt I've carried for so long seems to lighten like a heavy curtain pulled back to reveal the light of day.

Both of my father's hands are resting on my shoulders now. He tightens his hold with an unspoken ask for permission sitting in his eyes. After a moment's pause, I nod.

He pulls me into a hug. I stiffen at first, but then the fight drains out of me. I bury my face in his shoulder, inhaling his unfamiliar scent of clean linen and soap.

Footsteps sound from behind. I lift my head just in time to catch Kinsley rushing toward us. She wraps her arms around both of us but says nothing.

I lean over and kiss the top of her head. "Were you listening?"

She nods against me.

"I'm sorry you had to find out that way." Raw emotion coats my voice.

"I already knew all that."

I shake my head with my disbelief. "How?"

Kins does her typical snarky shrug. "I get what makes people tick. Seemed pretty obvious, if you ask me."

My father...my dad splits a grin between us. "You sure you don't want to study psychology instead?"

"Exactly," I blurt out.

Kins splits a grin between us. "Nah, too much drama."

Chapter Twenty-Nine

SOPHIE

It's wedding day.

And it's a gorgeous one at that. The air is crisp, and the sky is clear. No worries about rain so far. When I first arrived and saw the cabana over the walkway and the sage green sashes on the chairs, I teared up myself. But my emotions have been running very close to the surface since yesterday.

The sound of ocean waves hums in the background. The owner of the inn, Madison, set aside a room for us to use as the bridal suite. Mia's mother continues to fuss over Mia's hair, using her skills as a stylist to give her daughter an elegant updo.

As we help her with her dress, I think we're all trying not to bawl. Even Madam Tulard had tears in her eyes at the last fitting, saying it was her best creation yet. And that says a lot for a woman who supposedly designed a dress for someone in the royal family. I've yet to dig out the truth of that one, but I'm determined to find out—another great detail for that column I'm fighting for.

Marty said the paper's board of directors decided to take a serious look at my column proposal when they found out I had an offer on the table from US Hockey Magazine. So I'm hoping that means my dream is about to come true.

So what if I'm a failure at romance? I can still write about this quaint beach town that embodies it in so many ways. In a way, I could say I'm having a love affair with Sarabella, and that's enough for me. Really and truly, it is.

"Forget a thousand words. That's a face worth ten thousand."

Mia's voice snaps my attention back to the present. I glance at her reflection in the mirror before refocusing on attaching her veil in her hair like Madam Tulard showed me. "It's an emotional day."

She starts to turn around to look at me.

"Stay still, or you'll mess it up."

She lets out a *harrumph*. "Fine. Don't tell me what happened. I'll just imagine the worst and plot Luke Jameson's demise in the meantime."

For the first time today I smile. I may not have romantic love in my life, but I have a plethora of people I adore and consider my family. "Make sure they can't trace it back to you. I can survive another romance failure, but I cannot lose my best friend who's like a sister to me."

Uh oh...I started the waterworks.

Mia waves her hand in front of her face. "Oh no...I love you, Soph, but your timing really sucks sometimes."

I grab a tissue from the vanity and help her dab her eyes. "I'm sorry. Just know that I love you and...and I will always make sure I have backup mascara."

She giggles as she hugs me.

Madison pokes her head in the door. "All the guests are seated. Ready when you are."

I lock eyes with Mia, and we nod at the same time. Her mother and I finish arranging her veil, then touch up our lipstick before leaving the room and heading toward the breezeway. In a few minutes, I'll take my place under the wedding arch, followed by Mia, who will take her place next to Ethan, her soon-to-be husband.

And everyone will live happily ever after. The end.

But it's not the end. And, as wonderful as all that sounds, I'm trying not to freak out about seeing Luke sitting among the guests. That is if he's still coming. I have no idea since we're not talking anymore—he made that clear on the beach last night.

I squash the surge of tears trying to push their way out again. I've cried enough over that man, and today is about celebrating love and marriage.

The music shifts to a soft melody—my cue to start down the aisle. Ethan and his brother look so handsome at the other end of the breezeway. A subtle floral scent fills the enclosure, emanating from gorgeous arrangements of lavender orchids mixed with white peonies.

I take my place up front, proud of myself for not searching the guests for one hockey player in particular, and keep my eyes focused on Mia's entrance. The music changes to a modern rendition of the wedding march as she makes her appearance.

At Ethan's soft gasp, I smile. All the frustrations, hiccups, and delays fall away in this moment when everyone stands and watches the beautiful bride walk toward her groom.

Toward her future.

The thought sends a pang through me, which grows when I notice Luke in my peripheral vision. He's standing behind the seats, dressed in a light gray suit that contrasts with his burgundy shirt and dark brown hair.

He's gorgeous. My heart jumps to high speed so fast I almost gasp. Because he's not looking at Mia, he's staring at me, devouring me from afar. I close my eyes long enough to compose myself, then lift my chin and focus on Mia and Ethan.

Today is all about them and their new life together. And that I can be happy about.

The reception is a smash hit. Ironically, I think moving the entire event to the Sandpiper Inn and the Turtle Tide worked out better than our original plan. I suspected it might.

I scan the room filled with smiling faces, laughter, and couples dancing—I think Mia and Ethan have danced to every song. The taste of champagne lingers on my tongue as I revel at the sight of them glowing with their happiness.

I'm also daydreaming of the article I could write about a beautiful event like this if I get my column. Dominic and Madison could definitely expand their joint businesses into a venue for destination weddings. I can picture a two-page spread with pictures and everything.

A tap on my shoulder interrupts my thoughts. I turn around to find Payton smiling at me. His blue eyes sparkle at me, enhanced by the navy color of his fitted suit—an expensive-looking one, at that.

"Fancy a dance with a meager soul like me?"

I set my glass down on a nearby table. "I'd love to."

He spins me out onto the floor, quite adept in his moves.

"Payton, you're quite the dancer. Who taught you?"

He glances away for a moment. "My parents are the traditional sort. My siblings and I were required to learn."

"How many siblings?"

"Two brothers and a sister."

"That's right. You shared that during your interview. But you never answered where you grew up."

He scoffs. "Oh, it's just a small blip on the map in England. Nothing to really talk about."

Payton gave me the same brush-off when I did his interview. I haven't had a chance to dig a little, but I suspect there is definitely more to this man than meets the eye.

His eyes shift to something over my shoulder.

"May I cut in?"

I stiffen at the sound of Luke's voice. This would be so much easier if we never spoke or had contact again. Considering his last words on the beach, I assumed that's what he wanted. So why is he here, and why does he want to dance with me now?

Payton releases me, leaving me, once again, unpaired. "Of course."

Luke nods, then takes his place, pulling me closer so that our bodies touch. The ache in my heart quadruples to be so close to him yet feel so far away. I drop my gaze, unable to look at him. I can't face what I imagine I'll find there.

Or won't find.

"Sophie, are you going to look at me?" His voice rumbles out and wreaks more havoc with my heart.

"Why should I?" I glance to the side where Mia's sitting on Ethan's lap.

"Because I need you to see my face when I tell you how sorry I am."

After he walked away, I imagined every scenario of him returning and saying those very words. In one of them, he fell to his knees, begging me to take him back, which made me feel very vindicated. But none of it was real.

Swallowing my nerves, my emotions, and the ache threatening to choke me, I draw my gaze upward. His thumb caresses my cheek as he brushes away a lock of hair from my face, and it's all I can do not to close my eyes and lean into the warmth of his hand and relinquish my heart to him again.

As he searches my face, his eyes dart back and forth, appearing glassy as they do. Or could that be the reflection from the fairy lights draped around the room?

"You were right, Soph. I can't move forward while focusing on the past."

I work saliva into my parched mouth. "I'm glad you see that now."

"My father and I are talking things out."

My smile is tremulous but present, nonetheless. How can I not be ecstatic for him? "That's great. I'm so happy for you and Kinsley."

His expression shifts and turns more serious. "She's the one who looked for him. He never even saw the article."

"So your assumption—"

"Was wrong." He folds our clasped hands between us. "So very wrong... I'm so so sorry, Sophie. Will you forgive me?"

A tear slips down my cheek as I nod. "Yes, of course. I forgive you, Luke."

His brows draw together, forming a crease between them. "Does that mean you'll give us a chance?"

The longing in his eyes matches what I'd imagined in all those scenarios, but instead of throwing myself into his arms, I want to pull away. Like I said before, love has failed me three times already. In my mind, taking a fourth chance on Luke was my last try. And we've had three situations arise that have pushed us apart—the third one completely. I don't think I can risk my heart a fourth time.

I run the tip of my tongue over my lips as I search for words. "I don't know, Luke. I think I need time."

His mouth opens as if he's somewhat stunned, but then he swallows and bobs his head. "Will you do me one favor?"

Curious about what he would want, I give him a subtle nod.

"You're covering the next home game, right?"

I nod again.

"Wait for me at the door afterward."

"I don't think that's a good idea—"

"Please? After that, if you never want to see me again, I'll understand."

The intensity of his eyes wins over my indecision. "Okay. I'll be there."

He kisses my cheek, where the tear fell. "Thank you."

Still staring at me, he steps back and then turns and leaves the wedding.

I hold my hand to my stomach and inhale, then release a shuddering breath as I touch the place his lips just touched, knowing I'll never fully get over the hockey player who turned my world upside down.

Chapter Thirty

LUKE

I've never been so anxious for a game to finish. On the other hand, I'm nervous that the end of this game will also lead to the end of Soph and me. I want a shot at doing things right this time.

What if I walk out the door and she's not there?

No, she said she would wait, so I'm believing and trusting she'll be there. And hopefully, what I plan to show her will also convince her to give us a chance...like I've given my father.

We've done a lot of talking over the last couple of days. I admit, I blew up a few times, but now I have a better understanding of the demons he was fighting—how drugs became his only way of coping with what turned out to be an undiagnosed bipolar disorder and drug trafficking paid for them. This was also the real reason why he left—he was protecting us.

Prison helped sober him up and revealed he needed help, something the prison system managed to actually do for him. Never thought I'd hear someone say they were thankful they got put away.

And he made good use of his time, studying and learning how to be a plumber, which will come handy when he's released from the halfway house to live with me in Clearwater. Mom's house could use some work, and he needs a place to land. So it's a win-win for both of us.

Seeing Kinsley warm up to him was part of what pushed me to give him a chance. And to see Sophie was right. Family is precious, even if it isn't perfect, convenient, or ideal. Ours is a little messy at the moment, but we're getting there. We have an opportunity to build something new and to be the family none of us thought possible.

Doesn't mean it will be easy. I still have some anger to deal with and plan to get help with that. But the most important thing is, we have time.

I search out the seats where I know Kinsley and my father are watching and wave as I skate around the net and take position for a faceoff. We're down a point and need to win this one to make it into the Kelly Cup playoffs.

Kinsley does her usual 'I'm over it' casual wave with her elbow resting on her knee. No eye roll though and a big grin. I think this is the happiest I've seen her since our mother died. And I have to say, seeing my father grinning and clapping for me is…surreal. Not something I ever imagined would happen, let alone be possible.

I take position and wait for the ref to drop the puck. My opponent jumps at it, but I'm faster. After I pass the blue line, I pass the puck to Ethan, who may just have his head more centered on leaving for his honeymoon tomorrow than the game, but he's open and I need help.

He swipes it to Jayce who shoots it to Payton, making

me grin inside my helmet. The kid's come a long way in a short time. Kind of ironic to think of him in that light, considering I'm in a similar place. I have a lot to learn, but I'm ready and willing to leave the past in the past, and start living my life forward.

The crowd starts chanting.

Let's go Sun Kings! Let's go Sun Kings!

The puck zings back my way. I take the shot, sending it under the opposing team's goalie before he can bounce down to block it. The crowd's roar is almost deafening and many are jumping up and down in front of their seats as the guys and I make our pass by the players' bench, bumping gloves.

I do a sweep of the perimeter, just in case Sophie's at one of the camera holes. When I don't see her, I try to catch a glimpse of her up near the press box, but still no sign of her. My heart thumps even harder, anxious to prove to her I'm making better choices and taking steps for a future I'm desperate for her to be part of.

I want to make her proud.

That thought gives me pause as I take a turn on the players' bench. My mother was always the one I wanted to make proud. Kins likes to pretend she couldn't care less, but I always know she's rooting for me. And now my father is too.

But Sophie's the one I want cheering for me. And I want to be there for her too, encouraging her to keep reaching for her dream and celebrating when she does. Because I know she will. The people she works for are fools if they don't see how talented she is.

Gabe pats my shoulder. I shoot a grin his way. With only minutes left in the third period, I climb over the wall to take another turn on the ice. The score is tied, and I'd prefer this didn't go into overtime for obvious reasons. I've rehearsed what I need to say to Sophie so many times that if I don't get it out of my head, I'll explode.

Payton flies after the puck, steals it, and does a break-away. Ethan and I have his back as we skate after him. The opposing team can't keep up, so Pay makes an easy shot two seconds before the end. The horn sounds, announcing our goal, and the crowd goes nuts almost drowning out the whistle blow signaling the end of the game.

Wade flies down the ice to join the celly along with the rest of the team as we exchange hugs, pat backs and helmets, and grin like we just won the Kelly Cup. We're one game closer in our winning streak and feeling good about the future.

All the bad press about the Sun Kings is a thing of the past, thanks to how these guys have joined together as a team, and Sophie's articles. Kind of symbolic when I think about it. We're moving forward too, as a team united.

I can't wait to share that with Sophie, too.

That, and few other things…

I check my hair and suit one more time in the mirror.

Wade bumps me on the back. "Great game, my friend."

I chuckle at his exaggerated drawl as I adjust my tie. "Yes, it was."

"You joining us over at the Turtle Tide to celebrate?"

"Maybe later. There's something I need to do first."

"Does that involve a certain brown-eyed news journalist that has a love for pink?"

I temper my reaction to Wade's keen observations. I know him well enough that he wouldn't do anything but still, that he noticed Sophie elicits something primal in me.

"Most definitely."

"I'm rootin' for ya, bro."

I meet his gaze in the mirror. "Thanks. I'm gonna need it."

He pats my shoulder, then rests his hand there. "She'd be a fool to not want to be with you, don't ya think?"

"I'm hoping." I shoot Kinsley a text to let her know I'm about to walk out—our plan to time things so that I have a moment with Sophie before they show up.

With a deep breath for courage, I head toward the exit, but I hesitate when my doubt makes an appearance.

What if she's not there?

But what if she is?

I push the door open…and there she is.

Her smile is tentative at first, then widens some. "Hi."

I close the gap between us, but leave some space so she won't feel like I'm pushing her too fast. She said she needed time, and I plan to honor that, but I want her to have all the facts before she makes a final decision about us.

"Hi there." I fist my hands at my sides, resisting the urge to touch her face. "Thank you for waiting for me."

"Sure. Was there something you wanted to tell me?"

Is that hope I see in her eyes? I hold my hand out as an offering, letting her make the choice whether to take it or not. "Can we go somewhere more private?"

"Um, sure." She slips her fingers into mine, which amps up my hope meter.

The warmth of her touch settles the nervous energy ripping through me somewhat. This feels like a victory—

like that moment when I hit the puck and hold my breath, waiting to see if I make the goal.

I lead her out the door and around the arena along the same route we walked before. As we turn the corner of the building, Kinsley and my father walk toward us.

When I look down at Sophie, her brows draw together for a moment. She smiles, then glances up at me. "Luke, is that—?"

"Yeah."

As we stop, I hold my hand out to my father. "Sophie, I'd like you to meet my dad, Theodore Jameson."

He takes Sophie's hand and shakes it. "Just Ted, okay?"

Her smile flashes again, making her eyes tilt in that way I've come to appreciate...and love. "So great to meet you, Ted."

Kinsley rushes Sophie with a hug. "I'm so glad you're here."

Her expression turns tender as she wraps her arms around my sister. "Me too."

An ache hits my chest as I watch Sophie and Kinsley together. Right here, this is what I want. I know we still have a lot of things to work out with my dad, but family is everything and worth fighting for. So is Sophie.

My father gestures to Sophie. "I loved the article you wrote about Luke."

She blushes. "Thank you."

A twinkle gleams in his eyes. "She's quite the writer."

"Yes, she is." I turn to face her. "She's also the woman I'm in love with."

Sophie's eyes widen with her stare. Her mouth opens, shuts, then opens again, but she's not saying anything. As I reach out and entwine my fingers with hers, Kinsley tugs our father down the sidewalk to give us some space.

I didn't plan this part. I intend to tell my sister she can have anything she wants—including a car if I make it to the NHL—as a thank you for giving us this moment. But deep down, I'm afraid of losing Sophie. More than I realized. Something I'll probably need therapy for too, but I need her to know how I feel. No matter what.

She tightens her fingers with mine. "You love me?"

I lift our joined hands and kiss her fingers. "I hope that's okay."

Her eyes dart back and forth as she searches my face. Then she launches herself at me, hands wrapped around my neck as she presses her lips to mine. Instinctively, I crush her against me, returning her kiss with equal passion.

Our kiss turns tender, but then she buries her face against my chest and she's shaking. Is she crying?

I lower my mouth to her ear and whisper, "Soph, are you okay?

She nods vigorously.

"Are you crying?"

She nods again, then leans her head back to look at me. "You really love me?"

"I do." I smile as I run my finger along the edge of her bangs and down her cheek, memorizing every detail of her face. But it's what I see in her eyes that finishes me off. Sophie loves without reservations, qualifications or assumptions. I should be the one having a hard time believing she loves me despite all I've put her through.

"Are you sure, Iceman?" She runs a finger over the shape of my lips, sending heat through me.

I dip my head for another taste of her lips and hopefully convince her she's the only one I want. "Surer than sure."

She holds my face between her hands. "I love you too. You know that, right?"

"I do now." I tilt my grin. "I didn't want to assume."

She blurts a watery laugh and kisses me. "This time, assumptions are okay."

"Are you sure?" I ask, leaning in to kiss and nip at her beautiful lips.

Her eyes tell me all I need to know. "Yes, surer than sure."

Chapter Thirty-One

LUKE

Five Months Later

It's the final game.

The Sun Kings made it into the Kelly Cup finals, and I'm still here. Tampa Bay Lightning decided Jayce was the pick they wanted, and I was more than okay with it. I'm good right where I'm at with the guys I consider part of my expanding family.

And with Sophie. Thanks to the pieces she wrote about the team and me, plus USA Hockey Magazine offering her a job, the board of directors offered Sophie her own column in the Sarabella Herald Tribune. Like I said, the powers that be would have been fools not to cash in on her proposal for *Romancing Sarabella*.

She's been so busy writing dual features between the team and the new column that we've had to be creative in how we spend time together. And tonight, I plan to take advantage of the fact that she's here tonight and show her how much she means to me.

Nervous energy about the game and what I have planned shoots through me as I wait on the bench to return to the ice.

I scan the seats again to where Dad and Kinsley are sitting. They're both in on it and have my back. They'll make sure Sophie is at the press hole after the second period. I know it's a risk—a big assumption—but I'm fairly certain what her answer will be.

The Sun Kings have turned into a major attraction for Sarabella. Sophie's the one we have to thank for that. Her articles did exactly what the owner hoped for. Last year's scandal is long forgotten, and, thanks to the success of the exposure, the owner wants to add more people to our staff, including a full time PR person.

Fourth line heads to the bench as Payton, Ethan, Mathéo, and I take our turn on the ice. We spend most of the next minute chasing the puck and keeping the other team from reaching our goaltender, although Wade's done a stellar job blocking. Mathéo's the one to bring it home this time. The horn blows, and the refs signal the end of the second period.

As we skate by, Gabe hands me the box with a sheepish grin. "Go get her."

I do a circle of the rink to the other side, where I see Sophie with her camera at the press hole. Dad and my sister are standing behind her.

It's been an interesting five months with my father. A little rough at first for him to settle in, but then he got the hang of it. We're both doing some counseling to adjust. Kinsley joins our sessions remotely when she's away at school. She decided to spend the summer break at home so she could get to know Dad better. I'd like to think Mom would be proud of us and what we've accomplished so far, that she's watching over us and cheering us on as we become a family.

Kinsley jumps up and down when she sees me skating along the boards in their direction. Dad gives me a thumbs up, to which I shake my head. When I told him what I had planned, he got super excited and started making all kinds of suggestions on what to do. I reassured him that I knew the what, when, and how and that I had a plan.

As I get closer, I lock eyes with Sophie. She smiles at me in that way that tilts those gorgeous eyes, brimming with so much love the ache in my chest squeezes, then expands. I didn't grasp at first why she seemed so surprised when I told her I loved her. I mean, how can I not? She's amazing.

But then I began to understand all the bits of her heart, wounds and all. And as much as she's been part of my healing, I like to think I've been part of hers because nothing compares to the meaning she holds in my life. Not even hockey.

As I approach to press hole, she leans down, waiting for the kiss Dad and Kinsley told her I wanted.

But I shake my head as I get there.

Sophie purses her lips to the side as she straightens, her gaze questioning.

I glide down on one knee to the boards and open the ring box.

A rumble starts in the crowd, so I'm guessing the fans are starting to notice. And that's okay because, in a way, they've been part of our story. I never imagined that the first time we kissed through the press hole would lead us back here one day.

Say yes! Say yes! Say yes!

We both glance up at the stamping fans, shouting and cheering for her answer.

I swing my eyes back to Sophie as she leans in closer to the camera hole to hear me, her eyes full of unshed tears. The full force of everything she's meant and means to me hits me so hard I wobble on the ice.

"Soph, I'm a better man today because of you. And not only that, I have a family again. Something I never dreamed possible. But it's not complete without you. Will you marry me and make our family complete?"

With a sob, she nods and slides her left hand through the hole. I slip the ring on her finger, then rise and press my hand against the plexiglass where hers is, mouthing 'I love you' since there's no way she'll hear me now over the din shaking the place. I think the fans got a bigger show than they expected.

She mouths it back, then leans over again, her lips at the press hole, waiting for that kiss I promised.

And I gladly oblige. And I always will.

No assumptions needed.

vinci-books.com/offensivezone

She's my bodyguard. My fake wife. And the one woman I can't resist.

Being a pro hockey player is tough—but hiding that I'm royalty? Even harder. My family demands I return home unless I accept a bodyguard. My solution? A fake wife to protect my secret. But she's gorgeous, sharp, and completely off-limits… and I'm playing a dangerous game.

Turn the page for a free preview…

In the Offensive Zone with My Fake Bride: Chapter One

PAYTON

I've never been a fan of formal English gardens. Their structured beds, surrounded by short stone or brick walls, filled with topiaries and meticulously shaped shrubs, always felt too controlling to me. Not to mention the rows of flowers lined up like soldiers, as if they were trying to tell you what to do or how to behave in their presence.

Not something I share in mixed company, I assure you. And by mixed company, I mean royals and those who flock to surround them. Much like those stone walls, I never imagined I could wind up hemmed in like one of them.

But today, none of that seems to matter.

Funerals tend to have that effect on a person, I suppose. After the services for my cousin concluded, we returned to his estate for the reception—can you call something dour a reception when everyone would rather be received anywhere else but here?

Upon arrival, I made a mad dash for the gardens to escape the sea of sad faces—both genuine and fake, for the record. Yet, looking out over the perfectly manicured garden and various flowers giving their last hurrah with the imminent arrival of fall, I'm reminded of idyllic days as a child, playing with Sebastian in these very places.

One time, in particular, comes to mind—me chasing after my cousin and taking a turn too fast, which resulted in a nasty tear in my trousers from the aforementioned stone walls. My left knee still sports the scar from that fiasco. Maybe that's why I much prefer pursuing a puck in an open ice rink. The only obstacles are other players, and part of the challenge is to either maneuver around them or body-check them aside. The terrain is always changing, and I prefer it that way.

"Longing to be back on the ice, chasing that puck of yours?" My sister Emalia brushes by me, then perches on the short wall, edging a bed of roses ablaze in reds and yellows that remind me of my team colors.

I hum in the back of my throat in reply—my usual response when she annoyingly reads my mind. Practice starts in a matter of weeks, and I'd much rather be swinging a hockey stick than bracing for whatever curveball—sorry, wrong sport—slapshot life's about to send my way.

She crosses her ankles and folds her hands in her lap, already the picture of royalty. Losing Sebastian left a gap to be filled. Namely, Baronet of Tillendale. He never married and was the sole heir to his parents, who died much too young because of various health issues. Perhaps that's why our dear cousin lived life on the edge. He told me once he didn't expect to outlive the age his mother and father reached, and now he's proven himself right, much to my chagrin. And my sister's.

After slipping my hands into my trouser pockets, I

meander closer to where she's sitting. "When will you move onto the estate?"

"Later today."

"That's bloody fast."

She waves her hand in a casual gesture toward the small mansion behind me. "We waited most of the summer, hoping they'd find Sebastian lost at sea somewhere. There's a lot of work to catch up on."

I clear my throat. "I'm sure you'll have things back in order in no time."

She shoots a finely shaped brow in my direction like a bow ready to shoot an arrow, and the gleam in her eye forewarns me of its arrival. "Faster if my baby brother would stay and help his older sister out."

I knew she'd make one last-ditch attempt to sway me. Hearing that my cousin's yacht had gone missing was what brought me back to Tillendale, a relatively small and unknown town in the southern tip of England, of which my deceased cousin is—was—the Baronet.

A title now passed to my sister, making me heir apparent.

The sooner I'm on a plane back to the States, the better. Even as a youth, I never enjoyed the occasional formal functions that required my family's attendance. "The new season is about to start, and I have a contract to honor. The lads are counting on me."

"I know. But I had to try one more time. This won't be fun without you."

I scoff. "What are you talking about? Your favorite game as a child was to play queen. Unlike me, you are well-built for your new role, Em."

"Maybe, but I'd feel better having you close. Especially

since we're not sure Sebastian's accident was really an..."
She mouths the word 'accident' as if doing so would negate
the possible threat.

"Don't buy into those rumors so quickly."

She blinks, pursing her lips for a moment before speaking. "You heard what Mum and Dad said."

"Yes, I was in the room, but again, it could just be the ponderings and hearsay of their old cronies."

"Those old cronies, as you call them, have ties to MI5."

I lean toward her and lower my voice to a whisper. "So they say."

With a deep inhale, she turns her head to stare over her shoulder. "Still makes me nervous. I'd feel better if you were here."

Hearing the hint of fear in her words softens me. I sit down next to her and take her hand between mine. "I'm a hockey player, Em. Not a bodyguard. Your security detail will do a far superior job than I could with a hockey stick."

My attempt at humor doesn't seem to faze her as she diverts her stare to our clasped hands. "I don't need your protection. Just your support."

"That you already have, dear sister. I'm simply a phone call away."

She sighs in resignation. "Right."

Emalia lifts crystal blue eyes to mine as she squeezes my hand. Almost two years apart, my sister and I have often been mistaken for twins because of our shared features and coloring, although my hair is a shade darker than her sandy blonde locks.

"When will I meet this mysterious bodyguard you've hired for me?" I project a tone of humor to my words, more for my benefit than hers. I'm not yet keen on the idea of having a bodyguard, but at least we found a workable solution—one I hope will convince my teammates.

"At the airport. She'll meet the car there and make sure your pretty face doesn't get harmed in any way."

"I still don't see the necessity." The words slip out before I can stop them.

Frustration tinges her sigh this time. "Yes, we've been over this again and again, Payton. But it *is* necessary. You're now the heir apparent. You know how the system works."

I nod, clenching my jaw to prevent spewing my own suppressed irritation. When they finally declared our cousin had perished at sea, the wheels went into motion right away to pass the title to the next person in line—my sister, which then put me in the mix.

Initially, I was told I would have to quit hockey and move back to England. I resisted, stating that I had a commitment to fulfill. My contract with the Sun Kings has two more years left. And the powers that be could find nothing that would require my presence in parliament.

So, we made an agreement. I can return to the States as long as I agree to have a bodyguard with me twenty-four-seven. Never imagined she'd take my half-joking suggestion that said bodyguard should be a female who could pose as my girlfriend so seriously. After hours of hashing out ways to make this work, Emalia informed me she'd contacted a firm in London that trained and provided female bodyguards.

Then she had the nerve to outline her brilliant plan—her words, not mine—of me pretending I had a whirlwind romance over the summer and returned with a bride. I told her that seemed unnecessary, as couples live together all the time without involving a marriage contract. She insisted that despite our little deception—okay, major deception—

our family values needed to be upheld. However, I know for a fact my sister is a raging romantic because she's read romance novels as far back as I can remember. I'm almost certain she plucked this story of hers from one of her books.

Emalia lifts her face to mine and kisses my cheek. "Make sure you're a dutiful husband, little brother. You wouldn't want to upset your new wifey."

I growl in reaction to her tinkling laughter. "You're enjoying this entirely too much."

She holds her hands out and dons an innocent expression that might fool others but not me. "You always said you wanted to settle down one day."

Now she's playing dirty, repeating something I said after a nasty breakup last year. I rise and take a step back. "Yes, after I'm done living my life and doing the things I want to do."

Her face turns serious as she stands. "Sometimes we have to do what's required."

Em's words twist like a knife in my chest. She had to give up her medical practice to fulfill her newly acquired role of Baronet of Tillendale, which I know wasn't easy.

I take her hands and pull her up to hug her, but she remains stiff. "I'm sorry. I understand this has cost you more than it has me."

She softens and settles against me. "I keep wishing I'll wake up and find out it was a mistake. That Sebastian will walk in with that goofy smile of his and say it was all a joke."

I plant a kiss on top of her head. "I wish that for you, too, dear sister. I truly do."

She lifts her face to look at me. "I know you don't believe there's a threat, but promise me you'll do whatever your bodyguard tells you?"

Her gaze is relentless in her demand for my agreement, and her tone makes it clear she's left no room for arguments. I only hope my teammates in Florida will be none the wiser as to my true identity. I've done a fair job of avoiding deeper questions about my family. They only know I'm the third male to bear the name Payton Gerard Maxwell. That alone gave them more fodder than they needed in those first months of playing, but with every ribbing, I knew I became one of them, a part of the team. This new title development could change all of that if my ties to the monarchy were to become known.

The true test came last year when a photojournalist followed us for the entire season. I managed to avoid her questions about my familial origins, and thankfully, she didn't do much digging into my family. Not that she would have found much of interest. The Maxwell name was only second in line before now, and most people outside of Tillendale don't know or don't care about what title we might hold. Surely, this ruse won't be any more difficult than that.

"I promise." I strengthen my resolve to not let this become an issue as I hug her tighter for reassurance.

"Thank you." Her stern expression breaks into a gentle smile for the first time today, sending a spike of relief through me. Seeing my sister so troubled these last few weeks weighed heavily on me—probably what finally pushed me to concede to her insistence that I have a bodyguard.

Do I want to play a charade, deceiving my teammates, who have become like a second family to me? No. But I don't appear to have much choice. And I know deep down it's the least I can do for my sister, who's doing her best to accommodate me.

As she said, sometimes one must do what's required. I'm sure the long plane flight will give me plenty of time to get acquainted with my new fake bride and develop a plan to make this believable.

Unless I can figure a way out of this, that is...

In the Offensive Zone with My Fake Bride: Chapter Two

A wad of fabric sails over my arm and lands in a wrinkled puddle of my partially yet precisely packed suitcase.

"You need some shorts." My roommate Delilah dons the expression she normally saves for clients that says, 'Do what I say or die.'

If I were a client, I would comply, but I'm not. I tuck my index finger under the waistband and lift the shorts, studying the large floral pattern that makes my eyes hurt, before dropping them on the bed next to my suitcase. "I have plenty, thanks."

Which is a lie. I don't actually own a pair because, as a professional bodyguard, I'm rarely in a position to dress that casually. Unless a client requests we blend in more or the situation requires it, I opt for some version of my usual business attire. And one can never be over-prepared, something I learned during my very brief stint in the Army.

Once my tour ended, I knew I needed to pivot in a new direction. Intending to take a break and think, I wound up in London, thinking I'd explore Europe. That lasted barely a week before I went stir-crazy and decided I wanted to find some kind of job that would give me the same structure without the constant scrutiny of my gender.

That realization led me to Remington Security, which is owned by one of the best female bodyguards in the industry. And to meeting Delilah, who the firm recruited a year before me. She had a spare room, and I needed a place to land. The rest is history.

Del snatches the shorts off the bed and stuffs them into a gap between my extra pair of black shoes and the stack of pants, which are either black or navy. Another pile of neatly folded button-down blouses in shades of white, pale blue, or cream sits next to it. I add the matching jackets I'll need for this assignment but ignore her contribution because it's easier than fighting with her.

She leans over to study the contents of my carefully planned suitcase, then grimaces at me. "Doll, you're definitely going to need more attractive choices to pull this off. Isn't that part of this whole scenario? You're posing as his wife. Don't you think it will look strange if you always show up," she waves her hand up and down in front of me, "looking like a corporate exec with a stick up her bum."

"Shorts offer little protection in a scuffle, and I certainly can't run in flip-flops." I pluck the items out and toss them at her.

Using her well-honed reflexes, she snatches them out of the air before they make contact. Her grin turns positively evil. "Your principal is rather yummy, don't you think? Perhaps you should throw a negligee or two in there as well."

I roll my shoulders back. "It's a pretense, remember. Not real, in case you don't know what that word means."

"I'm perfectly aware of the meaning, Lil. I'm just

encouraging you to let your hair down a little." She points to my head. "Sometimes, I fear you have that ponytail of yours tied too tightly."

"It's a job, not a vacation, Del," says the woman who doesn't do vacations. Unlike my roommate, who plays as hard as she works, I have one modus operandi—work. I've accepted this about myself, and I'm good at it. But that's the job. When we're on assignment, it's twenty-four-seven. Can't let your guard down even for a moment because that could mean the death of the client. And that's a reputation killer.

She yanks out two pairs of jeans and a few shirts from one of my drawers and hands them to me. "Trust me, you're going to need some more casual attire. I spent a month in Florida for a job, and people there wear shorts everywhere. Even when dining at bougie restaurants." She pats the stack of garments. "These will do."

"Fine." I shove them into the small space left on one side. I could tell her I already packed two pairs of yoga pants and some athletic tops beneath my usual garb. My research revealed this was a popular trend at the moment—to look like you just came from the gym, even if you have no intentions of working out.

Her pout does little to diminish her striking Eurasian features. "And every assignment comes to an end. Why not extend your stay and spend some time on that gorgeous beach? What's it called again? Avocado something…"

"Mango Key Beach."

Del ruffles through two of my dresser drawers. "What about a bathing suit? Do you even own one?"

"I'll buy what I need there."

She darts out of the room, making me believe I can finish packing in peace, only to return, swinging small swatches of red fabric in each hand. "This is my favorite two-piece. Never fails to grab attention."

I grab her wrists before she can toss them in. "I'm supposed to blend in, remember?"

"Yes, during the job." She bounces her eyebrows and singsongs, "But afterward, it's all fair game."

I roll my eyes and snort, releasing her wrists so she can shove the vivid red two-piece—and the shorts—into a gap along the edge. "I'll make sure you get them back."

"No worries, luv. I have a spare."

A spare…like my client, Payton Maxwell, the third. I assume he's adjusting to his new role as a spare heir. The research I did on the Maxwells didn't look much different from what I imagine any average English family would look like. Parents married for almost thirty years. An older sister who worked as a pediatrician until she had to relinquish her partnership in the practice to take her missing, now presumed dead cousin's title of Baronet. Youngest and only son is a hockey player. I will say finding that out surprised me—not a typical profession for a Brit.

I zip up my suitcase and carry it to the door where my backpack is sitting.

"That's it? No books or special items?" She crosses her arms. "They'll never buy a new bride with no possessions?"

"I'll simply explain they're being shipped from the UK. Takes weeks. I'll be on my way back before they can start to question. Besides, no one's going to know the difference."

"What if he invites his teammates over?"

"I'm sure they don't go poking into his bedrooms, but I'll hang some of my clothes in his closet and leave some extra toiletries on his bathroom counter."

"You have that part all figured out, then?"

"As much as possible at this point." I tap my backpack.

"I made some preliminary notes and a list of things to discuss on the flight. That way, we can get to know each other and create a cover story."

"A whirlwind summer romance?"

I nod.

"Fell in love and eloped?"

I shake my head. "They're very traditional. Married at his parents' estate."

"Did they approve?"

Now, she's just being cheeky. "Yet to be determined."

She looks impressed as she shrugs. Then her eyes widen, and her mouth forms a circle all at once. Del dashes back into my room and returns with a white, strapless sundress I bought on a whim last year during a moment of weakness. I'd spent a month on assignment in the Caribbean only to return to the constant drizzle in London. I'd told myself then I needed a pick-me-up.

"Just a pretense." She yanks the tag off, giving me a sly glance. "You would have worn some kind of dress and surely brought it with you. Brides are sentimental that way."

Convinced she has ulterior motives, I lower my eyelids to study her micro-expressions.

"I'm not that easy to get rid of, doll. Remember, I'm part of your team on this assignment."

That's my one comfort in this unusual scenario. I grab the dress and stuff it into the front pocket of my suitcase. "Whatever makes you happy, Del."

She laughs. "And gets me off your back, right?"

"Affirmative."

Bodies move around the airport like ants swarming a nest. Delilah flew out the day before to check out the arena and the principal's apartment complex in Sarabella. Since the Maxwells are mostly unknown in the States, and a definitive threat hasn't been confirmed, she and I will operate as a basic team. Meaning, we'll tap into local resources if needed, which she'll establish as well.

I probably know this airport better than most who work here, but the people are always changing. After checking in and dropping off my bag, I scope the general areas from the entrance to security before backtracking to wait outside for my client.

Head constantly on a swivel, I make note of those lingering in the near vicinity. Most move quickly into the airport, carrying bags and suitcases with them as they scurry inside. Those don't concern me. It's the ones hanging around outside that have me watchful.

Like the tall brunette standing to my right, toting only an oversized bag. She crosses her arms and nervously searches the constant flow of vehicles moving through the passenger drop-off zone.

I suspect she's looking for the boyfriend she fears may be a no-show as she checks her cell for the umpteenth time. Mentally, I shake my head, recognizing the impending disappointment as the realization sets in. Indecision will follow next as she tries to decide whether to leave on her own and make the best of the situation. Or, if she's the ballsy type, to find the loser and tell him off.

Of course, there's the slim possibility that she's a hired killer, and this is all an act, but reading people is one of my strengths. My gut tells me she's exactly what she appears, so I move on, scouting the area while watching for the vehicle transporting my assignment.

Maxwell Payton, the third. I hope his insistence on meeting at the airport with the excuse that an escort would create unnecessary fuss isn't his way of being artificially noble. This charade of playing his wife will prove challenging enough as it is.

A black sedan pulls up to the curb, displaying the plate number I memorized from his family's credentials. Before the vehicle comes to a complete stop, the rear door opens, and my principal jumps out, slinging a duffel across his shoulders. For a moment, I'm transfixed by the contours and definition of his forearms as he adjusts the strap across his chest. The picture in his file showed him with short hair. Not the collar-length, tousled style he's sporting now.

I move in closer, prepared to make contact. But then he leans in through the open passenger side window and shakes hands with the driver, whose animated expression reveals pure delight.

"Thanks again, Bruv." The driver holds out a piece of paper and a pen, which Mr. Maxwell takes, then scrawls something across the white surface.

"My pleasure. And if you find yourself in the States, make a stop in Sarabella and say hello." He straightens as the car pulls away.

Not quite what I anticipated, then again, this is my first assignment with any kind of royalty. But I did expect someone softer and with more luggage.

I close the gap but keep a good three feet between us. "Mr. Maxwell."

He spins around. Momentary confusion flits across his face before his grin flashes into place. "Did you want an autograph as well?"

"No."

His smile slips a few notches as his gaze makes a subtle

assessment of me right down to my shoes. "Then you're the bodyguard, I presume."

"That's correct." I hold my hand out. "Lily Evans."

His brows tug together. "You're not British."

"No, I'm originally from the States."

He shakes my hand, then heads toward the terminal doors. I follow him, keeping my focus on every moving part surrounding us until he steps to the side into an enclosed area away from the throng of people.

"Mr. Maxwell—"

He stops and turns around. "Payton, please. I prefer not to feel as if I've stepped into my father's shoes, thank you."

I nod as I knew at some point I would switch to using his first name to fit the whole fake bride persona. Just didn't seem appropriate to start there right away.

"Of course. Payton. We have approximately forty-five minutes to go through security and get to the gate—"

He holds up his hand. "Look, I appreciate what my sister is trying to do here, but it's entirely unnecessary."

"But I've been hired—"

Again, he stops me by lifting his hand, drawing my attention to his forearms and broad hands with long fingers. And for a brief second, I wonder what he looks like in his hockey uniform on the ice.

"Yes, I know. Emalia filled me in, and I informed her I would go along with her little plan to appease her, but I don't need a bodyguard."

"She told me you'd say that." I scan our surroundings, keeping tabs on a few lingerers.

He pulls his head back. "She did?"

"Oh yes. In fact, she said you'd try to convince me to leave."

Finger pressed beneath his full bottom lip, he blinks in

thought. "I suppose I shouldn't be surprised. Emalia knows me better than anyone. But that just simplifies things, don't you think?"

"How so?"

Payton shrugs. "My sister already expects that I'll send you off. So that's settled, then."

"No. It's not." I shake my head as I say this.

This time, he sighs. "All right. Then I have a proposal."

I study his angular features—the pulse in his jawline, the set of his mouth, the pinch of his brows—he's scrambling for a way out of this. The least I can do is humor him until he finally realizes I'm not going anywhere. "I'm listening."

Hope flashes in his crystal blues, almost making me feel guilty that I'm about to kibosh his plan. "You can escort me through security to my gate. You can even wait until I get on the plane if you'd like. Then you'll have completed the most important part of your assignment."

"How do you figure?"

"Any threat," his brows lift, "if there *is* any threat, is here in the UK. Not in the States. So once I board the plane, you're free to go."

I shake my head for the second time, and I suspect it won't be the last. "Then we'd best get you to your gate."

In the Offensive Zone with My Fake Bride: Chapter Three

I should probably feel guiltier than I do, leaving my sister to deal with her new title and responsibilities. However, I know she'll be a whiz at it. She's built for it, whereas I am not.

Dealing with this bodyguard is proof enough of how out of my element I am in this scenario. At least she's agreeable to my proposal. Once I'm on the plane, I won't have to give it another thought.

Give my bodyguard another thought...

I lift my phone a little higher so I can study her without her noticing. She's sitting across from me, constantly watching either me or what's going on around us. I feel like I'm an ant in an ant farm, constantly under observation. The analogy even makes my skin crawl.

Though I will say Lily is madfit—our British term for 'hot'—for a bodyguard. I don't know exactly what I expected, but not this. With her light honey-brown hair pulled back into a ponytail, she appears younger. But that could be the light dusting of freckles covering her high cheekbones, which tells me she spends time outside. I could easily mistake her for a college student except for her attire, which seems more in line with a business executive.

She may be sitting, but my experience as a hockey player has taught me to be sensitive to a body about to change position or direction. As a forward, that's part of my job, so I can predict the best avenue to score a goal. And Lily is poised to move at a moment's notice, so that tells me she's athletic as well—another feature I find very attractive. Most of the very few women I've dated wanted nothing to do with the outdoors or any physical activity at all in some cases.

The flight attendant announces boarding is to begin, and since I'm flying first class, I rise and head toward the door. Lily follows close behind, still doing her job. Once I'm on the plane, I can relax for the duration of my flight without those hazel-green eyes watching me and everything around me. I'm still convinced my cousin's tendency for recklessness was his demise and therefore there's no credible threat to me. However, if I needed a bodyguard, I'm not sure I'd want one so breathtaking.

"Welcome aboard." The attendant smiles at me as I hold my phone out for her to scan my ticket.

As I look over my shoulder to nod my thanks to Lily, the attendant scans her phone.

I step to the side and face her. "What are you—"

Lily wraps her hand around my arm just above my elbow and, in one swift and impressive move, turns and propels me forward. "Let's not draw attention."

Once we get about twenty feet down the walkway to the plane, I stop and pull her aside, careful to keep my voice at a whisper. "What are you doing?"

Her gaze unwavering, she leans in and whispers, "My job."

"But you agreed to my proposal."

She waits for several people to pass by. "Actually, I didn't. I shook my head."

"But you said, 'We'd best get you to *your* gate.' Meaning my gate."

"Yes, your gate. And that's where *we* are."

I don't miss her implication or how she's handling me. A steady stream of travelers are now heading our way, inspiring a Hail Mary plan I'm begging the universe to let work. "Just go back and tell them you're sick or have a sudden family emergency."

Since timing *is* my strong suit, I launch myself in front of the latest pack of boarders, creating a barrier between Lily and me. Once on the plane, I stow my duffel and sit, watching the front to see if my bodyguard has decided I'm not worth the trouble or if she's as tenacious as I'm beginning to suspect.

After several people board and pass by, I pull out my phone and begin reading the book I started last night, doing my best to pretend that the movement next to me isn't Lily settling into her seat.

The small privacy door between the seats slides open. "Did you really think that would work?"

I exhale in resignation before lifting my head in her direction. Sunlight streaming through the tiny windows to my left highlights her hazel green eyes, making her irises appear almost backlit. The effect is captivating. "I'd hoped."

If that were true, then why do I feel somewhat pleased she didn't bail on me?

She leans forward, ruffling in her backpack, then sits back with a notebook and pen in her hands, which she promptly opens. "I made a list of things to cover so we can get our nuptials story down. The closer we keep to the truth, the better."

"Is this really necessary?" I probably sound like one of the petulant toddlers my sister used to treat, but I can't help it. I'm scrambling for some way to get out of this before I return to my *normal* life in Sarabella. When I threw the idea out about a female bodyguard, I honestly didn't expect Emalia to take me seriously.

She blinks at me. "Which part? Creating a believable story to keep your friends and teammates from knowing who you really are while I protect you? Or your continuous objections that are wasting valuable time and energy? Mostly mine."

"Well, when you put it that way…" This woman clearly doesn't like to be trifled with. I file that away, enjoying her forthrightness.

"Then let me rephrase. Let me do my job, Payton. That way, you can continue to do yours. That's the crux of this, isn't it?"

As much as I don't want to admit, she's right. I want to get back to the life I've worked hard to create outside of my family ties and responsibilities in England. Never mind that my sister outplayed me, which she's always excelled at.

"Fine. Let's get on with it. What's our story?"

An almost smug expression tilts her lips, which I find myself looking at more than I should. She's the enigma I never expected, that's for sure.

Lily folds back the cover of her notebook. "We met the first week you flew home for your cousin's funeral." She glances up as if to gauge my reaction. "Sorry for your loss, by the way."

The flash of compassion in her eyes twists something in my chest. I react with a curt nod. "Thank you."

302

She returns my nod and then refocuses on her notes. "What did you do that first week?"

I tilt my head back in thought to six weeks ago. "Let's see. I attended a polo match, had drinks at the pub with some friends, and…" I snap my fingers, "I helped my sister with her annual fundraiser event."

Lily taps her pen against her lips, drawing my attention there yet again. "Hmm, polo might work. Drinks with friends…perhaps I tagged along with one of them as a last-minute invite. That could work. What was the fundraiser for?"

"Underprivileged children. She started it not long after she went into private practice."

Something flashes behind Lily's eyes, then disappears with a smile that's decidedly forced. "Drinks with friends, it is. We wound up talking all evening and spending almost every day together after that."

She falls silent as she writes in her notebook. Does she not enjoy children or fundraisers? That seems highly unlikely.

I find myself wanting to learn more about her. Where did she come from, and how did she wind up being a close protection officer? What was her family like? Did she have any siblings?

"What about you?"

Her gaze jumps to mine. "What about me?"

"I should know details about you as well, correct?" I add a whimsical tone to my voice. "Seems odd that we talked for hours, yet I know nothing about you."

She checks her watch. "We met barely an hour ago."

"At the pub, the night we met. I'm practicing my part." I wink at her, just for effect.

A flight attendant stops next to my chair. "Would you like something to drink or something off our menu?"

I grin up at her. "Just some water, please."

"Are you sure I can't get you something more…enjoyable?" One side of her mouth lifts in a sly smile.

She's flirting with me. Normally, I'd engage and enjoy this rare occasion. In the States, one of the other guys on the team, such as Luke or Wade, would get the attention while I hung about like their wingman.

I swing my gaze to Lily. "I'm sure my wife would enjoy something."

The attendant's momentary flash of shock settles into a contrite expression. "So sorry. Of course! What can I get you?"

Lily's lips twitch up just so on the sides. "Some water, thank you."

The attendant nods, then turns around to walk back to the galley.

"Well done…husband." Lily's voice drops to a husky whisper.

If I weren't in on the ruse, I'd believe it myself. Suddenly uncomfortable, I shift in my seat. "Might as well start practicing now."

The flight attendant returns and hands us each a cup of water. I guzzle mine down, then hold my cup out to her. "I think I need a refill."

"Did you always want to be a hockey player?" Lily waits for my answer, pen poised over what I guesstimate to be her fourth page of notes.

In the last two hours, we've covered everything from

food and entertainment preferences to quirky details like my complete intolerance for anything sweet that's been salted— why eat it then? The entire purpose of eating a chocolate or a caramel is to enjoy its creamy sweetness. Why ruin it?

Yet, I still think I'm lacking enough details about Lily.

"I started playing as a child in a junior league and never looked back."

She tilts her head. "How did your parents feel about you wanting to make a profession of it?"

Not sure how this is pertinent to our convincing people we're married, but I don't mind answering it. "They've always been supportive of my choices, even if they don't entirely understand them."

Her mouth tenses for a moment. "That's nice."

"What about your parents? Do they approve of their daughter being in such a dangerous line of work?"

She clears her throat and studies her notebook. "They passed away when I was very young."

The twist I felt earlier in my chest returns twice as hard. "So sorry. That must have been difficult."

Her shrug doesn't hide the wariness I see on her face. "I don't remember much about them."

"Did your grandparents raise you, then? Mine like to play second parents to my sister and me, always nosing into our business." I finish with a chuckle.

She shakes her head. "My parents didn't have any family, so I grew up in the foster system."

I don't recall ever meeting someone who spent their childhood as an orphan. At the moment, I dearly wish I had some of my sister's diplomatic abilities.

"Sorry again." I let out a self-deprecating laugh. "I'm honestly not sure what to say."

"You don't need to say anything. It's simply the facts.

On the bright side, we won't have to make up any stories about meeting my parents. Makes things easier."

As much as I wish at times that my parents—and grand-parents—would show less interest in my life, I can't imagine not having them in my life. And my sister, of course, whose penchant for bossing me around is either her way of showing she loves me or her superpower. Maybe both...

I run my hands down the front of my trousers. "Right. So, what's your story then? Do I tell my teammates you're a...you know, a..."

"Bodyguard?" A gleam of mischief sparkles in her eyes. "After high school, I did a short tour in the Army, then moved into the private sector, doing security in London. It's vague but detailed enough."

"You mentioned keeping things as close to the truth as possible, so is that true?"

"Pretty much."

"Why did you leave the military?"

She studies me. "That's complicated. Let's just say I realized I wanted something different."

Color me intrigued and completely fascinated. I want to ask her to expound, but I get the sense she holds this close. If I planned to spend more time with Lily, I'd wait for her to trust me before asking her for details about her past. But somehow, I have to find a way to cut this arrangement short before I'm back with the team.

"Hmmm. I can relate to that. That's how I wound up playing ice hockey in another country. I wanted something different."

"But for different reasons, I'm sure." She says this with a finality that tells me the subject is closed.

The lights dim in the cabin, drawing our gazes upward. A yawn bubbles up before I can squelch it.

Lily closes her notebook. "Get some rest, Payton. We've covered enough for now."

I nod as I reach to close the small door between our seats, but she stops me.

"Sorry, but I need to keep eyes on you at all times."

"But we're on a plane."

"Whatever threat's out there—"

"If there even is one," I interrupt.

"A single moment of vulnerability is all it takes, Payton. Trust me on that." Her gaze never wavers as if to bring her point home.

Aside from the jitters now coursing through me, I confess I find the thought of her watching me as I rest somewhat unsettling yet comforting at the same time. On the ice, I can count on Luke or Ethan to have my back, but in life, I'm largely on my own in the States. Returning for Sebastian's funeral reminded me how much I'd missed our family gatherings.

And as my eyes close, shutting out a last glimpse of Lily's ever-watchful presence, I'm struck with the thought that she must feel the same.

All the time.

Grab your copy...
vinci-books.com/offensivezone

About the Author

Dineen Miller is an Amazon bestselling and award-winning author of both fiction and nonfiction, but only recently discovered she has a sublime addiction to writing and reading romantic comedies. In addition to these, she's been known to write romantic suspense and has dabbled with thrillers and fantasy.

Needing additional outlets for her creativity, she's designed several coloring books under her own name and under Hue Manatee Art, and has crocheted too many afghans to count. No, she does not have cats, but she is a dog-mom to two furry rescues that answer to wiggle butt and snuggle boy. And she's married to a punny guy, who thinks she's unique.

Acknowledgments

If you'd told me two or three years ago that I'd wind up writing hockey romcoms, I would have said you give me way too much credit. Yet here I am, working on an entire series.

And I love it! I not only love writing hockey romcoms, I love the sport too.

How did that happen? Well, I figured I couldn't write a hockey romance without understanding the sport, so I researched first, then realized I needed to watch a game. I jumped in right at the beginning of the 2024 Stanley Cup playoffs, and fell in love.

In fact, I'm trying to finish writing this page so I can go watch a game! How's that for true love?

A very special thanks and shout out to beta reader Charity Henico for her stellar input. I love you, girl!

Huge appreciation and gratitude to my launch team: Rita Mast Beachy, Tabatha Robinson, Koren Seago, Allegra Waldron, Traci Humes, Louise Bateman, Nikki Scheuermann, and Jess Barncastle. I'm so grateful for each of you, my friends. Your help and support to share this book means the world to me. You're truly amazing!

Great appreciation to my editors, Alice Shepherd and Judy DeVries for your keen eyes and encouraging words—

To all of you, lovely readers, thank you for taking the plunge with me into the first installment of the Romancing the Sun Kings series. I hope Luke and Sophie's story touched your heart and made you laugh. Life can be hard at times, and love is always the best remedy.

May you live authentically, love fully, and laugh often.